The Murder

of

Jeremy Brookes

Tony McFadden

Beach Nut Press

DEDICATION

For the seekers of truth.

At any cost.

DISCLAIMER

All characters in this book are fictitious. Any resemblance to real people is entirely coincidental. I don't care *what* he says.

This book is set in Australia, and written in Australia. It has Australian sayings and spellings.

ACKNOWLEDGMENTS

You're reading this due to the support of many beta-readers who have helped enormously. Thanks Al, Kay, John, Stephen.

Thanks also to the Northern Beaches Writers' Group, again, for their collective input to the opening chapters.

You're an awesome group of writers.

CHAPTER 1

Dan tapped the screen on his phone to wake it. 10:19 p.m. Half a pizza cooled on a serving plate at the centre of the corner table, in the small family kebab shop, an empty chair and plate across from him. There was a continuous flow of customers in the shop. A blanket of smell -- warm pizza, lamb skewers on an open flame, half a dozen rotisserie chickens slowly turning in a glass door oven – enveloped him. He picked a piece of pepperoni out of the melted cheese, then slid the plate a smidge away from him.

The owner, a matronly woman, hovered.

"A few more minutes, Sabrin. He's only twenty minutes late." He pointed at the serving plate. "And there's still half a pizza."

"Stewart likes it cold, does he?"

"Doesn't everyone?"

"I can box it up. What is he doing this time?"

"Old money croaked and the favourite grandson, due to get half the estate, is nowhere to be found. Stew's forte. Said he found him, and he'd meet me here at 10:00."

"He's late." Sabrin smiled and headed back to the kitchen. "Take your time. We close at midnight."

Dan reached for a piece of pizza, hesitated, then pulled his hand back. He tapped his phone again. 10:23 p.m.

Raucous laughter from the three bikies at the table next to him sealed his decision.

He took the plate to the counter. "Box this up, please." He licked the oils off his fingers. "It's always good, mate."

Kasheem, Sabrin's son, slid the half pizza into a take-away box and handed it back. "Tell Stew he still owes me $20 from last weekend's match. I'd do double or nothing on next weekend's game, but I don't like to take advantage of the elderly."

Dan laughed. "I'll tell him. Not the elderly part, thought. That's on you."

A scream and smashing glass shattered the night. Dan trotted out of the small restaurant and looked down the street toward his office. Two large men were grappling on the ground in front of a partially smashed in convenience store window. A small, wiry woman was trying to get between them, with limited success.

He walked toward them, slowly gathering speed. The two men had split and scrambled to their feet, the taller, bigger one squaring off with an older, but solid man with grey-flecked hair and a handlebar moustache.

Dan stared. "Son of a bitch. Stew?" The convenience store was across the street from Dan's office.

Despite his age, Stew was as hard as the rock he used to move, building walls and jetties for the stupid rich in the Northern Suburbs. That was almost a decade ago, before Dan took him on as his main guy in charge of finding missing persons. The hard slabs of muscle and grey handlebar moustache belied his animal cunning.

The big guy swung an elbow back at Stew's head. He blocked and mashed his fist into the larger man's solar plexus. "Down, boy."

The woman flailed, trying to get at Stew. Dan got between her and the fight. "Be careful. Either one of them would flatten you with one mis-timed punch."

"Tell your friend to stop."

Dan looked at Stew. He was holding his own. "He'll be fine."

The woman tried to get past. "Billy has friends."

"Billy? His name is Billy? What's your name?" He shuffled to keep between her and the fight behind him, pizza box tucked under his arm.

"Kat. His friends are at the kebab shop. Billy was trying to get cigs. You won't have a chance when they get here. Just let it go."

"How many?"

"Friends? Three."

"You look worried."

"He's going to beat me for not warning him you were coming."

Dan looked up the road toward the kebab shop. "Are his friends getting kebabs the same way Billy was getting the cigs?" Stew had Billy on his knees, face pressed up against the wall beside the kicked in glass.

"You should get out of here," said Kat.

"Stew, the lady thinks we should get out of here before the friends show up."

Stew stood back from Billy and let him stand. "We good here, Billy?"

Billy leaned his back against the wall and looked across the street at the office. A white signboard with blue 'McGinnis Investigations' occupied the space below the windows on the third floor. "Nah. This is coming back on you, one way or another." He nodded at the sign. "That's your mob, right?" He reached for Kat's arm. "Let's get out of here."

Kat pulled back. "I'm not feeling well. I'm going home."

"Like hell you are." He lunged for her and Stew drove a heel into the side of Billy's knee, buckling his leg.

"She wants to go home, mate. Stay down."

Billy growled something undecipherable and pulled himself to his feet, favouring one leg. Stew stood in front of him and kept a hand lightly on Billy's chest. "Don't do it."

Dan looked at Stew, then at the kebab shop. Three larger guys had just exited, the guy in front with a carry bag filled with food containers. The three were laughing and talking among themselves when the front guy saw Dan and Stew.

And Billy.

"Hey, Billy. What the hell is going on?"

Their pace picked up. Dan shook his head. "Ah, Stew, we gotta clear out." He looked at Kat. "Come with us."

Stew took a deep breath, pointed at Billy and shook his head. "One minute, boss." He drove a punch into Billy's gut, and when he doubled over, brought his knee up under the big guy's face. His nose disintegrated with a crunch and a spray of blood.

He watched Billy sink to the sidewalk and trotted across the street. "They're getting close."

Dan took Kat's arm. "Well?"

She looked at Billy. Blood pooled on the sidewalk as he pushed himself up. He wiped his mouth with his sleeve, smearing blood and snot across his cheek. "Stay here, bitch, or I'll thrash you."

Kat looked across the street at Stew, holding the door open. She looked at Billy's three friends approaching with increasing speed. "Okay. Let's go."

Billy's friends were only metres away. One peeled off to check on Billy and the other two dialled in on Dan and Kat.

"Hustle," said Stew. He hurried them through the door and pulled it shut, sliding the bolts into place just as the heavies reached the other side.

Kat flinched as they started banging on the outside. "I'm dead."

"Not tonight you aren't," said Dan. "Upstairs. Third floor."

Dan locked the office front door and led them in. "You hungry, Kat?" He dropped the pizza box on his desk.

She sat on the edge of his desk. "Thank you." She flipped the top of the box and took a slice.

"You have somewhere to go?" He wandered to the window. More 'friends' had arrived, most of whom Dan knew. Things were getting noisy. He looked back at Kat. "Do you?"

She shook her head. "We're up from Wollongong." She nodded toward the window. "Billy's my ride."

Dan scratched the back of his neck and looked at Stew. "No local friends?"

Kat shook her head. "I'll take the train back tomorrow. Can I crash here?"

"We're a business. No beds. There's a motel up the road." Dan opened his phone and scrolled through his contacts. "I think I've got their number."

"We're all going to be spending the night here if these lads don't piss off." Stew looked out the window. The friends had friends, and they were packing the street.

"You guys a detective agency or something?" Kat paced the office, looking at the pictures on the wall and the books in the book case. The computer screen on Dan's desk bounced 'McGinnis Investigations' like a one-sided game of pong.

"Or something." He opened the bottom drawer of his desk and pulled out three glasses. He held one up. "A drop? Either of you?"

Kat shook her head no. Stew nodded and Dan poured two fingers of whiskey and slid the glass across the desk. He poured a smaller one for himself.

"You have a successful business?" asked Kat. "It's not the shiniest set up I've ever seen." She pointed at the pictures behind Dan, along the top of a large horizontal file cabinet. "Hey, you used to play for the Rabbitohs?"

"A lifetime ago." He slapped his leg. "Knees took a hammering."

Kat raised an eyebrow. "Had a couple of pies, too, hey?"

Dan ignored her and pointed at Stew. "So, what happened, mate? What took you so long?"

"Last minute cold feet from the young lad. Wasn't that easy to find in the first place."

Kat looked back and forth between the two. "What are you talking about."

"A client hired us to find a missing grandson."

"Like a little kid?"

"No," said Stew. "He's in his mid-twenties. Twenty-six, or something."

"So then he's not missing, is he? He just doesn't want to be found."

"Gramps died and left him upwards of thirty million dollars. We were hired to find him."

Kat stared for a second. "Oh."

"I know, right? My grandfather was worth about a hundred bucks when he died," said Dan. "Hang on, Stew. What do you mean, cold feet?"

"He's living in one of those off-the-grid eco villages in the hills. One of those places the hippies went to die but didn't. He can make thirty bucks stretch a week, maybe longer. Thirty mill? I think it scared the shit out of him. Anyway, I talked him down. He'll be at the lawyer's office tomorrow morning, and we'll get paid tomorrow afternoon."

"Good." Dan finished his drink. "It's getting late. Early morning tomorrow."

"What's tomorrow?"

"Got an email from a spurned woman who wants to void a prenup. I've got a call with her early to arrange the details. Sounds like it's going to be a week of surveillance, at most. And we'll get paid what we'd normally charge for a month's work."

"She must be sure."

"She seemed like she was."

Stew glanced out the window. "What are we going to do about this?"

Dan and Kat joined him. Kat took a quick glance and backed out of eyeline.

Dan nudged Stew. "You want to come down with me and ask them to disperse?"

Stew grunted a laugh. "You gonna pay my medical bills? No thank you. There's a few guys looks like those skinhead fucks from the Gong. I'll take them one or two at a time, would love nothing more, but not a crowd that big."

Dan cleared his throat and looked at Stew. "Who's on tonight?"

Stew looked confused for a second, then smiled. "Wazza."

Dan nodded, slid through the directory on his mobile and stopped at the number he was looking for. He looked out the window at the dozen or so men on bikes lining the street while the call went through.

"Senior Constable Warren Peters speaking. This you, Dan?"

"Wazza, mate, I need you to do a drive by and disperse for me."

"Where you at?"

"Office."

"This late? I'm about five minutes out."

"I'd appreciate it. There's a growing throng of pissed off bikies on the road out front and I'm too tired for a fight."

There was a deep laugh on the other end of the phone. "What did you do with them? Steal one of their girls?"

Dan looked at Kat and smiled. "Maybe something like that."

"Is this a Raptor thing?"

"Oh, hell no. Just move them on. Thanks."

"Why don't you just go out the back?"

"My bike's out front. Was just stopping by for a minute. Things got away from me. Really appreciate this."

"No worries. Give me a couple of minutes."

"Cheers." He terminated the call and dropped the phone on his desk.

"I don't need saving," said Kat.

"We do," said Stew. "Only an idiot starts a fight he can't win."

"I'll stay a little bit, if that's okay with you." She looked at the crowd out front of the building.

"There's another exit. Takes you into the parking lot out back. Short walk to the train station." Dan nodded at Stew. "Walk her there?"

Stew sighed and threw back the rest of his drink. "Let's go, Kat."

CHAPTER 2

The boardroom was in the corner of the top floor of a thirty-story building on the Sydney Harbour. Two of the four walls were glass. The view, on most days, was spectacular. This day, the rain pounding the glass thrummed a muffled drumbeat and smeared the view of the iconic Harbour Bridge.

A marble-topped conference table occupied the centre of the room, a dozen ergonomic chairs evenly spaced around it. A larger expensive leather chair sat at the head of the table.

One of the double doors pushed open and Randolph Murray walked in. Tall, with a silver comb-over, his tie loose and his top shirt button open. He dropped a thick file folder at the head of the table, sat and spun in his chair to face the double doors. "Where in the hell is everybody?"

Mel Dvorak strode in, heels clicking on the wood floor. She sat at Randolph's right. "You're a couple of minutes early. Jeremy's on his way."

"Goddamned legal bullshit."

Mel smiled as she opened her laptop and connected it to the large plasma bolted to the far wall. She tapped a couple of keys and the front page of the *Oz Express* was displayed on the monitor.

The cover photo was of a tall, slim African-American -- Cassie Johnson -- who had moved to Sydney four years earlier. She had carried an all-female heist movie shot on the Gold Coast a year before that. It broke box office records and led to three movies a year until she decided to retire and spend her life and her money protesting the Australian government's immigration policies.

The non-flattering photo belied her beauty, and showed her flipping her middle finger to a police officer.

Mel adjusted the image so the full cover was displayed on the monitor. "Lot of content this week."

"I don't want a *lot* of content. I want compelling, can't-put-it-down content. Clickable content. Traffic driving content that lets me increase advertising rates."

"As long as it doesn't get you sued." Jeremy Brookes pulled out a chair and sat opposite Mel. He was pushing sixty but was still fit. His glasses were perched on top of his close-cropped greying hair. He dropped a tablet on the table and looked at his watch. "If you'd been here when the full editorial staff was here, Randolph, we wouldn't have to do this again."

Rand ignored him. "Get on with it, Mel."

She nodded toward the screen. "The cover. Nothing here to get legal in a knot."

Jeremy turned to the screen and adjusted his glasses. "I'll be the -" He stopped at the bold headline on the lower-right quadrant. "Really?" He pointed at the screen while looking at Randolph. "Are you shitting me?

You've changed it. You can't say that. *Peter Strange's Hidden Murder*? Who wrote this?"

She looked at her notes. "Barry. It's solid, JB."

"Like hell it is. A definitive statement like that exposes the company to libel. And we'd lose. And what in the hell are you talking about?"

Mel held out a page from her files. "It's alleged that Strange, when he was a kid, didn't pay attention to a child he was babysitting, and that child drowned in the bath."

"AACTA award winning Peter Strange?"

"You know another one?"

"Source?"

"Childhood friend." She raised her eyebrows. "Got a stat dec." She slid it across the table. It stopped, facing the right way around, in front of Jeremy.

"Go with it," said Randolph.

"No, no." Jeremy placed a finger on the sheet of paper. "One statutory declaration doesn't make it. You can't run it. I need to see the copy. How in the hell did copy get in that I didn't approve?"

"This is going out this afternoon." Randolph leaned back in his chair. "Mel has your signature on the draft, or it wouldn't be in the issue."

Jeremy furrowed his brow and looked at Mel. She smiled, nodded and held up a sheet of paper with a scrawl across the bottom. He leaned forward and reached for it, but she dropped it in the file.

"Is it just the blurb on the cover that's bothering you?"

"No. Well. But." Jeremy used the heel of his hand to wipe sweat off his brow.

Mel looked at Randolph and nodded. She started typing and the bullet changed to *What is Strange Hiding?*

"Thanks, Mel. How's that, JB? Better?"

Jeremy grunted and sat back in his chair, frowning. The picture taking up the cover of the tabloid finally registered with him. "Is that Cassie Johnson?"

"Yeah." Randolph tapped the conference table with his pen. "You need new glasses?

"What's the story behind her picture?"

"We'll get to that." He leaned forward, interlocked his fingers and rested his elbows on the table. "Where's the story about the Labor leader's -- who is it now? -- prostitute daughter? That's got to be on the cover. Needs to be prominent."

Jeremy rubbed the hair on the back of his head. "Come on, Randolph. Too far. *He's* fair game. Family is off limits."

Randolph shook his head sharply. "Mel, where is it?"

Mel highlighted the block of text on the right just below the magazine title. "Right here. *Poli's Prossie Problem*. Want it bigger?"

"I want it clearer. I don't want there to be any question about what we're saying. What's that fuck's name again?"

"Wilson."

Randolph nodded. *"Wanker Wilson and his Whore."* He gestured at the monitor. "Change it."

Jeremy clenched his fists. "He'll sue, Rand, and it'll cost the company a shit-tonne of money."

"It's *Randolph*, and he wouldn't dare. Change it."

Jeremy shook his head and looked at his employer. "What's going on? What is the end game? You think the publicity from a trial is better than advertising?"

"It'll certainly be cheaper. But he doesn't have the balls or spine to do anything about it." He jabbed a bony finger in the direction of the monitor. "I said change it."

Mel looked at Jeremy who shrugged.

"Doesn't matter what I think, apparently," said Jeremy.

Mel increased the font size and Jeremy watched as the block of text changed to *Wanker Wilson's Whore*. "Good enough?"

Jeremy pushed his chair back. "What do you have against him?"

"Wilson is a misguided, lefty, granola crunching mummy's boy who wants to open the borders for more immigration, shut down Manus and bring those fuckers here, raise minimum wage and increase corporate tax rates."

"It's the last one, isn't it?"

Randolph narrowed his eyes. "I hired you to warn me when I might get into trouble. I *didn't* hire you to *keep me out* of that trouble. It's my call. Warning heard and dismissed. Proceed."

"Tell me why Cassie's on the cover." Jeremy clenched his fists. "You know I know her. Are you provoking me intentionally?"

Randolph took a deep breath and shook his head. "It's always good to have someone on staff to act as devil's advocate. Helps test limits. You used to be good for that." He shrugged. "The last few months, though, you've been a real pain in the arse. You'd think I was putting out a women's magazine."

"You're over the line all the time now, *Rand*. Why is Cassie on the cover?"

"I think that's all we need you for, JB."

Jeremy scanned the cover, looking for the related blurb. He found what he was looking for, in medium size font, just below and to the left of Cassie Johnson's face. "Is that it? *Johnson's Johnson*? Really?"

"You know something I don't?"

"Jesus Christ. I've known Cassie since she moved here. The nicest person you will ever meet which, in your case, is not that difficult. She's given up an extremely lucrative career to help people. Why this?"

Randolph shrugged. "It sells copies. Gets me clicks. Millions of clicks. And that sells advertising. Which allows me to pay you an obscene amount of money to yell at me."

"And it's homophobic. Transphobic. Anyone who has seen her in that tourism poster in the bikini *knows* she doesn't have a cock, excuse my French."

"It sells."

"I'm not signing off on that." Jeremy flipped his tablet cover closed. "No way in hell." He leaned forward. "What's the story? I guarantee you I didn't sign off on any story about Cass."

"You were tied up with something else," said Mel. She leaned back and crossed her arms. "I read it through. It scans. We're not out on a limb."

"Your marketing diploma serves you well."

"Sarcasm doesn't look good on you."

"What in the hell would you know?" Jeremy pointed at Randolph. "This goes to print, I'll be representing Cassie in the lawsuit against this shithole company." Jeremy's face was pomegranate-red. He started coughing and pulled a handkerchief from his pocket and wiped his mouth.

Randolph had a small smile on his face. "So, you and this Cassie are an item?"

"We're friends. I won't stand for this, mate. I've been putting up with more shit than I'm happy with for far too long."

Randolph squinted his little eyes and regarded Jeremy. He crossed his legs and picked at an invisible piece of lint on his trousers. "I've had the feeling for some time now that you're unwell, that you'd rather be somewhere else. So go be somewhere else for a little while."

Jeremy folded the hankie and dabbed at his lips. He stood and slid it in his pocket. "I quit."

"That's done." Mel scrolled down. "This block of text could be a bit larger, but then it draws attention from the Strange story. Do you want it larger, or leave more negative space than we usually do?"

Randolph ignored her and leaned forward. "Quit? Jeremy, you're just overtired. You look pale. Take a couple weeks. Head to the Whitsundays. I've got a place on Hamilton Island. Take your wife and spend a couple of weeks there. Maybe invite Cassie along for a three-way, if your lovely wife is up for it."

Jeremy shoved his chair to the table, picked up his tablet and opened the door.

"Go fuck yourself, *Randy*." He pulled his phone out of his pocket. "I'll see you in court." He called his wife. "I'll see you in a couple of hours, hun. I just quit. It's time."

"Oh, Jeremy, sit down and stop being a goddamned fool." Randolph's demeanour had shifted from annoyed-genial to terse. "We have an employment contract. You need to give sufficient notice. Take time. Calm down."

Jeremy's voice was loud enough now to echo through the office. "Take my contract, crumple it up in a little ball and shove it up your bony, cheap arse." Jeremy stood a little taller. "It's refreshing seeing you for what you really are. I thought, for the longest time, that this -- all this that you do -- was driven by greed. I was wrong. You're evil. Your satisfaction comes from ruining people. You'd get just as much satisfaction if you were dirt poor."

Randolph smiled. "You're wrong. It's all about the money. By any means. Where'd you find your balls, mate?"

"You're done, Rand. Finished. Over. See you in hell. I'll ruin you financially." He put the phone back up to his head. "Honey, we should have done this months ago. Love you."

Mel watched the door swing shut behind Jeremy. "He seems upset."

Rand pressed a speed dial on his mobile phone. "I should have punched that fuck in the throat." He gripped the phone tight enough to whiten his knuckles. He pressed it to his head. "I need you and Robert in here now."

"What are you going to do?" asked Mel.

Two thick-necked men walked into the conference room, one a half head taller than the other.

"Gerald, Robert, I've got a bit of a chore for you."

They nodded.

"Find Jeremy tonight, in the shadows, and tune him up."

"How hard?" asked the taller one.

"Hard enough he doesn't come in tomorrow, Gerald. Or the next day. Understood?"

They looked at Mel, nodded and left.

Mel watched them go and scribbled a note in her pad. "The cover picture staying as is?"

"Has the bitch paid?"

Mel shook her head.

"Then her picture stays on the cover and the story stays in."

"She's stubborn, and doesn't seem to care about her career. She may never pay."

"Does she have a pet?"

Mel flipped through pages in a file folder. "Yeah. A terrier. Rescue dog."

Rand nodded. "If she doesn't pay this time, do the dog. And let her know what's coming." He took another picture out of his folder; a young, rising local star just off the back of a surprise indie hit. He jabbed the image with his finger. "We got the goods on him yet?"

"By the end of the week. Promise."

"Discrete?" Randolph slowly closed the folder.

"Out of town mob. Way out of town. They think it's a broken marriage thing."

"And how much am I going to pay?" He smiled at Mel.

"The very barest minimum," she smiled back.

Randolph closed the folder and squared it on the table. "Are you bringing anyone to the dinner on the weekend?"

Mel shook her head. "Danni has an away match this weekend in Perth. She's leaving with the team Saturday morning. I'll be going to the function stag."

"Still with that?"

"What?"

"You're a beautiful woman. Any *man* would love to go out with you."

Mel sighed and stood. "I'll catch you later."

Jeremy pushed the door open and stepped out of the pub at the top of the hill on Harris Street. He took a deep breath and smiled wistfully. The rain had washed the streets clean and the spring air was fresh. The blow up with Randolph had jacked his adrenalin. The hormone had filtered through his system though, and he felt unsteady. Tired. He fumbled his phone out of his pocket and sent a text to his wife. *5 minutes.*

He looked ahead at the park, soft lights illuminating the benches about a hundred metres ahead. He and his wife had a standing date, once a month, a bottle of wine and a pizza, looking over the harbour. He walked downhill toward the park, the occasional shop lights illuminating his path. He swallowed back some bile. His stomach had been acting up for…he thought for a minute. He couldn't remember. Nerves.

He entered a dark patch beside a couple of closed shops. A small lane ran between them, access to the trash bins. As he stepped in front of the lane a hand grabbed him by the arm and pulled him into the dark. He heard a weapon cock as he stumbled to the ground.

"Come on. Stand up and give me your wallet."

Jeremy strained his eyes in the dark. A figure his height blended with the shadows.

"Wallet."

Jeremy took a deep breath. He slowly reached into his suit pocket and pulled out his slim billfold. "Take it. My watch?"

"Keep it." Light from the street glinted off the barrel of the revolver as the mugger motioned Jeremy to the back of the lane. "That way."

Gerald and Robert stood across the street, in line with the alley. They watched

Jeremy get pulled into the dark alleyway. Gerald looked at Robert and moved to take a step off the curb when he was stopped by a flash and a muffled report. The killer stepped out of the dark, looked up Harris Street and left.

Robert placed a hand on Gerald's arm. "Let's go. Job's done."

CHAPTER 3

"Who are we tonight?" asked Dan. He stood in the middle of their inventory room, a manila envelope tucked under his arm.

Andy Smith pushed through and grabbed a pack of A3 sized magnetic signs. He was slightly shorter than Dan, but had at least ten more kilos of muscle on him. "One of those telco construction subcontractors." He handed the signs to Dan and grabbed some hi-vis vests and hard hats. "We'll blend right in."

"That'll work." Dan tucked the signs under his arm with the envelope and grabbed a vest and hard hat. "What's this?" He picked up a small box about twice the size of a key fob and took it with him downstairs.

He slapped a sign on each side of the van and crawled in the back seat.

"Terry, what's this?"

Terry was the only one small enough to fit comfortably in the space behind the row of seats. He sat on a stool in front of a video monitor, headphone cans off one ear. "Cool piece of electronics. It jams key fobs. Blocks the signal. Good if you want to stop someone from locking their car. Or unlocking it."

"Beryl know you bought it?"

"I'll, erm, let her know tomorrow."

"You better, or I'll be the one catching hell." He placed it in his pocket. "We set up?"

"We're ready to go. Haven't done a group all-nighter in yonks." He looked past Dan into the front of the van. "Where's Stewie?"

Stew wrenched open the front door and climbed behind the wheel. "Call me that one more time and I'll cut you, kid."

Terry laughed and spun back to the monitor. "Sure thing, gramps."

Andy hopped in the front passenger seat. The van settled under the increased weight. "We going, or what?"

The van pulled away and Dan settled in his seat. He slid the papers out of the envelope. "Okay, lads, this is an easy job. Good coin. And because it might take a week or two to retrieve our equipment, we're listening and recording live." He handed pages to Andy and Terry. "Layout of the ground floor is on one side, and upstairs on the other. We've been promised a clear hour, but get in and out in thirty, just to be safe."

"She's sure a night of recording will get what she needs?"

Dan nodded. "She's going out of town, she says. She's positive he'll have his girlfriend over tonight. We get the recording and she'll get the divorce and half of what he owns. And we get a nice payday for a night's work."

Stew stopped the van at the mouth of a cul-de-sac in Kirkham, a high end community just outside of Campbelltown. "What are we looking for?"

"The target is the house at the end of the road." He checked a note. "A 1955 Benz 300SL Gullwing is our cue. When it leaves we go in."

"Alarm system?" asked Terry.

"If there is, you can disable it, right?"

"I can bypass most types, boss."

Stew slouched down in his seat. "Car's coming through. Damn. That's a five million dollar set of wheels. How much are we getting for this?"

"It'll pay office rent for a few months. Move in, Stew. We're good to go."

Dan picked the lock on the front door and stepped to one side for Terry. The youngster rushed in with a small bag of electronics and stopped, a confused look on his face.

"Ah, boss, there's no alarm system."

"Don't look a gift horse. Spread out and hit it. Back here as fast as possible."

Stew and Terry headed upstairs, each with bags over their shoulders. Andy took his bag to the kitchen and Dan entered the lounge room. He took a recorder-transmitter out of his bag, slid the switch to the 'on' position and stuck it to the frame underneath the sofa.

He repositioned the sofa and picked up a framed picture on the fireplace mantle.

"Kitchen and pool room are finished. And by pool room I mean the room with the giant-assed indoor pool," said Andy. He took the picture. "This guy looks familiar."

"Yeah. Didn't realise he was the target. Seems like a nice guy in the movies."

"He's an actor." He placed the picture back on the mantle. "Can't believe anything they say."

Dan frowned. "Should have been told."

"Job's a job, man. You finished in here?"

Dan adjusted his bag. "You take it. I'll do the garage. Meet you in the van."

Dan slid the van door shut and tapped Stew on the shoulder. "Let's go. Turn right at the end of this road, then right again. There's a house being built behind this one. We'll park in its drive. We made great time, guys. Twenty-three minutes."

Stew followed the directions and pulled into the drive of a partially constructed house.

"Anywhere here. Set up the listening positions and start recording." Dan looked at his watch. "She said he'd back at 8:00. We've got a few minutes."

Terry pulled on a set of headphones, listened for a second, and shook his head, smiling. "We got out of there just in time. There's a crowd showing up." He typed a command and three monitors came alive, quartered with four live camera feeds on each.

"Audio?"

Terry tapped his headphones. "Loud and clear." He took the headphones off and dropped them on the table. "How long we gonna sit here?"

Dan checked the video streams. The man from the photo on the mantle was pouring drinks in the lounge room. Two women were sitting on the sofa, one in an overstuffed chair. The actor handed drinks to the three women, then sat between the two on the sofa. He opened a cigarette holder and removed a flat glassine packet. He closed the cigarette holder and tapped a pile of white power on it.

"We'll have more than we need in less than an hour, is my guess," said Dan.

Stew rolled the truck into the company's parking spot behind the office. The clock on the dashboard ticked over to 11:15 pm.

Dan opened his eyes and took in the surroundings. "Okay. It was a good night. Unload into the lab and look at it in the morning. We're well ahead of schedule." He opened the passenger door and hopped down and came face to face with Billy.

"Where's Kat?"

Dan rubbed his face. "I'm too tired for this shit, mate. Go home."

Billy crossed his arms and looked down on Dan. "Kat."

Stew walked around the front of the truck and joined Dan. He smiled when he saw Billy and the splint on his nose. "You're looking good. I walked her to the station. That was a couple or three days ago. She said she was heading back to the Gong." Stew leaned forward and sniffed. "I think maybe she's tired of you being on the piss all the time, mate."

Billy gave Stew a two-handed shove in the chest.

Stew barely budged. He smiled as he looked up. "She's not here, mate. Ya better leave before you piss me off."

"I'll be back."

"Bring friends." Stew laughed as Billy walked out of the parking lot through a walkway to Queen Street. He slid open the side door and took crate of electronics from Andy. Dan reached in his pocket and dropped the key fob jammer in with the rest.

"When are we pulling the equipment from the target's house?" asked Andy.

"I'll get a call sometime in the next week or so. Not a big deal. They're hidden well," said Dan.

"Couple of bills worth of equipment."

Dan laughed. "I'll add them to the invoice if we don't get them back. She's good for it."

The *Oz Express* was folded lengthwise beside Dan's morning cup of coffee. Terry picked it up and sat on the edge of the desk.

He snapped the tabloid and made a show of reading the front cover.

"Cassie Johnson. My favourite movie star. A babe who looks gorgeous and can kick some serious arse." He nodded at Dan. "You saw that space movie she was in, right? Had that battle with about a dozen aliens and she cleaned them up with two double headed axes. Poetry in motion. The choreography was exquisite."

Dan grunted. "Last movie I saw her in was that one that was like a Beverly Hills Cop remake. Too bad they killed her at the end. That was a franchise just waiting to happen."

"It's movies. People come back all the time."

Dan cocked an eyebrow. "She was shot at least fifteen times. She ain't coming back. She retired a year or so ago, anyway. Why are we talking about her?"

Terry pointed at the front page. "You think she has meat and veg?"

"Don't care. I liked her movies. And she seems to be a genuinely nice person. Too bad she retired, but she opened up that homeless shelter and food kitchen in Sydney a month or so back. Doesn't really matter, does it?" Dan looked away from his monitor. "Are you finished scrubbing the recorders? If not, finish them. And if you're done with that, make sure all the video equipment is ready. Is Andy back yet?"

"Anytime now. He had to pop in at the bank."

Dan grabbed the tabloid back from Terry. "Get him to double check all the equipment when he gets in."

"You don't trust me?"

"I trust you fine. Andy's going to be relying on that equipment next time he uses it, and he has to be happy with them."

Terry scratched the back of his neck and smiled. "Tell him I'm in the lab when he shows."

Dan tossed the tabloid on the desk. "Go."

He heard the front door open and looked through his office door at the entrance, expecting Andy's bulk to fill the doorway. A woman came in and stopped at the front desk. Beryl listened to her for a minute, then turned and caught Dan's eye. He nodded and waved her in.

The woman looked to be in her late forties or early fifties, tall, with a slight build, dark brown shoulder-length hair and an angular face. She was dressed like she just came from the gym, water bottle in one hand and a folder in the other.

She stepped tentatively into Dan's office, tucked the folder under her arm and held out her hand. He shook it and pointed at a chair.

"I'm Dan McGinnis. I run the show here. Have a seat."

"Sally Brookes. And I'm pretty sure the woman at the front desk who looks like your mother runs the show." She sat and placed the folder on Dan's desk. She glanced at the *Oz Express* and frowned.

"What brings you here?"

Sally nudged the folder toward Dan. "I want you to investigate my husband's murder."

"That's police work. And we've agreed to stay out of each other's way."

Sally nudged the folder a little closer. "I'm not happy with the cops' conclusions. They finished too fast. Didn't dig hard enough."

Dan leaned back in his chair. "That's not how things work. I -- and my firm -- have a healthy working relationship with the police. Second guessing them is not a way to keep it healthy."

"Read the file. This happened in Pyrmont. Virtually downtown Sydney. Miles from here. The Campbelltown Local Area Command won't give a shit what you do."

Dan looked at her for a beat, then slid the file onto his lap, leaned back and opened it. "You're very matter-of-factly talking about your murdered husband. When did this happen?"

"Three days ago." She nodded at the tabloid on the desk. "The day before that rag came out."

"Not that long, then."

"Different people grieve in different ways. And I'm more angry than anything else right now. Read the file."

"Tell me about it while I read."

Sally took a mouthful of water from her bottle and leaned back in her chair. "My husband works -- worked -- at the publishing company that prints that rag. He was one of four or five lawyers on staff to make sure no lines were crossed."

"Tonnes of lines are crossed every issue."

Sally nodded. "Yeah. He was getting burnt out telling that rat bastard Randolph Murray not to publish things and having them show up in the next day's paper."

"So why didn't he quit?"

"He did. The day he was killed. I'm positive that Randolph silenced him."

Dan looked up from the file. "This says straight mugging. Dragged into a dark lane off Harris street and shot." He looked up at the ceiling for a second. "I remember this. There was a load of press."

"Nobody likes a shooting in a recently gentrified neighbourhood."

"Take it they didn't find anything?"

"Just a regular old mugging. Which is bullshit."

Dan grimaced and dropped the folder on his desk. "The guy had other lawyers. Why would he want to kill your husband, just because he quit?"

"He didn't just quit. He was on the phone with me when he quit and I heard him tell Randolph that he was going to ruin him, financially and any other way he could."

"I'm sure he's heard that before."

"Probably not from a guy who kept copies of every legal document he created."

Dan placed his hand on the file. "I know what the police say happened. What do you think happened?"

Sally sniffed. "He still had his watch on. It was a Patek Philippe. It wasn't cheap. Any thief worth his salt would have taken that, too."

"Maybe they were interrupted."

"No. Jeremy was shot cleanly between the eyes. Instant death." Her voice caught. "Whoever did that wasn't in a rush."

"I'm very sorry for your loss. But I don't think I can help you."

"I can pay double your daily rate."

Dan slid the folder back across the desk to Sally. "It's not the money. We're in the middle of an all-hands case right now." He looked at his watch. "The calendar is really full."

Sally shook her head. "No. Not good enough. You're the fifth agency I've met with. You've got to help me."

"I'm truly sorry."

Sally sighed and collected the file. "Do one thing for me, okay? Meet me at the morgue tomorrow. I'm making arrangements to collect my husband's body."

"You think that would convince me?"

Sally stood and shrugged. "Maybe if you talk to the Medical Examiner." She dropped a card on Dan's desk. "This is the address. I'm going to be there tomorrow at 10 a.m. If I see you there, I'll see you there."

Dan watched her leave the office and heard her walk down the three flights and out the door.

Terry walked in with a keyboard under his arm. "So, we taking that lady's case?"

"You bugged my office?"

"I left one of the transmitters on your desk." He grinned and picked it out from behind Dan's monitor. "Testing its range. All good." He sat across from Dan. "So, the lady's case."

"Not really a case. It's a mugging gone bad."

"She was really insistent."

Dan sighed. "She's grieving. Denial is a stage of grief."

Terry crossed his arms. "That was anger I heard. She's pissed."

"Another stage of grief. And we're booked up." He looked at Beryl standing in the door, scowling at him. "I don't have time and it's a guaranteed loser."

"I didn't say anything," said Beryl.

"You didn't have to."

She glared at him. "Meet with her tomorrow."

CHAPTER 4

Sally circled the block twice before finding a parking spot by the Glebe Morgue. She turned off the engine and sat for a minute, hands gripping the steering wheel. She took a deep breath and got out. As she reached for the morgue door a hand reached past her and opened it.

"Allow me," said Dan.

A brief smile flicked across her face. "Thanks for coming. I didn't think you would. I thought you were too busy."

"The case that should have taken a week was wrapped up in a night. My team is putting the case docs together. I had nothing to do. Thought a ride into the big city would be fun."

"The woman at your front desk insisted you come, didn't she?"

"That's Beryl. And yes." He nodded toward the interior of the morgue. "So are we going in?"

She navigated the clearances required to view her husband's remains and a morgue attendant led her and Dan into a viewing area. They were met by the Medical Examiner.

"You're here for Jeremy Brookes' remains?"

Sally nodded. "This is Dan McGinnis. He's helping me investigate my husband's death."

"I'm Doctor Tobias Woods." He shook Dan's hand and handed him a business card. "Let me know if there's anything I can do to help."

Dan slid the card into his shirt pocket. "Thanks, Doc."

"Wait here," said Dr Woods. "I'll be back in a second." He left and the door slowly hissed shut. The room was not much larger than a big walk-in closet, white tiled and sterile. In addition to the door recently exited by the attendant there was what looked like a giant letter slot in the opposite wall.

Sally rubbed her arms. "Cold."

Dan raised his eyebrows. "Better that than too warm, down here." He slid his hands into his pockets and hesitated. "How was he killed?"

"Shot."

"Got that yesterday. Where, exactly?"

"In a dark lane in Pyrmont."

Dan looked at her. "Seriously."

"In the head. Between the eyes." A small smile passed across Sally's face. "He didn't get my humour either."

"That could be messy," said Dan. "You sure about this?"

"This isn't the first time I've seen him since then." Sally took a deep breath and let it out slowly. "Small calibre. All the damage was inside." She pressed her index finger against her forehead, just above the eyebrow line, directly above the bridge of her nose. "Right here."

"So the bullet was recovered?"

"It was. There was no ballistic match to anything in their systems." She rubbed her forehead. "It was immediate, instantaneous death. So I've been told. That's the only thing that gives me comfort."

The door opened and the attendant came back in. "Are you ready?"

Sally nodded and the attendant opened the door on the opposite wall and pulled out a gurney on rails. A male body, sheet up to his neck, came through head first.

"I'll leave you. Let me know when you're finished." The attendant left and the door hissed shut again.

Sally's breath caught. "Jeremy." She reached out and gently placed a hand on her husband's chest. "I'll miss you."

Dan kept his hands in his pockets and leaned forward, looking closely at the entrance wound. It had been cleaned up in the morgue and the incision to remove the scalp and top of the skull for the autopsy was clearly evident. He squinted and adjusted his position to get a closer look. "Stippling."

"What?"

He pointed at the head wound. "It's cleaned up a lot, but there's stippling. Powder burn. And a stellate pattern around the entrance wound. The muzzle was held against his head when the shot was taken." Dan glanced at Sally. She'd gone pale. "Sorry. I thought the police would have told you that already."

Sally shook her head. "They took a picture and said they're working the case, but I got the impression it would end up in the bottom of some detective's desk drawer."

"So you want my team to find the mugger?"

Sally pulled the sheet over her husband's face. "I told you, it wasn't a mugging. I want you to find out who murdered him."

Dan rubbed the back of his neck and stepped away from the body. "What makes you think it wasn't a mugging?"

"Again, like I said, he had his watch on when he was found."

Dan shrugged. "So? Muggers don't like to hang around. In and out. Go before anyone sees you. Probably was happy with what was in the wallet."

"A couple of hundred dollars. The watch was worth at least two thou. A mugger would have taken the watch. And my husband was coming to meet me with a pizza. No pizza box." She shook her head. "I'm wasting my time."

"Maybe. Not sure what you think I can do that the cops can't. They've got the labs and the manpower."

"And are overwhelmed with cases and won't give my husband's death the attention it deserves." Sally waved at the doctor through the window and her husband's body started sliding through the wall back into the morgue. "So will you help me or do I go somewhere else?"

Dan watched the body slowly disappear into the wall. "I would need a copy of the case file and I'd like to see where it happened."

"So that's a yes." It wasn't a question.

"It's not a no. How far away from here was," he rubbed the corner of his eye with his index finger, "Jeremy killed?"

Sally took out her phone, opened a mapping app and navigated to the location. "What's your mobile number?"

Dan told her and she sent the location to his phone. He opened it and nodded. "I'll see you there in fifteen minutes."

Dan stopped on Harris street and turned off his bike. A car door opened across the street and Sally got out. She had a large manila envelope tucked under her arm. Dan waited for her to cross to his side.

She handed him the envelope. "The police files."

Dan opened the flap and looked at the contents. There was a bundle of recently photocopied pages held together with a large holdback clip. "How'd you get this?"

"Not relevant." She pointed at the lane half a block up the hill. "We're going there."

Dan checked for surveillance cameras at the front of the shops as they walked side by side up the hill. "This would have been four days ago, right?" He looked at his watch. "Three and a half."

"Four days tonight." Sally stopped at the entrance of a lane between a Japanese restaurant and a Persian one. A piece of police tape attached to the Japanese side flapped in the light breeze. The area looked to be used solely for trash bin storage.

Dan wrinkled his nose and stepped into the gap. He opened the flap on the envelope and slid the pages half out. He thumbed through them until he found a crime scene sketch. He oriented the page and himself until he'd sorted out the geometry. He pointed at the back wall, a dark brick. "Over there."

Sally nodded, but stayed where she was. She leaned against the side wall, watching Dan.

"Doesn't make sense."

"Lately much of life doesn't." Sally slowly walked into the lane. "What are you talking about?"

"Your husband was found dead the very end of the alley, up against the back wall."

"I know. So what?"

Dan turned, back to the wall, and looked out toward the street. "He'd have to swap places with the mugger. Killer. And they would have passed each other in fairly tight quarters." He slid the drawing back into the envelope and tucked it under his arm. Four dumpsters lined the north wall of the lane. He lifted the lid of the one furthest in and looked in at the contents. "This hasn't been dumped in days."

"According to the report, the crime scene techs went through all of them."

"Find your husband's wallet?"

Sally frowned. "No, it was taken. I'm sure I told you that."

Dan lifted the lid of the next dumpster. "You did. Typically muggers take the cash and cards and dump the wallet."

Sally shook her head. "What have I been telling you? This *wasn't* a mugging. Someone killed him and did a piss-poor job of making it look like a mugging. Are you going to find the killer for me?"

"I can't say this was an entire waste of time. I got a nice bike ride in this morning. Beautiful day. You know it takes over an hour to get in here?" Dan took a breath as he stepped out of the lane. "So let's make the best of it. Where's a good place for coffee around here?"

"Just down the hill. Freshly made pastries, too."

"Let's go and you can explain to me who you think did this."

Sally ordered while Dan sat at a table outside. He slid the papers out of the envelope. He put the crime scene sketch to one side and looked at the photos. Jeremy was crumpled on the ground, half-leaning against the back wall. There was little blood. A small amount had leaked out of the hole on his head, but the instantaneous brain death stopped the heart just as fast.

Sally came out of the coffee shop and sat across from Dan, who stacked the photos together and tried sliding them back in the envelope.

She put her hand on his. "Don't worry about it. I've looked at the pictures. Enough times I could probably draw them from memory."

Two cups of coffee and pastries were placed on the table. Dan placed his hand over the images until the server left.

"Don't take this the wrong way, but you seem pretty cold about your husband's death."

"I don't have time to be hysterical."

Dan watched her eyes while he took a sip of coffee. "What do you do for a living?"

"I'm a neurosurgeon. Based out of North Shore Hospital." Sally took a pastry and slid the plate toward Dan. "Have one or I'll eat them all."

"A brain surgeon? I've never met one of those before. And Jeremy was a lawyer." He picked an egg tart off the plate and bit into it.

"Yes, we make," Sally paused. "We made a good living."

"Past tense? You left your job?"

"Taking a sabbatical. I'm due for a break."

"Planned before…?" Dan let the question tail off.

Sally sipped her coffee. She stared at him a minute before she responded. "No. I need to figure out who killed Jeremy. I can't operate on other people's brains if I'm distracted."

Dan finished off the egg tart and wiped the corners of his mouth with a napkin. "Makes sense. So let's get to the brass tacks. You seem really convinced this wasn't a run of the mill mugging, which implies that you've got some idea who did this."

Sally smiled wryly and shook her head. "I think he pushed way too hard at the office. They're ruthless. The things I know they've done for profit." She took a deep breath. "But I might be wrong. I'd rather you looked at this fresh. From ground zero."

"Okay." Dan considered her for a moment. "What was Jeremy doing in this neighbourhood?"

Sally pointed vaguely over her shoulder. "Jeremy works in Pyrmont. We'd get together in the park down by the water every month or so. He'd bring the pizza and I'd bring the wine. Rain or shine. It was usually a lovely night." She looked down. "He didn't make it."

Dan slid the papers into the envelope, closed the flap and handed them back to Sally. "You don't need my help. You seem to be doing a pretty good job yourself." He stood and finished his coffee. "Thanks for the snack. I've got a business to run. My condolences, and I wish you the best of luck."

Sally stood. "I wish you'd reconsider. I can't do this alone."

"You don't have to, Sally. The police are well equipped to sort this out." Dan's phone rang. He looked at the display and diverted the call to voicemail. "Best of luck, and thanks for considering my company." His phone chimed with a voicemail notification.

Sally took the envelope and pressed it into Dan's hands. "Take it. Read the police report. Give it a couple of days. Don't say no yet."

Dan sighed. "No promises." He slid the envelope inside his jacket and zipped it. "I'll call you in a couple of days."

Dan walked back up the hill to his bike. His phone started ringing again, as he approached it. Same number. He popped in his earbuds. "McGinnis Investigations."

"Dan. I'm disappointed."

"Join the long list. Who is this?"

"I hired you to void my prenuptial agreement."

"Oh, right. Disappointed, why?"

"One of your team, I think it was Andy Smith, sent me files and a summary from your surveillance last night."

Dan smiled and pulled on his helmet. "Disappointed we took so long?"

"Speed is only of value when the content is quality. This was shite."

"That's bullshit. I was on hand while it was collected. Drugs, hookers, some activity between consenting adults that's fine behind closed doors, but would be more than ample grounds for divorce. It's all gold."

"We can't use any of it. Nothing in the so-called evidence you sent violates the pre-nup."

Dan straddled his bike and placed his thumb on the starter. "Then send it back. I'll be invoicing you for the electronics we had to leave in the house." Dan terminate the call, swore under his breath and started his bike. "Fucking hell."

CHAPTER 5

Dan stayed off the motorways on the trip south back to Campbelltown. The file was pressed against his chest, held in place by his zippered leather jacket. His phone was in a cradle between the handlebars, playing Evanescence. He stopped at a red light, flipped open his recent calls and dialled Stew.

"What's up, boss?"

"Our client just called and she's very pissed off. Who put the package together?" Dan released the brake and accelerated with the traffic.

"Andy did. It was good though. Usual package. Never had a complaint before." There was a pause. "What was the problem?"

"Specifically, I'm not sure. Generally, she said there wasn't anything in our surveillance that would trigger the pre-nup."

Stew laughed on the other end of the line. "Damn. One hell of a pre-nup. That kid did fucking near everything. And we've got video *and* audio."

"You double check Andy's pack?"

"Not that I have to, but yeah. I sat with him while he pulled it together. Really good content."

"She's not paying for it."

"The bitch."

Dan chuckled and downshifted into a corner. "I'm invoicing her for the electronics. Ask Beryl to pull the inventory list together and write it up. I'm going to deliver it personally."

"You got it. When are you back?"

Dan looked at the time on his phone. "Forty-five minutes. Make sure everyone is there. We need to discuss some things."

"*Some things.* Sure."

Dan terminated the call and accelerated around a taxi. The symphony of angry horns brought a smile to his face.

Randolph sat back in his office chair, tablet on his lap. Mel sat across the desk from him, watching the mirrored images from his tablet slide across a monitor on the wall.

He scrolled slowly, stopping at an image of the young actor, bent over a glass-topped coffee table, snorting white powder through a rolled up fifty dollar bill.

He tapped on the screen. "The cover." He looked at Mel. "Tell him that's the cover unless he can come up with the necessary funds to keep it from being the cover. He's got forty-eight hours."

"The amount?"

Randolph thought for a minute. "Let's make it interesting. He's been banking off the 'boy next door, squeaky clean' image for a good long while. How much is it worth for him to keep his snow snorting off the front page?

Start at a million. Bump it up if he squawks."

"That's a steep starting price."

"I'm getting impatient. My retirement account isn't growing fast enough. Call him today."

Mel smiled and tapped her pen on the desk. "Sounds like a plan."

Dan rumbled to a stop in the parking space beside the surveillance van. He dismounted, walked around the back of the van and ran into Kat.

"This is getting ridiculous. I thought you went back south."

"I did. Then Billy did, too. I'm trying to avoid him. He's getting clingy."

"And...?"

Kat shuffled her feet. "Well, you were nice before. Not many nice guys around anymore."

Dan shook his head and walked past her. "No. Not interested. You're a big girl. You'll be fine." He unzipped his jacket and pulled out the envelope. "I've got work to do. There's a nice kebab shop down the road."

Dan bypassed his office and entered the conference room. The rest of the team, including Beryl, were sharing pizza and beer. He tossed the envelope on the table, grabbed a beer out of the fridge in the corner and put a slice on a paper plate. He dropped in the chair at the head of the conference table and twisted the top off the bottle. "Andy, how did you fuck this up?"

Andy choked on his mouthful of beer. He wiped the suds off his chin and looked around the table. The others were quietly laughing. "You prick. It was a perfect package. I can't help it if that's a normal day for him."

Beryl slid a sheet of paper across the desk. "The electronics are still in situ. I added an inconvenience margin."

Dan read the figures and smiled. "Thirty percent?"

"She pissed me off. So now what?"

Dan shoved the envelope to the centre of the table. "Maybe something here. Sally Brookes and her husband Jeremy had a date once a month in the park at the bottom of Harris Street in Pyrmont. He grabs a pizza at the pub on the top of the hill then meets her in the park where she has the wine." He cleared his throat. "Four days ago she waited in the park while her husband was killed in an alley half way there."

Stew tipped the envelope up and spread the papers across the table. He grabbed the crime scene photos. Andy and Terry poured over the police report. Dan watched them for a couple of minutes. Papers and pictures were passed among them. Beryl grabbed the crime scene photos from Stew and spent a considerable amount of time examining them.

"Thoughts?" asked Dan.

Stew stroked his handlebar moustache. "This is a mugging gone bad." He picked the crime scene sketch from the table. "What are we supposed to do with it?"

"Sally is convinced the mugging was staged and that he was a targeted kill."

"Based on what?"

Dan shrugged. "She's convinced. Wants to pay us a bag of money to prove it."

"There's nothing to prove. You met her this morning. Did she tell you who she thinks killed her husband?" Terry flipped through the pages of the police report.

"The turd who runs *Oz Express*."

Stew snorted. "Crock of shit. Waste of time case."

"Yeah, well, she's going to pay us, and we've just lost a pretty good paying gig." Dan reached across the table and took the police report from Terry. He stacked it with the rest of the papers and photos and butted the edges together. He slid them back into the envelope and handed it to Beryl.

"What am I supposed to do with this?" she asked.

"Copies, please. Four sets. Five, if you want to be involved."

"Come on, boss," said Andy. "This is a waste of time. There's got to be better things for us to do."

"Not right now, no." Dan leaned forward. "Look, even if we determine for the lady that this was a straight up mugging gone bad, we'll be providing a service to her. It'll let her rest easy, get off the conspiracy theory, if nothing else."

"What did you find out this morning?" asked Beryl.

Dan shrugged again. "Not much more than this. Her husband was walking to the park. He didn't make it. Got dragged into the lane and shot. Took his wallet but not his very expensive watch."

"Did they find the wallet at the scene?" asked Beryl.

"No. I asked the same."

Beryl collected the envelope. "I'll make some copies."

Dan stood and paced. "So, let's do it this way. We'll investigate this like it was a mugging, but with a bit more vigour than the cops appeared to have."

Stew groaned. "It's way the fuck up in Sydney. I left for a reason. Too busy. Too big. Too many arseholes."

"Who are you afraid of running into, Stew? What's her name?"

Stew stuck two fingers up at Andy. "Piss off, mate."

Beryl came back in and distributed copies of the report to the four men. "So where do we start? We're investigating this, right?"

"We are." Dan took the report and flipped it open. "The victim worked at *Oz Express*. I'll swing by there and see what I can find out about his work environment. See if there's any history we should know about. Wife seemed to think there was friction there." Dan chewed the inside of his lip for a second. "I've seen what they publish and it wouldn't surprise me." He rubbed an eye with the heel of his hand. "Let's not piss around. I'll see if I can get a meeting with the main guy. Terry, Andy, if the company had anything to do with this, it wouldn't have been the main guy. Security or a third party would have done it. You two scope out their security and see what you can find out."

Beryl sucked air between her teeth. "You're never going to get a meeting with the big guy, whatever his name is."

Stew looked up from his phone. "Randolph Murray."

"Think you can find out where he's having dinner tonight?"

Stew smiled. "Piece of piss. Shouldn't take long." He returned to his phone and started typing. "Tomorrow night good enough for you, boss?"

"What's tomorrow night?"

"He's going to be attending a business dinner at the casino. I think I can get you in."

"That works."

"What's my role in this?" asked Beryl.

Dan smiled. "I need a website set up for a sports management company. I'm the CEO."

"How deep?"

Dan scratched his jaw, thinking. "He's a media guy. He'll dig a bit. Medium depth. What can you do in twenty-four hours?"

"It'll be passable. Won't take that long."

"Good. I want you to go over the police report with a fine-toothed comb. See if there's anything squirrelly in it."

Dan returned to his office and took Doctor Wood's card from his shirt pocket. He checked the email address and sent the doctor a request.

CHAPTER 6

Andy stopped the hired black Escalade at the entrance to the casino. Terry jumped out of the front passenger seat and opened the back door. Dan stepped out, black suit, white shirt open at the collar and no tie. He nodded thanks to Terry and walked up the steps to the entrance. A sign inside the hotel casino directed attendees of the business function to an escalator to a floor of banquet rooms.

Dan walked up the escalator stairs into the casino. The banquet rooms were on the far side. The path through the casino was a maze, wending its way through blackjack, roulette, poker and craps, enticing -- or trying to -- those walking through to the other side. Dan paused near a blackjack table and watched for a bit. There were four players having horrible luck, one hitting on seventeen. He shook his head and kept walking.

Signs at the far side pointed to a ballroom and the sports function that Dan would have been attending as a guest of honour if it was a decade earlier.

A security guard approached Dan at entrance to the banquet room. "Invitation, please?"

Dan presented his phone. "Electronic version only, I'm afraid. Late addition to the gala." He opened his mail app and scrolled to the invite and expanded the bar code. He tipped the phone sideways and held it out for the scanner.

It beeped and the security guard looked at the scanner's display, waited for a response and nodded. "Good to go Mr McMaster. You're at table thirteen in the back."

He stepped into the large room and took stock. It was a standard layout - - a few dozen round tables evenly spaced over the floor, with a podium on the stage. Banners advertising the function ran across the top of the stage and large monitors on either side played highlights from the latest Grand Final.

A smaller monitor near the door displayed the seating arrangements. Randolph Murray was at table two. At the front.

Dan scanned the table markers until he found 'Two'. Randolph was there, drink in hand, with two other couples. Three seats were empty. A quick glance at Table Thirteen showed him it was still empty. "Perfect."

He casually walked to Randolph's table and took a seat to his right in front of name card that said M. Dvorak. The seat beside him had the name card D. Newman.

Randolph leaned back in his seat and looked at Dan. "I think you're at the wrong table, young man. That seat is for my Chief of Staff."

Dan stuck out his hand. "Absolutely, sir. I'm at table thirteen."

"So head back there before I alert security."

Dan smiled. "Absolutely. It's just, I'm such a huge fan. The way you've built your media empire is a - a - a model for what I want to do."

"You have me at a disadvantage. You know who I am. Who are you?"

Dan looked at his hand, still not accepted by Randolph, and pulled it back. "Daniel McMaster, sir. I run a sports agency firm. McMaster Elite."

Randolph started typing on his phone. "Never heard of you."

"Not surprising," said Dan. "We're small and boutique. Below the radar right now. But I want to expand."

The man across the table, a lean, angle-faced man in his forties with slicked back hair, laughed. "I like this guy, Rand." He stood and extended his hand across the table. "Name's Brad Harriman. I own the -"

"Yeah, the Hobart Warriors. Not doing bad for their first year."

Brad nodded. "Thanks. Also got a stable of horses and I own my own financial services company. You're right picking this guy as a model. He's done well." He squinted and cocked his head. "Do I know you from somewhere?"

"I don't think we've ever met."

"You ever play? You look like a front rower what used to play for the Rabbitohs."

"Not me, mate. Is this your wife?" A much younger blonde woman, made up within an inch of her life, sat beside Brad.

Brad looked confused for a second, furrowing his brow. Then he glanced to his left and smiled. "Yes. Julia. Third, actually. Pretty, isn't she? We met at the opening game last season." He pointed to the other couple at the table. "Toby and Eliza. Toby's got a good gig with HSBC making a shit-tonne on derivatives or futures or something like that. Eliza owns an art gallery in Newtown."

The look of distaste on Toby's face wasn't hidden. "Sit down, Brad. You're embarrassing yourself. Mr, what was it, McMaster? Stay away from Brad. Unless you want the ATO crawling up your arse."

Dan put his hands up, waist high, in surrender. "Straight arrow here." He sat back down. "Not looking for any illegal shortcuts. That's why I wanted to talk to you, Mr Murray. You have a reputation of making deals to get things done."

Toby grunted and shook his head. Dan glanced at him and turned back to Randolph. "You put confronting information in your newspapers and magazines. How do you manage to keep from getting sued?"

"Truth is a defence."

Dan nodded. "You must have a good legal team."

Brad laughed. "His guys are animals. A legal team like you wouldn't believe. And if he can't get them in the courts, he'll get them in the streets."

Randolph closed his eyes and took a deep breath. "Like Toby said, don't listen to Brad. He's a fool."

"A rich fool," said Brad.

"There's rich, and then there's rich." Randolph pinched the bridge of his nose. "What is it you exactly want, Mr McMaster?"

"Just some guidance, Mr Murray. A friend of a friend works for you in your legal department. I know you probably don't know the guy. Jeremy Brookes. Thin guy. Kind of a terrier, last I talked with him."

"When was that?"

Dan scratched his chin. "Oh, almost a year ago, I reckon. At a party where his wife was being honoured for a new brain thing she'd done."

Randolph returned to typing on his phone. "Your company website doesn't mention anything about travelling in such rarefied circles. What took you to that function?"

"Well," Dan shrugged, "one of my clients' mother is Director of Nursing at Royal North Shore. He went along as her date. I tagged along because who doesn't like a free meal?"

Randolph nodded. "Were you close?"

"No." Dan stopped. "*Were*? Why past tense?"

"I'm afraid Mr Brookes was killed not that long ago. I understand from the news that he was mugged in Pyrmont. Not that far from here. Careful on your way to your car."

Dan slumped back in his chair. "Really? Damn. He was such a nice man. His wife must be distraught." Dan blew out a breath. "I suppose I should give her a call." He leaned forward. "Was he in the middle of something with you?"

"His work had nothing to do with his mugging. In fact, he had quit that day. Walked out of an editorial meeting."

"Huh." Dan retrieved his phone from his pocket and started typing in its browser. "When was this?"

"I really can't remember, Mr McMaster. And it doesn't really matter."

"I found it." Dan held up his phone. "This was the cover just after he was killed. Did he quit over this?" The cover of *Oz Express*, with Cassie Johnson, filled the screen. "Was it the cover? Or one of the stories?" He shook his head. "None of them look good. I'm surprised he lasted as long as he did. Did he threaten you before he left?"

Brad reached across the table and tipped the phone so he could see the screen. "Oh, that was a great issue. You think that hottie," he snapped his fingers, "Cassie what's her name's got man junk?"

Randolph frowned. "The headline is *Johnson's Johnson*. How in the hell could you forget her name? And it doesn't matter if she does. As long as it sells issues."

Dan shook his head and slid the phone back into his jacket pocket. "Maybe you're not the role model I'm looking for."

"Oh, I'm pretty sure I'm not. And I'm pretty sure you don't own a sports management company. Why are you really here? Is McMaster your real name?"

"Looking into Jeremy's murder. Trying to map out his last day." He pointed at Randolph. "You appear to have played a large part in it."

Randolph looked around, raised his hand and signalled security. "Mr McMaster, or whoever you are, get the hell out of here. "

Dan slid back his chair and stood. "No need for security. I'm sure we'll talk again, Randy." He set a path to avoid the security intercept and made it to the door. He nodded at them and made his way down the escalator.

He reached the bottom and sent a text from his phone: "*Coming out. Be ready.*"

Randolph was turned in his chair. He watched Dan leave one set of doors as Mel came in a second set. He continued watching Dan's departure until he disappeared out of sight on the down escalator. He turned back to the table and acknowledged Mel. "Goddamned security in this place. Some ass-hat came in pretending to be someone else, implying I had something to do with JB's mugging."

"Who?" asked Mel.

"Some big fuck, said his name was McMaster something or other. I'd bet a thousand that wasn't his name."

"He knew JB?"

"Said he knew him. Said he was investigating his *murder*. Tracking his path on the last day he was alive."

Mel toyed with her napkin. "Why would he be talking to you?"

Randolph shrugged. "JB worked for me. He was killed after work. Nothing else. Don't get paranoid." He looked at his watch. "When does this thing kick off?"

CHAPTER 7

"Have fun boss. We'll be right here. Let us know when you're on your way out and we'll have the truck ready." Terry hopped back in the front seat of the Escalade and watched Dan walk up the steps into the hotel casino. "Where to now?"

"We park and wait while he's meeting Rand. What else?"

Terry brushed his had along the leather arm rest. "We take this baby for a spin. You think Dan would ever get one of these for the company?"

"We're not taking it for a spin." Andy pulled into the end of the long drop-off lane and tucked in behind a Mercedes S Class with two large men in well-cut suits leaning against it. "That's Randolph's car. Been doing some recce. Got a play?"

Terry chewed his lip for a second. "Well, if we're not testing this thing out…" He cleared his throat. "We brag about the bad asses that we are and see if they rise to the challenge."

"Seriously? The best you've got?" Andy shook his head and smiled as he cut the engine. "That's pathetic, mate." He made a point of looking at Terry's slight frame. "And 'bad-ass'? Really?

"What's your plan then, old man?"

Andy smacked Terry's chest with the back of his hand. "Follow me, don't push too hard. Don't be the young bull."

"Whatever that means."

"Old bull and young bull are on top of a hill looking down at all the cows for their taking. Young bull says to old bull, let's run down there and screw one of them. Old bull says, let's walk down and screw them all." He slapped the younger Terry on the back. "Don't force things."

"Got it." He shook his head as he opened the car door. "You don't think I look bad-assed enough?"

"Another six hard months at the gym, and maybe," Andy opened his door. "maybe someday you can grow up big like me." He flexed his bicep, straining his suit jacket. "If you eat all your greens and get your sleep."

They closed their respective doors and approached the Randolph security team. The two brutes noticed them and came to full alert. Both had shaved heads, low body fat and very, very tight suits. Gerald held out his hand. "Don't approach the vehicle."

Andy tapped himself on the chest. "Me, Andy. You?" He tipped his head close to Terry. "Talk to them like they're a breed of white ape. Small words, short sentences. It'll speed things up."

Terry chuckled. "Me, Terry. Me like big truck."

The tall guy placed his hand on his chest and said, "Me Gerald. You're nothing at all like a big truck. Now back the hell off before we turn the two of you into pretzels."

"Hang on, pal. We're just trying to kill some time. Our boss is in at this gala thingy and so is yours, I assume." Terry swaggered up to the Mercedes. "Gotta kill a couple of hours, right?"

"Kill a couple of yours?"

"What?"

"Right, sorry." The big guy put his hand on his chest. "Me, Gerald. You, fuck off."

"That is absolutely unnecessary. We're birds of a feather."

"Flock off, then," said Gerald. He stepped closer, looming over the much smaller Terry.

Andy inserted himself between the two. "Hey, Gerry. Chill, mate. Just mucking around."

Gerald stretched his neck. "Never 'Gerry'. It's Gerald. Go back to your truck."

"Terry, these guys don't want to play." Andy leaned close to Gerald and spoke quietly. "You're the meat for Randolph Murray, right?"

Gerald stood implacably, hands crossed in front of his groin.

"Nothing? You see, *my* guy is in there," Andy jerked his thumb toward the casino, "trying to hook up with your guy. In a business deal, of course. Not hook up like, hook up. And since we're going to be doing business together, I reckon it would be good to get to know each other."

The other guy stepped forward and pushed Andy back. "You reckon?"

Andy smiled and held his hands out in surrender. "Hey. No need for that. What's your name?"

"Beat it."

"Come on, now, joking aside, I've got a question," said Terry. "Help us out, maybe. We really are in the same line of work. Your guy has more power and visibility than our guy, but our guy's been moving up fast. What should we look out for? It's been pretty easy so far, wouldn't you say so, Andy?"

"Mice nuts, really. Drive him around. Our presence has been the

53

deterrent. Haven't to any more than glare at people to keep them out of our way."

"And out of our boss's way." Terry leaned forward. "You ever have to get physical?"

"Stay in my face and you'll find out," said Gerald.

"Come on, Gerald, ease up on the guys. We were beginners once, too," said Robert. He held out his hand. "Robert. We've been watching and taking care of Randolph for a couple of years. Don't mind Gerald. He's a bit of a tight-arse." He looked over at his partner. "He should relax on nights like this. It's an easy one. Unlikely we'll get ambushed sitting in front of this place."

"You get ambushed often?"

"You know what the guy does for a living. He makes a lot of enemies. What does your boss do?"

"He's got a sports management company. Small one. Building it up."

"So he probably hasn't pissed many people off."

"Some sports franchises, maybe," said Terry. "And if he gets bigger, probably definitely. You ever run into some heavy hitters?"

Robert shrugged. "Haven't met one I couldn't manage yet." He nodded toward Gerald. "The two of us are pretty adept at minimising the mess."

"You're the smarter one, right?"

Robert raised an eyebrow. "Don't tell *him* that." He walked toward Dan's SUV. "Nice wheels."

"It'll do. What's the worse you've come up against?"

"Oh, that's not something I'll ever talk about with you. And it's unlikely you'll ever get yourself in that type of situation, not with the kind of business your guy is in."

"Your guy is just a media guy."

Robert chuckled. "That doesn't quite cover it. More money in extorting those primping twats he puts on the cover. *That's* what gets hairy. A beat down or two usually pulls them in line."

"You're fucking kidding me," said Terry. He leaned close. "What kind of money do you guys get? You hiring?"

"What do you mean?"

Terry leaned back. "What do you think I mean? My guy pays shit. The job is boring. You sound like you get all the funs. Your guy hiring?"

Robert cocked his head and looked Terry up and down. "Bit of a pencil neck, Terry. I don't think, and please don't take this personally, but I don't think you could punch your way out of a robust spider's web. Knock down someone my size?" He chuckled and shook his head. "Ain't gonna happen."

"Hey. I'm wiry. Got some special ninja skills. I might surprise you." He raised his hands in a karate chop stance. "Wanna throw down?"

Robert looked at his surroundings. The high-end vehicles. Couples in expensive clothes. "Listen, kid, I don't want to hurt you, or embarrass you in front of your friend."

Terry looked over at Andy, leaning against their Escalade. "You're just worried Andy will jump in. Don't worry about that. He's lazy. Doesn't like me that much. Probably would *like* to see me get smacked around. Not that I would be. I can hold me own." He cleared his throat. "So what kind of stuff do you guys get into?"

"Above your pay grade, kiddo. Now fuck right off."

Terry stepped closer to Robert and lashed out and slapped him on the forehead. "Fuck off yourself."

Robert grabbed Terry by the throat and squeezed. "You little piss-ant. I'm going to crush your larynx and watch you suffocate to death."

Gerald grabbed Robert by the arm. "Jesus. Ease off, mate." He looked over his shoulder at the security watching them. "Not now."

Robert release Terry and stepped away. "Yeah. The little shit got me cranked."

Andy pushed himself off the Escalade and tapped Terry on the arm. "You don't look good, mate. You okay?"

Terry rubbed his neck. "You didn't see that?"

Andy's phone chimed. *Coming out. Be ready.* "Let's go, Ter. Good talking, lads. Got to run. Boss is coming out."

Gerald looked at his watch. "Three hours early."

Andy shrugged. "I go where I'm shoved. Catch you later, maybe."

Terry ran to the passenger side of the vehicle and stood by the back door massaging his throat. Dan trotted out the sliding doors and down the steps, a couple of security close behind him. Terry opened the back door and Dan slid in.

"Let's get going, guys."

Andy had the Escalade started and was beginning to pull away as Terry hopped in the front seat. He twisted to talk to Dan in the back. "Something you said?"

"More like who I said it too. You find out anything from the help?"

Andy left the drop-off area and accelerated into traffic. "They're not angels. Very hard lads. This Randolph guy isn't afraid to crack heads when needed."

Dan nodded. "Not surprising."

Terry rubbed his throat. "You really didn't see what that guy did?"

"I don't know what you're talking about."

"What, were you playing Angry Birds or something? That guy had me by the throat. Said he was going to kill me."

"Did he kill you?"

"Besides the point. What the *hell* were you doing?"

"Hey, guys." Dan leaned between the seats. "You're both okay. Let's get out of here. I got what I want."

CHAPTER 8

Dan knocked on the door and waited. He heard floorboards creak inside, then Sally peered through the curtains and opened the door.

"So good to see you. Does this mean you are going to take the case?"

He held up an index finger. "Not quite, but almost. May I come in?"

Sally stood to one side. "You want to see Jeremy's notes, his papers, his calendar, that sort of thing, correct?"

"I guess that's pretty obvious. Is that a problem?"

Sally motioned for him to sit in the lounge room. Dan sat in a stuffed chair. Sally sat on the sofa at right angles to him. "You've talked with Randolph already, haven't you?"

"We bumped into each other last night. We spoke a bit. I don't think he likes me much."

"He doesn't like anyone. Do you think Jeremy's work will help?"

Dan shrugged. "It can't hurt. There isn't enough from the initial discussions I've had to convince me, but I'm willing to be convinced." He looked at his watch. "It hasn't been a week. Do you think they've cleaned his office out yet?"

"I'm supposed to stop by tomorrow and pick up his personal effects."

"Which means they'll pack the office at the end of today. It's not even noon yet. Let's go."

Sally stopped at the reception desk in the *Oz Express* media offices. Dan stood to her left and slightly behind. She waited until the receptionist was off the phone before she spoke. "Good morning. I'm Sally Brookes. I'm supposed to be picking up my husband's personal effects. Jeremy Brookes."

The receptionist stared at Sally for a second, then past her to Dan. He fumbled with his handset and dialled a number. "Hi, Larry here. Reception. Uh, Mrs Brookes is here for her husband's personal effects. She isn't scheduled until tomorrow."

He listened for a minute, then looked up at Dan. "No, she's here with someone else."

"This is my brother," said Sally. "Dan. He's here to help me."

The receptionist nodded and spoke into the phone. "Her brother." He nodded and then spoke. "Okay. No problem."

He replaced the phone on the cradle and smiled sadly at Sally. "You know where his office is, right? Mel said you could get his belongings. She'd come out to see you, but she's got an editorial meeting to attend."

"That's okay." Sally nodded at Dan and walked to her husband's office. The name plate on the door said *Jeremy Brookes, Legal*. She slid the plate out of the frame and dropped it in her purse. She paused with her hand on the doorknob, then twisted it and entered.

Dan followed her in and closed and locked the door behind them. "You put on a show of going through his personal effects and I'll look at the work files. Take your time. I'm going to need a box for anything interesting we want to secrete out of the building."

A smile cracked Sally's face. "Like secret squirrel stuff."

"Kinda sorta."

An hour later Dan followed Sally out of the office. Sally carried a box with personal effects: a bowling trophy, a couple of stress relief balls, a personal desk lamp, family pictures flat on the bottom. Her purse sat on top.

 Dan carried a large potted plant.

"Thanks for this, Dan. I didn't realise how difficult it would be."

"No worries."

The receptionist stepped out from behind his desk and held out a hand. "Sorry, I've got to check."

Sally glanced back at Dan who stepped up beside Sally.

He held out the potted plant. "What to check it out?"

"No, that's fine." Larry pointed at the box. "Just need a peek in there."

"I'm not going to steal your fucking office supplies." Sally tipped the box forward. "Look all you want."

The framed pictures had slid forward. On top, partially obscured by the bowling trophy, was a picture of Sally and Jeremy embracing on a beach, sunset in the background. "Yeah, I'm just doing my job. Everything looks okay. We're really sorry for your loss."

Sally jerked the box back upright. "Right."

Dan smiled at the receptionist. "Thanks, Larry. You've been very helpful."

Dan placed the potted plant on the kitchen counter and Sally placed the box on the dining table. She removed the trophy, stress balls and framed pictures and put them to one side. Dan retrieved the three file folders from the bottom of the box and placed them on the table. He took off his leather jacket and hung it on the chair and sat. He spread the files in front of him.

"Can I get you a cup of coffee?" asked Sally.

Dan opened one of the file folders and looked up. "That would be great. Black please." He slowly flipped through the pages, reading Jeremy's notes in the margins. He folded a couple of corners over and put the folder to one side. Opened the second and did the same. Sally placed a mug of coffee in front of him, on a coaster, as he opened the third.

"Thanks."

"Find anything?" She sipped her tea.

He lifted the first page and read some hand-written notes in red pen. "Jeremy hated his job."

"Really?"

He looked at her. "You're surprised? For real?"

"Not surprised. I knew, but he was never explicit." She sat at the table across from him. "What did you find?"

He gestured at the other two files. "Dozens of cases where Rand was pushing for one scandal or another to be published and Jeremy pushed back. Usually unsuccessfully." He closed the file in front of him and pulled the first he had opened. "Libellous stories about Australian, American and European celebrities. He lets it run for a few weeks, then prints a retraction. At that point it's too late; the issues and advertising has been sold and the money made off the scandal."

Dan flipped to a page deeper in the first folder. "It looks like he's started extorting some of them, too. When the facts are real -- when he's got solid evidence to back up the scandal -- he presses for substantial amounts of money to kill the story. Sometimes he kills it after he gets the money, sometimes he publishes anyway. Jeremy kept a record of all of it."

Sally shook her head. "That's not enough. There's nothing that says

Randolph knew about Jeremy's notes. No motive."

"Not yet."

"You think there might be something?"

Dan closed the folder and sat back in his chair. "It doesn't smell like a mugging gone bad. Too many things off-kilter." He shook his head. "But I haven't found anything, so far, that points to anyone in particular." He placed his hand on the files. "Certainly any of the extorted or defamed celebs could target him, but that's kind of farfetched. They wouldn't necessarily know of Jeremy's involvement."

"And none of them would have the wherewithal to get their hands on a gun. Pampered, the lot of them."

He sighed. "Let me take these files back to my office. I'll have the team pour over them, see what we can find. I'll give you a call later tonight, okay?"

She nodded. "Stay and finish your coffee though."

Dan cradled his cup with both hands. "Why did Jeremy stay there?"

"He was an idealist. He was the very first day I met him. It was a frog in the pot scenario."

Dan raised his eyebrows.

"You know. He was in cold water that slowly heated up and he didn't realise the predicament he was in until it was too late. Randolph started pretty legit."

"Then slowly slid into the slime."

"That's about right," said Sally. "And he dragged Jeremy along with him."

"And Jeremy's role?"

"At first it was just him. Passed muster on the stories. Made sure there was legal footing. The enterprise was small and it couldn't afford lawsuits."

"And then he grew," said Dan.

"Slowly, over a few years. Then 2009 happened." Sally sipped tea.

"Black Saturday?"

She waved that away with a shake of her head and placed the cup on the saucer, rattling as her hand shook. "No. That was a terrible thing, but Randolph played that straight. Later in the year. Early August. A bunch of dawn raids in Melbourne snagged an Islamic terror cell. They were planning suicide attacks on Holsworthy Barracks."

"I remember. Seems pretty straightforward," said Dan.

"You'd think. Rand is a piece of shit, though, so he milked the Islamic part of the story for weeks. The usual bullshit about all Muslims being terrorists, and he whipped up a frenzy that lasted over a month, leading up to the September 11 anniversary."

"What a dick."

Sally pushed her cup and saucer back. "Jeremy wasn't happy with the tripe Rand was publishing, but the public sentiment was what it was, he didn't have to push too hard. I think that was the turning point for him."

Dan tipped back the last of his coffee. "Interesting story, but nothing in it to justify Rand as a suspect." He closed the folders and stacked them in a pile. He pulled on his jacket and started the zipper, then slid the folders inside. He zipped the jacket closed, trapping the files. "I'll have a closer look at these in the office. I've got a smart team. I'll give you a call later tonight. Thanks for the coffee."

"It wasn't just a mugging, Dan. Rand Murray had something to do with it, I know it. He was targeted and the cops aren't doing anything about it."

Dan smiled apologetically. "No guarantees. I'll call you tonight, one way or another."

CHAPTER 9

Dan dropped the files on the conference room table. "So, what do you have?"

The whole team was there. Beryl sat to his left. Further down on that side was Stew. Andy and Terry were on his right.

"What's the goal here?" asked Beryl. "What are we trying to do?"

"We're seeing if there's any point in looking into the case of the murder of Jeremy Brookes. Or do we believe the cops, that it's a mugging gone bad. Have you found anything that might challenge that?"

Beryl rested her hand on the police report. "Something bugged me the first time I read the report -- no pizza box."

Stew sighed. "Kinda weak."

"And there's something else." Beryl drew a three-sided, long narrow rectangle on the whiteboard, representing the alley. She drew a stick figure at the closed end of the box and rectangles along one of the long sides.

She pointed at the stick figure. "Jeremy was here, all the way into the box canyon. It's like he was stood up against the wall." She pointed at the rectangles. "These dumpsters mostly block the path to the back. To get back there, he would have had to traverse that narrow space. Or, more accurately, the mugger would have to move him back there. In close quarters."

She picked up a red marker and placed a large 'X' over the drawing. "A mugger would take the money and run. If he was going to shoot, he wouldn't move the guy to the back of the alley to shoot him. He'd shoot him where he stood."

Dan nodded. "You're right. It doesn't make sense."

"Plus," said Beryl, "Jeremy still had his watch. A very nice watch."

"Thief maybe just wanted cash. Didn't want to fence an easily identifiable time piece."

"That's thin," she said. "A fence would maybe only give them ten cents on the dollar, but it's free money. They would have taken the watch. I certainly would have. It's beautiful."

Dan slid the three folders to Stew, Terry and Andy. "Beryl makes good points. Not a mugging gone wrong. I buy it."

Andy opened the folder in front of him. "What's this?"

"Jeremy's notes. As many as we could smuggle out of his office. Jeremy was the head of legal for Randolph Murray's publishing empire. Lately Jeremy's been on Rand's bad side," said Dan. "Look, I agree that it's a no brainer that something strange happened when Jeremy was shot. Too many inconsistencies, not just a mugging. I don't know who killed him, but I think our client is right. To a degree."

Andy sat forward. "Wait, she's our client now?"

"I think it's interesting enough to pursue. She's fixated on this Rand guy being behind her husband's death. Not sure about that, but this beats investigating pre-nup violations."

"It's way the fuck up in Sydney," said Terry. "I don't have contacts up there."

Dan smiled. "Stew already used that whine. An opportunity to expand our footprint. Plus, we're going to lose money on the Callum Ryan thing."

Stew was flipping through one of the folders. He shook his head. "This guy is horrible." He jabbed his finger on the page. "Printed patently untrue information about two of the Green party members and only retracted it when they backed off a bill against a coal mine one of his buddies was opening in FNQ. The day the bill went through, the paper printed a retraction and threw one of their junior reporters under the bus." He flipped forward a couple of pages. "Looks like that particular journo is now filing police blotters in Darwin."

Terry pointed at a sheet in his folder. "Same kind of thing here. Jeremy's notes are brutal, though. Surprised he stayed there as long as he did."

Beryl grabbed the file folder from Stew. "No indication that Rand thought Jeremy a threat, right? Nothing that points to him or *Oz Express* as the perp behind the crime. So this would be a full on investigation. Could take the five of us off everything else for a couple of weeks." She turned to Dan. "She willing to pay that much?"

"We'll find out soon enough. You're right. A lot of shoe leather required for this. Investigating what the police have already investigated, in an area we don't normally operate." He looked at each of his team in the eyes, holding the gaze for a few seconds with each. "This will be full on. We may end up with a no decision."

"Hey, if we can at least put enough together to convince the cops something is wonky," said Andy.

"Fuck that." Terry slapped the folder closed and shoved it down the table to Dan. "If that arsehole is in *any* way involved I want to tank him. Hard."

Dan smiled and nodded. "All agreed?"

Nods and mutterings of assent came from around the table.

He placed his hands palms down on the table. "Excellent. We start tomorrow morning, here, with a kick-off meeting. Beryl, hang around for a few minutes. The rest of you can take off."

Andy handed his folder to Dan, who placed it on the one Terry had slid back. He added Beryl's to the pile.

"You want me to put together the costing?" Beryl flipped open her pad and poised her pen.

"Yeah. A week's worth. Assume a few days overnight in Sydney each, including you. The usual expenses. There's going to be a lot of leg work. I'll put a plan together tonight."

"Electronics?"

"I'm going to need to insert some in unfriendly places, so mostly covert stuff." He smacked his hand on the table. "Shit. Most of that is still in that kid's place. We'll have to use what we've got." He looked at his watch. "Can you get me a ballpark number within the hour? I'd like to sew the client up before we end for the day."

"Not a problem. I'll email the numbers to you."

"Thanks."

Beryl left and Dan stood and wiped her drawing off the whiteboard. He thought for a second, then started listing the activities planned for the next week, and who would be performing them.

Half an hour later Beryl came into the meeting room and dropped a sheet of paper on the table. She looked at the whiteboard filled with notes. "I emailed it, too. Thought you'd be gone by now."

"Still sorting out the details." He added a note, then stepped back. "It's a start." He picked the paper off the table and looked at the numbers. "Cost or with margin?"

"Our time plus twenty percent on the expenses."

Dan nodded. "Great. Thanks again. Go home, see you in the morning."

"See you tomorrow, boss. Turn off the lights when you leave."

Dan chuckled and sat at the head of the table. He waited until Beryl left then scrolled through his phone to the number. He put in his earbuds and called.

"Sally speaking. Is this you, Mr McGinnis?"

"Good evening, Sally. And it's just Dan, okay?"

"You're taking the case?"

Dan picked up the paper. "I had a long chat with the team, weighed the pros and cons, and assuming we can come to an agreement on terms -"

"Jeremy had a very healthy insurance policy, plus neither of us have been working for free for quite a long time. I don't care how much it's going to cost."

Dan smiled and placed the paper on the table. "Dangerous words. You're lucky my accountant isn't on the line." Dan cleared his throat. "We're kicking off tomorrow morning and will head up there tomorrow afternoon."

"So you *do* think Randolph is involved?"

"Don't know," said Dan. "But we are convinced it wasn't just a bad mugging. I'll give you a status update in a couple of days."

He signed off and scrolled through his contacts again. "Warren, mate, need a favour."

"Another drive by and disperse? How'd that go?"

"Thanks for that. No. I'm looking for a contact in Sydney PAC. Looking into an incident in Pyrmont."

"That's way out of my jurisdiction, mate. Yours, too."

"You know some people who know some people, though, right?"

Warren sighed on the other end of the line. "I'll see what I can do."

"Tonight, right? I'm heading up there tomorrow. Need to know who to talk to."

"I said I'll see what I can do. I'll ping you with what I find out. You owe me."

"I will if you come through. Thanks."

Dan terminated the call, placed the phone in camera mode and took a picture of the whiteboard. "This is going to be interesting."

CHAPTER 10

Dan parked his bike on St John's Road in Glebe, just outside Sydney's city centre, and a block away from the Glebe police station. He checked his watch. Warren had set up a meet with a Detective Sr Sergeant at a coffee shop. A Detective who might know something about the case. Dan was about ten minutes early. He left Beryl to run the kick-off back at the office.

He stepped up to the barista. "Large flat white. One of those banana nut muffins, too, please."

"Sure. Name?"

"Dan. I'll be at an outside table."

"We'll bring it out. Want the muffin heated?"

"Hell no. Thanks." Dan handed cash to the barista.

The barista's laugh followed Dan to the outside table. He unzipped his jacket and placed a file folder on the table. It was a beautiful late November day. Mid-twenties at 9:00 in the morning and cotton clouds in the sky.

The coffee shop was jammed between other two and three story buildings lining a narrow road. A post office branch was across the street, next to a community center advertising yoga classes for suburban mums and badminton on the basketball courts.

He checked the message from Warren again. He was waiting for a Detective Senior Sergeant Bruce Chang. Warren had sent a head shot, but it looked at least ten years old.

A server brought out a mug of coffee and a small plate with the muffin.

Dan placed his phone on the table and made some space. "Thanks."

The server looked at the photo on the phone and smiled. "You looking for Bruce?"

"We're catching up. Having a chat. He's a regular, is he?"

A middle aged, slightly gone to pot Asian man pulled out the chair across from Dan. He had a wispy fifteen year old's moustache. "I am." He smiled at the server. "The usual, Di. Thanks." He settled into the chair and stared intently at Dan.

"Detective Chang, I presume?"

"The one and only. Warren says you're okay. A real White Hat. Like an Australian Dudley Do-Right."

Dan leaned forward and extended his hand. "Who?"

"It doesn't matter. Says you're good. To a fault."

"I am. Are you?"

Chang half stood and shook Dan's hand. "He didn't say?"

"He didn't say."

Chang sat back in his chair, half a smile on his face. "Huh. Well. What can I do for you? Something about a case we handled poorly?"

Dan slid the file folder part way across the table. "I'm not saying it was

70

handled poorly. I'd just like another take on it."

Chang flipped open the file, glanced at Dan, then started reading. He turned the pages one at a time, every couple of minutes.

Dan sipped his coffee and picked at his muffin. "Don't want you thinking that *I* think you didn't do a good job. Just think there might be an alternate view."

Chang nodded without looking away from the file. "Uh-huh. Sure."

"So, there are some aspects of this case that make me and my colleagues believe it was a targeted hit, not a mugging gone bad."

Chang looked up, dead smile on his face. "Kinda figured you'd think that, Dan. You wouldn't be travelling all the way up here to pat me on the back and whisper sweetness in my ear." He closed the folder and pushed it back toward Dan. "Which brings me to my first question: What brings you hell and gone from the sticks you normally reside in?"

Dan pointed at the file. "Victim's wife wants us to take a closer look. She doesn't think the official report is complete."

"And she went all the way down to Campbelltown to find you? Don't you wonder why?"

"Why, what?"

"Why'd she drive an hour south and retain a small PI agency when there are barrels full of them around here?"

Dan shrugged. "Her money's as good as anyone else. Better than some, I'd guess."

"Were you her fifth or sixth choice?"

"I didn't ask." Dan smiled. "She said fifth."

"Hmm." Chang pointed at the police report and left his finger on the paper. "And how did you get a copy of this?"

"From my client. I wouldn't know how she managed to get it."

"You know, technically you shouldn't have this and technically I could keep it, but I expect you've got a copy. Or copies." He slid the file back to

Dan. "A bit of a head start for you, with the police report," said Chang.

"And the autopsy report." Dan closed the file folder and tucked it inside his jacket. "Were you actually involved in the investigation?"

"A couple of my Detective Constables were. They briefed me. Guy's walking down Harris street and gets dragged into a dark lane and is robbed and shot. Or shot and robbed. No difference."

"True," said Dan. "Can't dispute the facts. But you missed a couple. Facts, that is."

"What else do you need to know?"

"The guy had a pizza. Did you find a pizza box anywhere? And his watch. Worth a couple of grand. Still on his wrist when your boys showed up."

"One was a woman."

"What?"

"One of the detectives on this case is a woman. And those 'facts' aren't relevant. The mugger grabbed the pizza, if there was even a pizza, and was scared off before he could take the watch. So what?"

"Kinda weird, if you ask me."

"What are you trying to find?" Chang leaned back as the server delivered a cup of tea and an orange poppy seed muffin.

Dan pointed at the muffin. "You eat enough of those you fail a drug test, you know that, right?"

Chang pulled the top off the muffin and laughed. "Maybe if I eat a dozen of them in one sitting." He dipped part of the muffin top in his tea. "So like I said, what are you expecting to find?"

"Don't know. Looking into it as much as we can. The wife thinks the guy's employer was pissed at him." He slid his case folder across the table to Chang.

Chang chewed the muffin and opened the file. He read through the top page, then stopped chewing. "Randolph Murray? You're gunning for Randolph, mother-fucking Murray? Been nice knowing you, man. He's going to disassemble you."

"So you've run up against him before?"

"Not personally. I've still got a job. You know what they say: Don't pick a fight with someone who buys ink by the barrel."

"It's all online now."

Chang sighed. "Worse." He washed down the muffin with tea and wiped his lips with a napkin. "I can't stop you from doing whatever you're going to do. Wouldn't think of it. But I can warn you that you're in for a battle if you're going against The Rand."

"*The Rand*? Seriously?"

"Look, *you* wanted to see *me*. I can't offer any other insights on this so called mugging gone bad. No, we're not going to reopen the case. Randolph didn't kill him. He wouldn't get remotely close to getting his hands dirty. And if he had someone kill the victim -"

"Jeremy Brookes."

"Right. Brookes. If Rand wanted Brookes dead, the number of cut-outs between him and the actual killer would fill the Opera House. So good luck with that." He pulled another piece off of the muffin. "Anything else?"

"A man gets killed and the first thing any competent investigator checks -"

"- is the wife." Change nodded. "Detecting 101."

"According to your file, she has an alibi. She was in the park with a friend, waiting for her husband."

"As I was saying. If it's not the wife, and everything else looks like a mugging, it's a mugging."

"Who was the alibi? There's no name in the file."

"She is a prominent woman. Since it checked out we agreed to keep the name out. And no, I'm not going to tell you."

Dan pulled the file back and closed it. "Fine. So you don't mind if my team and I poke around in your jurisdiction?"

"Would it matter if I did? You're going to do it anyway. I'm here every morning at 10:00. At least the days I'm on duty. Pop by if you want a muffin. Next one's on me." He wiped his face and stood. He brushed the crumbs off himself. "As far as the Sydney PAC is concerned, this is a closed case." He nodded and walked back toward the station.

Dan watched him leave. "Huh. Well, that's the cops, then." He took a mouthful of coffee and scrolled his contacts. He found the number he was looking for and poked it.

"Sally Brookes speaking."

"Sal, Dan here. I'm in your neck of the woods and thought maybe we could catch up. Did Jeremy have a laptop?"

There was a pause on the line. "Sure. Where are you?"

Dan told her the name of the coffee shop. "It's right around the corner from the Glebe police station. That's close to where you live, right?"

"I know the place. It's walking distance. I thought you were coming by in the afternoon."

"An appointment brought me in early. It's not too much of a problem?"

"No, none. What do you want Jeremy's laptop for?"

"I won't know until I see it."

Sally sighed. "Okay, fine. I'll be there in five. Can you get Di to make me a large flat white?"

"Sure. See you soon." Dan hung up and popped into the cafe. "Di, right? Diane? Can I get a large flat white for the table?"

"Sure thing. You know my name, what's yours?"

"Dan McGinnis."

"Of the McGinnis Book of World Records?"

Dan chuckled. "Haven't heard that since high school. I'll be outside. Thanks."

He sat down as Sally came around the corner across the street. She had a laptop bag over her shoulder. She saw Dan, waved and trotted across the narrow street. She sat at the table as Di came out with the coffee.

"Hey, Sally. Dan's meeting all the old regulars."

"Thanks, Di." Sally waited until the server left, then opened the bag and handed the laptop to Dan. "This won't be much use to you."

"Why's that?" Dan opened the laptop and was greeted by a login window.

"I don't know his password."

"Secretive?"

"We respected each other's personal space." She smiled. "Seemed like a good idea at the time."

Dan tried a couple of passwords and slowly closed the lid. "I've got a clever guy on my team that will have a look at it."

"There wouldn't be any work related info on it. Not sure how getting into it will help."

Dan slid the laptop into the case. "On the off chance his death is not work related. There might be something on this thing that helps." He closed the case. "Tell me about him. Not work information. Personal information. What he liked doing in his spare time. Hobbies. Passions. That sort of thing."

Sally sniffed. "If I'm honest, he was pretty boring. His work was his life. We enjoyed movies and the odd show at the Opera House. We'd take three or four weeks overseas trips every year."

"Where'd you go last time?"

Sally absent-mindedly turned her coffee cup in its saucer. "July. Japan. Spent three weeks there and then a week in Seoul. It was our first time for both places. I really enjoyed the time together. Jeremy works so hard. Worked so hard. He'd come home from the office and spend another three or four hours reviewing copy, defending the organisation from lawsuits, generally covering Rand's arse. It was a thankless job."

"I'm surprised he didn't go somewhere else."

"I told him the same thing, many times. He felt he was the only thing standing between Rand and a lot of destroyed careers."

"Quixotic, I think."

"Maybe." Sally sipped her coffee in thought. "So what's next?"

"I met Randolph under less than ideal conditions last night. I need to see him in his office." He looked at Sally. "I need your help."

"What were these less than ideal conditions?"

"I crashed a banquet he was at. Pissed him off, I think." He grinned. "Nah, I definitely pissed him off. I won't get in without help."

Sally nodded and placed a call on her mobile.

"Hello, Mel. I need to see the boss for fifteen minutes." She listened for a minute, then held her hand over the mouthpiece. "This afternoon okay?"

"Sure thing," he said.

"This afternoon at 2:00 would be great. Thanks." She ended the call and smiled at Dan. "Easy. They're feeling very guilty. I think they have a reason to be."

Dan checked the time. "Four hours." He tapped the laptop. "Time enough to get this back and meet you…where?"

"Outside of their office." She scribbled an address on the napkin. "You know the place? Pyrmont near the fish market. About a kilometre from here."

"I can find it." Dan folded the napkin and slid it into his shirt pocket. He tucked the laptop into its case and stood. "Thanks. I'll see you then."

CHAPTER 11

Dan idled to a slow roll into his parking spot and turned off the bike's ignition. The immediate localised rumble of his bike was replaced by a distant, but growing, rumble of, by his ear, at least six bikes. He dismounted and turned to wait for their arrival.

Billy was in the lead, sitting low, looking hard in the harsh daylight, despite the flab and the t-splint on his nose. Six others, in two rows of three, rolled along behind him. Dan glanced up at the windows on the third floor, then back at Billy and his friends.

"Ah, shit. This is the last thing I need right now." Dan stood facing the seven approaching bikers, feet shoulder width apart, hands loose in front of him.

Billy dismounted and walked toward Dan. He spread his hands out as Dan tensed up. "You look nervous."

Dan nodded toward Billy's entourage. "You're coming in hot. If I'd known, I'd have brought friends, too."

He heard the back door slam behind him. Stew stepped up on Dan's left and Andy on his right.

"Right here, boss," said Stew. He cracked his knuckles. "I think the three of us can take them."

Billy shook his head. "I know you pack a wallop, gramps, but no, that's not why I'm here."

"Too bad." Stew bunched his shoulders and relaxed. "I'll have to relieve the tension some other way."

"Go whack off, gramps. Your boss and I gotta talk alone."

Stew took a step forward. "Right. Seven against one isn't very sporting."

"Surprised you can count that high." Billy waved at his entourage and they started their bikes and rode out of the lane. "So it's three against one now. But I'm not here to fight. Let me talk to your boss alone."

"It's okay, guys. I'll be up in a second."

Andy clapped Dan on the shoulder. "We'll keep an eye on you."

Billy waited until Stew and Andy had entered the back entrance. "It's about Kat."

"Lovely lady. You shouldn't hit her."

"That's none of your fucking business.."

"I'm not going to look for her, if that's what you want." Dan leaned against his bike and crossed his arms.

"You do that sort of thing, though, right? Find missing persons?"

"Uh-huh. Sometimes. Pays the bills. But if we think the client intends harm on the missing person, we don't. Ever. For any price."

Billy balled up his fists and took a step toward Dan.

"That's not helping your cause, mate." Dan stood up off his bike. "And you should probably piss off now before I do something I probably won't regret later."

Billy stood rigid for a second, then backed off a step. "We'll talk again."

Dan waited until Billy was back on his bike and on his way out of the lane before he opened the saddlebag and retrieved the laptop. He walked into the office, heading directly to the conference room. Stew was at the window, packing up a directional microphone. Andy and Terry sat on one side of the table, Kat and Beryl on the other. Dan slid the laptop across the table to Terry.

"Hello, Kat."

Beryl handed her another tissue. "Why didn't you take the case, Daniel?"

Dan scratched at his jaw and looked at Stew. "She heard it all?"

Stew smiled. "Every word, boss."

"He called her a bitch." Dan leaned down and looked in Kat's eyes. "He called you a bitch. AND, you told me, he hits you. Why would I take that case?" He sat down beside her. "You're better than that."

Beryl took Kat's hand. "Let's get you cleaned up and find a place for you to stay tonight."

"Thanks Beryl." Kat wiped her nose.

Dan interrupted their departure. "Kat, I want to talk to you in a couple of minutes, okay? The rest of you, stay here."

Stew finished packing the surveillance gear and sat at the table. The door swung shut behind Kat and Beryl and he leaned forward. "We going after Billy?"

Dan scoffed. "Nope."

Terry opened the laptop and wiped his finger across the touchpad. "Who's is it?"

"It belongs to Jeremy Brookes. Look for anything that shows state of mind over the past three or four weeks. Just mine the thing."

"I've got to get into it yet. That might take a minute or two."

"How long is a minute or two?"

Terry shrugged. "I'll have to brute force the password. Which will take as long as it takes. Hopefully the guy didn't have a thirty character password with alphas and symbols. He's old. It was probably 'passwerd' with an 'e'. I'll get started on it." He carried the laptop into the audio/video lab and rummaged through one of the drawers. Dan followed him in. "I've got a thumb drive around here somewhere that'll do the trick."

"Can you set it up to do that brute force thing while you do something else?"

"Super easy. So what exactly are we expecting to find in this Brookes case? He was shot. The cops, I'm assuming, still think it's just a bad mugging."

Dan tossed a business card on the table. "Detective Chang is happy that it's an open and shut case. Can't say he seemed too interested in any alternative theories."

Stew walked in and picked up the card and grunted. "He's pretty good."

"You know him?"

"Bumped into him a couple of times in my past life on the North Shore. Wasn't a Detective back then. Constable. Out of Chatswood at the time. Good cop, though. He picked up the son of one of my customers for shoplifting. Emmanuel something. Kid couldn't shut up. I had a talk with Chang and got him to drop it as long as I kept the kid clean. Got him to lift rock for me." He chuckled. "The kid really put on some beef. Got hooked on weights. Turned into a gym rat. Chang's a reasonable guy."

"Maybe he's getting sloppy as he gets older." Dan scratched his jaw. "Got nothing new from him, though."

"So what next?"

"I'm going to need some covert surveillance equipment. Audio definitely. And a couple of small video if I get a chance."

"Store or send?" asked Terry.

Dan thought for a minute. "Store."

"We going in tonight? I'm going to need to get some sleep this afternoon. Still shagged from the last one."

Dan shook his head. "I'm taking them with me to a meeting with Randolph Murray this afternoon, hoping I get a chance to insert them somewhere."

Terry's hands froze above the keyboard. "Murray?"

"That's fucking nuts, Dan," said Andy. "Insane. While he's in there?"

Dan shrugged. "If I can get him out for a minute, I obviously will. But assume I can't. Get and prep the best, smallest, most covert devices we've got."

"Most of the good shit isn't here. We'll do what we can. How are we getting in?"

"No 'we', Andy. Just me. And Jeremy's wife."

"We'll be outside."

Dan tugged at his lower lip. "I don't think that's a good idea. I've got to assume he's got security. You guys met some of them. They'll be watching the outside. They'll pick you up in a heartbeat."

"Come on, boss. I'm insulted. We're better than that."

Dan checked the time on his phone. "I need to head back in an hour. Gather the electronics for me. I'll be back shortly. I've got to talk to a girl about a guy."

"It'll be ready."

Terry looked up from the laptop. "You don't need what I find before you go, do you?"

"Not really. Why?"

"This brute force thing could take hours."

"Take your time. Get in. Don't need it today. I'll be back in an hour for the other stuff."

Dan and Kat slid into a booth, across from each other, at the back of the kebab shop. Kat looked around nervously, her glance flitting from the door to the dark interior.

"You okay?"

Kat stopped the surveillance and leaned forward. "I don't want him to find me."

Sabrin placed gyros in front of both of them. "Lamb for the lady, chicken for the gentleman."

"Thanks Sabrin." Dan leaned back and waited until she'd left. "So why this Billy guy? He's a bit of a dick. Drunk most of the time and he fucking hits you. Immediate disqualification in my books."

Kat shook her head. "It's been over a month since I let him hit me. He wouldn't dare now."

"Okay, I'm confused."

"Don't be. Thanks for the food. I think I'm going to head back to Wollongong. I've got a job I've got to get back to. You see Billy, tell him I have no interest in him anymore, okay?"

"I can do that. Easy." He took a bite of his gyro and wiped his mouth with a napkin. "So what do you do for a living?"

"Graphic arts for an advertising company. They pay me to doodle. It's a pretty good gig." She slid her sleeve up her arm and showed him a tattoo of a bumblebee. "I do a bit of freelance work for the ink shops, too."

"That's nice. I'm going to stay out of your business, okay? If you need help, ask for it, but otherwise, you're strong enough on your own. You cool with that?"

Kat nodded while she chewed. "I appreciate that. I think I'll be okay."

"You will be." He waved his hand around the table. "This is all paid for. Take your time. I need to run back into Sydney."

Terry placed three small audio recorders and two video transmitters sat in the middle of the meeting room table. Dan picked up one of the video transmitters.

"No local storage with this. No good unless we're parked within a block of the building in the van."

"Exactly."

"No." Dan put the video transmitter back on the table. "Too big. We talked about this. Lowest profile. They collect, I'll get back in later, and we'll analyse. Only transmit if the device is very small."

"Kinda hobbling the investigation, boss," said Andy. "But if that's the way you want to do it."

"Not so much 'want' as need to. It'll take a bit longer. And I need to find a way back in to collect. But it's all about risk mitigation right now." Dan picked up one of the audio recorders and flipped it over in his hand. "I need a way of sticking this under her desk, on behind a sofa. I don't know what I'm in for."

Andy stepped out of the room for a second and came back with a roll of tape and a pair of scissors. "Old school. Double sided tape." He cut short pieces off the roll and prepped the three audio recorders. "Good to go?"

"Good to go."

Andy added tape to the two video transmitters. "And you're taking these, too."

Dan shook his head. "Look, I -"

"Fuck that. If we can't manage a street sit for a couple of hours, we shouldn't be doing this, shouldn't be working for you. I've set the audio up to transmit, also. You won't be as pressed to collect after the fact." He sat back. "The laptop -- how do you want the data?"

"Once you get in, you know best. Filter to get anything related to his interactions with the head of *Oz Express*. Or his minions. Don't care so much about personal stuff. Looking for a motive."

"Most motives are closer to home. You told me that yourself."

Dan took a deep breath. "You're right. Trawl the whole damned thing. Let me know what you find. I've got to run."

Andy tapped the table. "Uh, boss?"

"What?"

"Need the address where you're going to be. We'll be right behind you."

"I'll send you all a text." Dan opened his phone, grabbed the piece of paper with the office address and started typing with one hand. "See you there."

CHAPTER 12

Dan met Sally in the front foyer of the *Oz Express* headquarters.

"Just in time," said Sally.

"How are you playing this?"

"Truth. Grieving widow wants to talk to the boss about finalising things with the company. You're coming as my assistant."

"Lawyer, maybe. Has to be something that aligns with whatever he thinks I am from the last run-in."

Sally smiled. "Then let's keep with the truth. You're a private investigator I hired. I'll just lie a little about why I hired you."

"Truth it is, then. You lead, Sally. We'll play it straight."

Stew parked the surveillance van in a lot across the street from the headquarters. "Close enough?"

Andy pivoted out of the front passenger seat and squeezed into the back. "Should be." He sat in front of the recording equipment. "Jesus, it's tight back here." He leaned down and looked out the back window of the van. "We're harbourside. Pretty sure a douche like Rand will have a harbour view office." He turned on the three audio receivers and the two monitors for the cameras. "How long, do you think?"

"He just walked in the front," said Stew. "Give it a bit."

"We're not going to know if it's not working, or if we're out of range, or if he had to shut them off because there was a security sweep."

Stew narrowed his eyes and open his mouth to retort when a scratchy noise came through the speakers. "Ya spoke too soon. Clean it up."

Andy adjusted a dial that rotated a small directional antenna on the roof of the van until Dan's voice came in clear. *"You lead, Sally. We'll play it straight."*

Andy pressed the record button. "Let's eavesdrop."

Sally checked her watch as she stepped up to the reception desk. "I've got a meeting with Mr Murray. I'm Sally Brookes. Mr McGinnis is with me."

The unnaturally blonde woman flashed her impossibly white teeth in a tight smile. "Go right in. He's coming from another meeting running a couple of minutes late. He'll join you shortly." She pushed a button under her desk and the office door popped slightly open. "We're all so terribly upset about what happened to JB. Can I get you some tea? Coffee? Water?"

"We're good," said Dan. "Thanks."

He followed Sally into the expansive office. Thick carpeting muffled their footsteps. Two sides of the office were glass walls overlooking Sydney Harbour. Vertical louvred blinds were pulled open to a view of the Harbour Bridge. Dan walked to the window and looked down. "I can see the van.

Perfect."

He took the three audio devices out of his pocket, pulled the covering paper off the double sticky tape and stuck one under the top lip of the desk. He moved the blinds to one side and placed one at the bottom of the window near the floor, obscured by the blinds.

He tossed the third one in his hand, looking around the office. Sally sat in a chair across from the desk. A large potted tree of some sort sat in a corner by the door. Dan walked over and dropped the third and final voice recorder in the pot just as Rand walked in the office. The door swung open and blocked Dan from view.

"Why are you here, Sally? Hasn't everything been resolved? Is there something left for me to do? I'll get my assistant in here."

Dan pushed the door closed and slowly walked across the thick carpet to the desk. "Sally has hired me to look into her husband's murder. We won't need your assistant."

Rand turned. "Murder? I thought it was a -" He registered Dan's face. "Mr McMaster, or whoever you are." He sighed and walked around his desk and sat. "What the fuck are you doing here?"

"It's Dan McGinnis. And it's like I said. Sally retained my agency to investigate her husband's death."

"I don't believe it was a mugging," said Sally. "Dan and his team are going to help me prove it."

Rand leaned back in his chair and crossed his arms. "Occam's razor. It was a mugging gone bad."

Sally leaned forward and jabbed down on the desk with her index finger. "Too many inconsistencies."

"Hey, I'm the first to inflate a story for sales value. I'll make up shit about anyone to sell a story." He tapped his nose. "But I can always see the truth in the lies. And the truth about dear old Jeremy is that he was mugged on Harris street and the impatient thief killed him."

Sally choked back a sob.

"Sorry, Sally." He shook his head. "No, fuck it, actually I'm not. Stop chasing delusions. Jeremy is dead and there's nothing you can say or do to bring him back."

Dan leaned forward and crossed his arms on Rand's desk. "Agree to disagree. Sally's convinced me it's not simple mugging. I'm investigating." He leaned back and opened his hands, palms up. "Where's the harm in me investigating? It's not your money."

"No, but it's hers and you're fleecing her. You, sir, should be ashamed of yourself."

Dan snorted. "You're one to talk."

Sally knocked on the table. "Hey, can it, both of you. Randy, when in the hell did you ever care about anyone other than yourself? I've retained Dan's agency and it's none of your business. I'm here so we can find out what Jeremy was working on before he died."

Randolph looked at Sally, then at Dan. Then back at Sally again. "It's Randolph. What do you actually expect to get from me? He was one legal hack of many, trying to keep my figurative arse out of legal jeopardy. Wasn't even one of the best in the stable. Sorry to be blunt, Sally, but you know me. I don't hold back."

Dan put his hand on Sally's arm. "Maybe you should, once in a while."

Sally jerked her arm away and wiped a tear off her cheek. "What exactly did Jeremy do for you?"

Rand sniffed. "I already told you. Sum total of his role. Kept my arse out of legal jeopardy." He shrugged. "More accurately, kept my company out of legal jeopardy. I'm protected. You're his wife. You should know this."

"How did he protect *you*, I mean.?"

"I could publish an article that says you eat live kittens and kick puppies and fiddle three-year old girls on the Opera House steps and the lawsuit couldn't touch me." He smiled.

Sally shook her head. "I don't know how he lasted here as long as he did." She clenched her jaw muscles. "Why did you take this meeting? Do you enjoy doing this?"

"Don't waste your time, Sally. He does," said Dan. "He enjoys it very much. I'm pretty sure a lot of this is him trolling us." He stared at Randolph. "I've got a couple of questions for you."

Randolph looked at his watch. "I've got six and a half minutes until I need to be on the telephone with the Prime Minister." He smiled. "Ask whatever you want. I'll answer what I'm comfortable answering."

"Did you have an amicable relationship with Jeremy?"

"Amicable? He was the legal headache to almost every story I wanted to run. So no, not entirely *amicable*. But he was doing his job."

"Doesn't really answer my question. Would you buy him a flat white if you bumped into him at a coffee shop?"

"No. I don't drink coffee."

"Again, not what I asked." He leaned forward. "You like it straight, no bullshit. How much did he piss you off? Enough to have him killed?"

Rand tipped his head back and laughed. "Oh, my. You're serious. I don't have to kill anyone. I can drive them to suicide. I can ruin anybody's life, given the right motivation and a little time. Information is everywhere. And manufactured information," he tapped the side of his head, "is limited only by my imagination." He sniffed and leaned forward. "So don't piss me off too much, Mr McGinnis. I'm sure I could have you on the ropes in a matter of weeks."

"I have no doubt you'd try. Was there anything in the past week or two that boiled over to more than an angry word or two between you?"

Rand waved his had dismissively. "He was always angry. He didn't like my," he paused to find the words, "imaginative way of grabbing eyeballs. The cover grab and headlines need to be compelling enough to entice the reader to turn the page. Or, as is more common these days, click through to the story."

He leaned forward, resting his elbows on his desk. "I make no apologies. It's a business. The more clicks, the higher the advertising rates. The people I target can afford it and believe me, they are not that clean." He looked at Sally, then back to Dan. "Anything else? I've got a phone call to make."

Andy lifted the headphones off his head. "Damn. That guy is a grade-A douche nozzle."

"Keep recording," said Stew.

"Of course." He checked the switches and nodded to himself. "Not a rookie, mate."

"Look sharp. Boss is arriving."

The back door opened and Dan and Sally stepped up into the truck. "You got all that?"

"The guy's a massive dick," said Andy.

"Ironically, he's probably got a small one. Nice and clear?"

"The three audio channels are clean. We'll hang around and record whatever happens in that room. Something tells me you won't be getting back in there again." Andy pulled a chair out and motioned Sally toward it. "You okay?"

She settled into the chair, let out a shuddering breath and finger-combed her hair back. "I've only heard stories. Jeremy would tell me how much of a pain in the arse he was, but this first-hand experience was something else." She pinched the bridge of her nose. "He's a monster. He and Jeremy certainly didn't get along."

"He didn't seem too broken up about your loss," said Andy.

"He's a sociopath," said Sally.

Dan shook his head. "Bordering on psychopath, but there's more than one psychopath sitting in a CEO's chair." He picked up the set of headphones and held one can to the side of his head. "Silence. He's not in the office right now." He put the headphones back on the table. "You guys head back. We're not going to get anything from this guy."

Andy looked at Stew.

"Well, boss, Stew and I were planning on spending the rest of the day picking up what we could. The battery should last another six hours on those things."

"And then hit one or more of the city clubs, right?"

Stew shrugged. "Why not?"

Dan considered for a second. "Why not. Call me if anything incriminating comes up." He rested his hand on the door. "Sally, let's go grab a coffee and chat."

The door was yanked opened, catching Dan off balance. "What the…?"

Gerald stood in front of Dan. He held out his hand. The three audio devices, in pieces, were in in his palm. "These are yours, I assume, mate?"

Dan looked down on him from the truck interior. He put his hands behind his back and leaned over, pretending to examine the pieces of plastic in his hand. "Have we met?"

"I've met your buddy Andy, there. At the Star. Heard about your interaction with my boss. I'm not too fucking pleased about that, but I'll let it pass for now." He lifted his hand fractionally higher. "You want these?"

"What are they?"

Gerald shook his head and closed his fist. He tightened his grip, the muscles in his forearms bunching. He opened his hand again and there were twice as many pieces. He threw them into the truck, shards of plastic and electronics skittering across the metal floor. "I think they're yours. Mr Murray asked me to tell you politely to fuck off and don't come back." He dusted the remaining fragments of plastic off his hand. "And if you do come back I'll make sure you regret it. Have a nice day."

Dan watched him walk back to the office building. "Well, lads, no point hanging out here any longer. I'll see you back at the office. Sally, we need to have a quick sit-rep chat over coffee before I go back to my office."

"Shit." Andy turned off the electronics, put the protective cover on the front of the equipment and stored the headphones and cables. "So much for beer on the waterfront."

"It's over-rated anyway," said Dan. "Maybe next time."

Gerald knocked lightly on Randolph's office doorframe. "Boss, they've left."

Rand looked up from his papers. "Thanks. You thoroughly destroyed them?"

Gerald held up a clenched fist and smiled. "Crushed to dust. They won't be able to recover anything off of them."

Rand nodded and turned back to his papers. "Excellent. I'll be in the office until at least 7 tonight. The afternoon is yours."

Dan carried two takeaway coffee cups to the table in the shopping centre food court. "It's probably crap, but it's got caffeine."

Sally took a test sip, wincing. "What do you want to talk about? The meeting with Rand was a bust."

"Maybe it was a bust. It was good insight on the man. But I don't have anything from that conversation that makes me think he's responsible, directly or indirectly, for Jeremy's murder."

"So you think it was just a mugging gone bad, then." It was a statement, not a question.

"No, I don't think that anymore. Someone definitely targeted your husband. But I don't have enough evidence to say Rand had anything to do with it."

Sally slumped over the table. She lifted the cup to her mouth and sipped. "This is terrible. So what now?"

"Terry, one of my guys, is trawling through your husband's laptop as we speak. I'm hoping he finds something there." He held up a hand. "Something that may not have anything to do with Rand. We're going at this with an open mind."

"That's fair. What else?"

"Jeremy had a home office, right?"

Sally nodded and took another sip of coffee. "A small one. I haven't been in there since his death."

"I'd like to go through it. I'll bring one of my team. Can we meet there tomorrow afternoon? Say, around 2:00?"

Sally nodded. "You know my address. I'll see you then."

CHAPTER 13

Kat was leaning against the front door when Dan arrived at 8:00 in the morning. She was wearing a sweatshirt with a UNSW logo, tight, faded jeans and a pair of bike boots. She had a small backpack over her shoulder. When she saw Dan approach she stood upright and adjusted her pack.

She pointed at the door over her shoulder with her thumb. "You're still locked up."

He looked at his watch. "It's 8:00. Kinda early. Beryl isn't in yet."

"But I want to talk to you, not her."

Dan yawned and nodded. "Let's get breakfast."

"I'm kinda tight on money."

"My treat."

Dan led Kat to a cafe half a block down the road and pointed her at a table. "Poached eggs on toast and a coffee okay?"

"You're buying. Whatever."

She shucked off a windbreaker and hung it on the chair and sat. She was picking at a hangnail when Dan returned.

"So, what do you want to talk about?"

"A job."

"I'm confused. You've got a graphics art gig in the Gong, freelancing for the inkers. Yesterday you were heading back home and everything seemed okay."

Kat toyed with a tube of raw sugar, tearing off the end and pouring it into her cup. She slowly rolled up the paper tube, then looked up at Dan. "I need a change. I need to get out of that environment. I keep falling into bad habits."

"I'm not a social worker. And I don't give charity to individuals." He held up a hand. "I'm sympathetic to your problem. Really. But I'm not sure how I can help. I don't have any open spots, I'm not planning on expanding, and even if either of those events happened, you don't have the skillsets I need in my business."

"How would you know? You've met me twice. Neither time under the best of circumstances. Let me intern with you for a couple of weeks. Show what I can offer."

"Well, you're persistent. No guarantees. Two weeks only. If it doesn't work out I don't want a lot of grief when I send you packing."

"Understood. Standard stuff. We got a deal?" She held out a hand.

Dan ignored it, took a pen from his shirt pocket and wrote two email addresses on a paper napkin. "Full name, date of birth, tax file number. Email it to Beryl and copy me. Call the office after 1:00. Beryl will let you know one way or another." He stood and smiled. "Good luck."

Dan tapped on Beryl's desk as he walked in. "You'll be getting an email from

Kat shortly, I expect. Do a background on her and make sure there aren't any outstanding arrest warrants, will you? If she's clean she'll be interning for a couple of weeks."

"I already got it. Interning doing what?"

Dan shrugged. "We'll see. She's keen. Good at graphic arts, it would appear. When Andy and Stew come in send them to the meeting room. We need to catch up."

"And Terry?"

"Tell him to leave the laptop and whatever he's pulled from it on my desk. Thanks."

Dan grabbed a whiteboard marker off the meeting room table and wrote three headings on the whiteboard: *Means, Motive, Opportunity*. He sat at the table and stared at the board.

"Lotta blank space up there, boss," said Stew as he sat.

"Might be able to put something up for motive, and I have no doubt he could kill someone, or have someone do it for him. Not a clue if there was opportunity. We need to nail that down."

Andy sat beside Stew. "You make him for this? If we were doing this from scratch, like we're supposed to, I doubt this Randy guy would be on the radar more than half a tick." He scratched his chin. "We really should be doing this from scratch."

"I agree. You and I are heading to the family home this afternoon. We're going to tear through anything in his office. This morning I'm reviewing what Terry pulled off the laptop, and you and Stew are going to sit on Rand's muscle. Track them and see if you spot anything out of the ordinary."

"Loose or tight?"

Dan thought for a second. "Tight. See what happens when they feel a bit of heat."

Stew stood and nodded at Andy. "Let's go, kid."

"I'll text you the Brookes' address," said Dan. "Meet me there at two."

Andy smacked Stew on the shoulder. "I'm only five years younger than you, mate."

Stew chuckled. "Let's go, kid."

Beryl waited for Stew and Andy to leave, then walked in with a couple of sheets of paper. "Kathrine Eloise Brady. Twenty-four years old. A few misdemeanours five years ago, but nothing since. Taxes are current. She's been regular with her rent in a small one-bedroom apartment in Gwynneville." She looked at Dan. "That's a suburb in North-West Wollongong. No nasty debt problems. Two low limit credit cards that aren't overdue. Currently has her own business that's barely keeping her in noodles."

"What do you think?"

Beryl shrugged. "I'd need to meet her for an hour or so to get a read. Looks good on paper, though."

"When she calls at 1:00, set up a meeting with her. Tell her it's a personality interview. Take her out to lunch, or tea, or whatever you think might be enlightening." He stood and wiped the whiteboard clean. "I'll be in my office reading through Terry's analysis. Try to shield me from distractions, okay?"

Beryl scooped up the papers. "Sure thing boss. What's she going to do here?"

"Maybe you'll be able to tell me after you meet her." He laughed as she grunted in assent and walked out, shaking her head.

Andy sat behind the wheel, idling at the kerb in front of the *Oz Express* offices. "This is stupid."

Stew peeled the wrapper back on his lamb kebab. "What is?"

"Say you're personal security for a high end client who sits in his office on the thirty-fucketh floor all day. What do you do? Nothing. Sit around, update Facebook, troll people on Twitter, get soft, lose your tactical awareness. And we're sitting out here, wasting our time. Two hours, so far.

They're going to be in there all day."

Stew pointed with his half-eaten kebab. "That's them, right?"

Gerald and Robert had just left the main doors and trotted across the street and got in a late model sedan.

"What do ya think," said Stew around a mouthful of food, "those guys are up to? Getting boss's lunch?"

Andy put the car in gear. "It's about time. Tight follow, right? Bring the heat?" He swung in immediately behind their car. "Let's ride their arse."

"Why not? You were starting to get on my nerves, whining about them staying in all the time."

"Yeah, well." Andy shrugged and tailgated the security team's car.

They rounded a corner a car length behind. "They *have* to notice us," said Stew. They took another left hand turn into a dead-end street.

"They noticed us," said Andy. He rolled to a stop behind them. Gerald and Robert got out of their car and turned back toward Stew and Andy.

"Let's go." Stew opened the passenger door at the same time Andy put the car in reverse and started backing up.

"Fuck, kid. Trying to kill me?"

Andy jammed on the brakes. "Right. Sorry. Let's go."

"You were going to run?"

"No. Hell, no. Looking for a place to park." He rolled his shoulders. "Let's do this."

Gerald and Robert walked down either side of their car toward them. "What in the hell are you two up to?" asked Gerald. "You've been sitting outside the building for the last two hours. Not too fucking obvious."

He squinted, then pointed at Andy. "You again? First the casino, then the spy van." He looked at Stew. "You replaced the skinny kid with an old man? Wow. They make them stupid out in the sticks."

"I was in the spy van, too." Stew smiled and swapped places with Andy. "You take the friend. I want to have a word with this mutt."

"You sure?"

"It won't be a fair fight, but I'll take it easy on him."

"Really? The guy looks big. British accent. Probably ex-SAS or something like that."

"His youth and enthusiasm isn't a match for my cynicism and lack of fucks to give with respect to the damage I do." On the last syllable he lashed out with his right hand, fingers extended, and jabbed Gerald hard in the throat.

Stew grabbed him as he struggled for air. "Easy, easy. Relax. Didn't hit you hard enough to kill you. Your trachea is spasming. I don't think I fractured anything. You'll be right in a second."

Robert lunged forward and twisted his body, swinging an elbow toward Andy's head. Andy rolled out of the way, the elbow contacting his cheekbone just below his eye.

"Oh, you son of a bitch." He rolled back with his own elbow and smashed Robert in the face. He kicked the side of his leg and followed Robert to the ground. He pressed an arm against his neck, putting all of his weight on his carotid. "You. Arsehole." He bounced his weight on Robert's neck. "Fuck. You."

Robert scrambled at his arm, the efforts getting weaker until he passed out.

Andy pushed himself to his feet. "You good, Stew?"

Stew nodded and eased Gerald against his car. "Stay there. Tell your boss we're keeping our eyes on him." He looked at Robert, semi-prone on the ground. "What the fuck?" Then he saw Andy's face and he started laughing. "He tagged you? You're growing a mouse, mate." He nudged Robert with his foot. "You didn't kill him, did you?"

"Knocked him out. He'll be fine." He touched his cheek. "Better than me. I've got a date on the weekend."

"You're still pretty."

"Fuck you." He nodded toward Gerald, leaning against his car, trying to catch his rasping breath. "One punch?"

"Not even a fist." He checked his watch. "Coming up on 1:00. You're catching up with Dan at the client's house, right?"

"Shit, right. I forgot. He's not going to let me live this eye down."

"It's been a long time since you got tagged." He got in the car. "We're splitting up. So either I take the car back and you ride pillion with the boss…"

Andy started the car. "Oh, hell no. I'll drop you at Central and you can take the train back. Nice relaxing trip."

"I can catch up on a book."

Andy snorted as he pulled from the curb. "You can read?"

"You want matching mice, kid? I can pop you from here."

"You good with the train?"

Stew lifted his arse and dug out his wallet. He checked through the plastic until he found the transit fare card. "I'm good with the train. Take me there, Jeeves. See you when you get back."

Gerald steadied himself on his car and tried slowing his breath. His head throbbed. His throat hurt. Every breath brought a stabbing pain like trying to swallow glass. He forced himself to stand completely upright and take a deep breath. "Jesus Christ." He staggered to the back of the car. Robert had rolled to his hands and knees and was trying to stand. Gerald grabbed him under the arm and helped him up.

"What the hell just happened?" asked Robert. He rubbed the side of his neck and winced. "That's going to bruise."

"We gotta tell the boss about this," said Gerald.

"Do we have to?"

Gerald scowled and dialled.

"Well, Gerald, did you handle them? Are they backing off?"

Gerald pressed the phone to his head and walked a few paces away from Robert. "They caught us by surprise, boss."

"What are you saying?"

"We underestimated those guys. They took us both out with a couple of well-placed shots." Gerald closed his eyes and tipped his head back. "So I'll get a couple more guys. Four or five more. We'll find them again and let them know -"

"Took you both out? Jesus CHRIST. How much do I pay you again?"

"Came at us from behind. Didn't have a chance. I'll get a crowd and track them down wherever they are and erase them."

Gerald heard Randolph sigh on the other end of the phone. "I'm going to call him first. See what the hell it is they want."

"You won't have any luck."

"YOU DON'T FUCKING TELL ME WHAT I CAN OR CAN NOT DO." Randolph took a deep breath. "I'll call him. I'll talk to him. If you need to gather an army of equally incompetent FUCKS and pay him a visit, I'll let you know."

CHAPTER 14

Dan raised a hand to knock on Sally's door and it opened. Sally stood to one side and motioned him in.

"I thought there were going to be two of you," said Sally as she led him into the lounge room. "Have a seat."

Dan checked his watch. "Should be right behind me." He smiled when there was a knock on the door. "Like I said."

"Wait here. Make yourself comfortable."

Dan sat back in a supple leather chair and took in the surroundings. A bookcase on one wall showed heavy use, books stacked on their side mixed with upright, an organised chaos. A framed photo of Jeremy and Sally on a cruise ship balcony hung on the wall beside a wedding photo, taken when they were both much younger.

A large hardback coffee table book was open to large glossy pictures from somewhere in the western USA.

Dan stood as Sally came in with Andy. "So, what can I do for the two of you?"

Andy had a black eye and some abrasions on his knuckles. Dan glanced at him and raised an eyebrow, then pointed at the book. "Grand Teton?"

Sally sighed and closed the book. "Yes. Jeremy and I were planning a trip there next month. It never happened."

"Sorry to hear that. We need -"

She interrupted. "- to see Jeremy's office?"

Dan nodded. "That would be great. Lead the way."

Sally walked them to a small office in the back of the house. A mahogany desk sat in the corner below a small window. A computer monitor and keyboard were attached to a docking station. She stood at the door and didn't enter.

He pointed to a file cabinet beside the desk. "Locked?"

"Nope. The house is secure enough. Can I get you boys coffee?"

"I'm fine. Andy?"

"No. Maybe beer a bit later."

Sally smiled. "I'll let you two at it. Let me know if you need any help understanding anything he's written."

Dan waited until Sally left and turned to Andy. "What in the hell happened to your face?"

Andy smiled. "You should see the other guy." He held up his hands. "Nothing. Stew and I had a close tail on Rand's guys, um, Gerald and Robert. Big units, as you know. British. Probably ex-SAS. They, uh, didn't take kindly to us sitting in their back pockets."

Dan looked closer at the bruised eye. "It's usually nothing, or a lot more when you get in a scrap."

"This was very close to nothing. Caught an elbow when Robert turned on me. Stew and I took care of it. Wasn't looking for a scrap." He rolled his shoulders.

"Right." He pulled open a file drawer and lifted out all the folders. "You take these and see what you can find in here that would indicate a beef large enough to get him killed." He handed the folders to Andy and opened the next drawer. "I'll look at these."

Andy started sorting the documents into piles on the floor. After a while he looked up at Dan. "What did Terry find on the laptop?"

"Nothing, yet. Still trying to open it."

"What about the calendar?"

Dan shook his head. "We'll see it when we see it." He nodded at the piles of documents on the floor. "What do you have?"

Andy sat back on his heels. "Okay. Four piles. Biggest one contains nothing of importance. It's fortunate that it's the biggest pile. This next one contains files directly related to his wife. Insurance policies, travel plans, that sort of thing. The third pile are threats he's received from people the magazine wrote about. Not many, considering the trash that ends up in the magazine, but that's not too surprising as his name wouldn't be widely known."

"The fourth pile is threats from Rand?"

Andy shook his head. "Threats *against* Rand. From Jeremy. Not threats of physical violence, but legal threats. Started about three months ago. Some of them are very explicit."

Dan held out his hand. "Let me see."

Andy picked three off the top of the pile and handed them to his boss. "Lawyers are very good with words."

"As you'd expect." Dan read the top page and chuckled. "*I will ensure that the legal community is aware of your disdain toward the profession, and your overwhelming need to bury anyone who opposes you, and will expose the methods by which that burying happens. The legal loopholes you use,* *while technically not illegal, will paint you and your organisation is such poor light that advertisers and investors will flee. It is my sincere hope that my efforts will bankrupt your company **and** you, leaving you penniless."* He turned the page over to look if there was something on the back. "Damn."

"That was one of the nicer ones." Andy continued going through the pile of unsorted documents. "You find anything?"

"Nothing as good as that. Not yet. This drawer is mostly financial. Their old passports. Receipts for pistol club membership dues. For both of them. Mortgage papers. Old tax returns. They weren't hurting for money, that's for sure. No signs of blackmail or extortion or anything like that."

Andy picked another sheet off the small pile. "This stuff is pretty inflammatory. Do you think it was enough to push Rand to have Jeremy killed?"

Dan looked at the closed door. "Maybe. Rand seems to take a lot of this in stride. Though the threat of rendering him penniless might get a rise out of him."

Dan scratched his chin. "Maybe. Still weak."

"It's motive, boss. The two meatheads are means. Opportunity?"

"We need to find out what the muscle was up to that night." Andy checked the calendar on his phone. "That was five days ago, right?"

Dan clapped him on the shoulder. "Take off. I'll get copies of those nasty ones and head back to Campbelltown. See you there."

"Sure thing, boss." Andy pulled himself up and left. Dan followed with the handful of pages from the threat file.

Sally met him at the office door. "You find what you need?"

Dan held up the pages. "Do you have a copier?"

Sally took the pages and fanned through them and nodded. "He told me about these. I warned him about poking the bear. I'll scan them and email them to you, okay?"

"Thanks." Dan stepped out on the front porch. "Andy and I will take a rain check on the beer. I need to get back to the office."

He unlocked his helmet from his bike. Andy was parked behind him. "How did Stew get back?"

Andy grinned as he got in his car. "Train."

Dan grunted. "Musta loved that."

"He didn't seem to mind. Said he had a book he wanted to read on his phone."

"Wow. See you back at the shop." He put his headphones in, started the latest podcast and pulled on his helmet. "Drive safe, mate." He started his bike, giving Andy a wave as he accelerated away from Sally's house.

He rolled smoothly through the surface streets until he hit the M5 South. Midday traffic was easy and the trip was almost hypnotic.

He was halfway back when his phone rang. It was in his pocket. He didn't like blind answers. He sighed and depressed the button on the headphone cable. "Dan McGinnis, McGinnis Investigations."

"Have I caught you at a bad time, Mr McGinnis?"

"Randolph? What do you want?" Dan gripped the handlebar tighter. "And how did you get this number? I only give it to clients."

"I have resources. I'm very disappointed that you attempted to bug my office, Dan. Almost as disappointed as I am that you're poking your nose into Jeremy's mugging."

Dan eased past a large truck. "I don't really care what you think. I work what I work. Why are you calling me?"

"Two of your men attacked two of mine earlier today. Unprovoked. From behind. I want an apology from both of them immediately and you to back off the wild goose chase you're on."

"Unprovoked? And from behind?" Dan chuckled. "That's not what they told me. Told me your guys were a couple of bitches. Dropped like a hooker's underpants. Get it through your fat skull, Randy, nobody takes me off a case until I'm finished, and I'm not finished."

"I'm concerned for the welfare of a former employee's spouse. You're leading Sally Brookes on. You're letting her believe a fantasy and you're taking her money knowing that there's nothing to the narrative. Back off. Back off or I'll make sure you don't work another case this year."

"That's a pretty specific threat. It's like six weeks. So I'll be okay to work a case next year?"

"You should be out of the hospital by January."

Dan chuckled. "Piss off, mate. Stay in your lane. You might think you've got influence over some people, but I don't give a rat's what you think." He slowed as he exited to Campbelltown off the motorway. "Stay you, you douchebag." Dan terminated the call and returned to the movie review podcast he was listening to.

Randolph jammed his finger on the "End" button. "What a fucking arsehole. Jesus." He made another call. "Get the extra men. Get the message across. Don't get arrested."

Dan parked beside the van. Andy and Terry were inside inventorying the contents. Dan slapped his hand on the side and stuck his head in the door. "Where's Stew?"

Andy looked at his watch. "Train's in in about ten minutes."

"Should have been here by now."

"The vagaries of the NSW Transit system. Someone was dancing on the tracks at Redfern, daring the trains to run him over. Took the cops a little while to clear the thing. He messaged me half an hour ago. What's up?"

The sides of the van rumbled as motorbikes rolled into the parking lot.

Dan turned. "Uh, guys, we've got company."

Billy and his biker friends rolled up, a car in their wake. Billy dropped the kickstand and turned off his bike. The car behind his crew stopped and

Gerald and Robert stepped out. Dan did a quick count. Billy plus the two in the car plus Billy's friends made six.

"Kat's kinda busy, Billy."

"This is just a funny coincidence. Not looking for Kat at this moment. My new friends are paying me a couple of bills to rearrange your face, which I will enjoy doing." He leaned forward. "Don't tell them, but I would have done it for half of what they paid. If you can still talk when we're finished, tell Kat I said hi."

Dan made a show of looking over Billy's head. "You lost three of your friends. Didn't they want to take part in the fun?"

"Got something else to do, and we don't need them."

Dan pointed at Gerald and Robert. "Those guys are your friends?"

When Billy turned to look, Dan smashed him on the side of the head with his elbow, like a close right cross. Billy's legs turned to jelly. "Andy, Terry, get out here and help me." Dan stepped over him and tackled the next guy off his bike.

He was on the ground, punching and driving his knees into the man he tackled when someone kicked him in the ribs, driving the wind out of him. He grunted as he rolled away from the kick and looked up at Gerald. "Mistake, mate."

The bikers were off their bikes and overwhelming Andy and Terry. Andy was fully engaged with two and Robert, while Terry was valiantly doing his best against the third.

Billy was still a pool of unconscious smelly leather on the macadam.

Dan slid sideways out of Gerald's reach and bounced to his feet. "Big, big mistake."

Gerald rubbed the front of his throat. "Your old guy caught me by surprise. Not going to happen again."

Dan chuckled and inched a couple of steps closer. "I doubt that. Stew's a sneaky fucker."

Gerald's eyes flicked over Dan's should, then back to Dan. He smiled. "Really?"

"I'm not falling for that. What do you think I am, an idi -" Something hit him on the back of the head and Dan's knees buckled and he fell into darkness.

Throbbing behind his eyes and a metallic taste in his mouth.

Sun on his face.

Dan groaned and opened his eyes, squinting. He was sitting on the ground, back against his van. Andy was to his left, also just coming to, and Terry to his right, out like a light.

The bikers were gone, the rumble of their bikes fading in the distance. Gerald and Robert stood in front of them. Robert had a length of pipe in his hand, stained with blood.

"Yes, I think you're an idiot." Gerald leaned forward. "You're not dead because I don't want you dead. Drop the case."

"Tell Randolph to -"

Robert kicked the bottom of his foot. He raised the pipe. "So we kill the fat fuck now?"

Gerald restrained him. "We had instructions. Leave him alive."

Robert pointed the pipe at Dan. "Until next time. Idiot." They walked back to their car and pulled out of the parking lot.

Terry stirred. He groaned and opened his eyes. "Ow. Damn." He held his head. "What in the hell just happened?"

Stew walked around the corner at a comfortable walking pace, face down looking at something on his phone.

"Oh, shit," said Dan. "We'll never hear the end of this."

CHAPTER 15

Dan followed Stew up the steps to the office. "I'm getting too old for this shit."

"You've been too old for this for at least a decade. Sorry I wasn't there. Looks like you guys had fun."

Dan brushed his hand against the back of his head and winced. "Not so much. What are we going to do about this?"

Stew held the door open for Dan. "We'll be meeting them again, I'm sure. Next time we won't be so nice."

"We?" Dan nodded at Beryl. He walked slowly into his office. "I'll keep that in mind." He eased into his chair. "Keep an eye on Terry, okay? He had his bell rung hard."

"Sure thing." Stew sat across from him. "What was it about?"

"Rand doesn't like us pressing him. Really doesn't like it." He took a bottle and two glasses from his bottom drawer. He poured a healthy two fingers in each glass and slid one across the desk to Stew.

Dan sat back and sipped on his. "And if Rand doesn't like us pressing, there must be a reason for it."

Beryl knocked on the doorframe and entered without waiting for a response. She dropped a copy of the *Oz Express* on Dan's desk and put her hands on her hips. "Recognise this?"

Dan pulled the paper closer. The full page cover was a black and white photo of Callum Ryan, young actor, snorting a white powder through a rolled up banknote. Dan pointed at the picture. "This is that kid we tried to get the pre-nup details on."

Stew pulled the paper closer. "And that's from our surveillance. What in the hell is going on, Dan? We working for these slime bags now?"

Dan pulled the paper back and looked at the picture intently. While examining it he snapped his fingers. "Get Terry."

Beryl mock saluted. "Aye-aye, captain."

He flipped through the paper to the article on Callum. There were more pictures. They all looked familiar. He closed the paper and threw it on his desk. "Son of a BITCH."

Terry limped into the office as the paper hit the desk. "W-what's going on, boss?"

Dan nodded at the paper. "The pictures in this -- rag -- of Callum Ryan. The cover and another half dozen on the inside."

Terry picks up the paper. "Yeah?" He looked at the cover and opened the paper, then immediately closed it and looked at the cover. "Hang on. This is ours." He flipped rapidly to the story. "These, too."

"Exactly," said Dan. "Take that piece of trash rag and find out exactly from which tapes, what time markers, these fuckers took these snaps from."

Terry looked through the paper. He folded over corners of the pages with Callum Ryan's photos.

"Terry?"

He looked up. "Yes, boss?"

"You okay?"

"I'll be fine. Want another shot at those son of a bitches." Terry hustled out of the office with the paper under his arm.

Dan leaned back in his chair and looked at the ceiling. "That prick."

Stew leaned forward and topped up Dan's glass. "We get paid for that?"

"Oh, fuck you. Don't remind me." He slapped the desk. "What in the hell was her name again?" He picked up his phone and scrolled through his call history until he found the number he was looking for. He stabbed the number and pressed the phone to his head.

It rang twice and a woman's voice answered. "You've got a copy of the paper?"

Dan leaned forward and pressed the phone harder to his ear. "What kind of game are you playing?"

"No game."

"We provided video and audio recordings of this young actor with the understanding that you were looking for a divorce."

"And there was nothing there."

"Yet you take the video and sell screen grabs to the *Oz Express* to ruin the relationship anyway."

"I absolutely did not do that."

Dan clenched his jaw muscles and tightened the grip on his phone. "So tell me how the pictures got on the front page of the daily shit rag."

"I was expecting your call because I knew you'd be upset at the photos. Imagine, someone taking your hard work and plastering it all over that rag, hurting that young man's career."

"I don't give a shit about that 'young man's career'. I want to know how the pictures got in the rag. I have a copy, and you have a copy. I know nobody in my house sold them, so it must be you."

The woman on the other end of the phone laughed. "Well, I didn't sell anything to anybody."

"Don't destroy any of your emails, voicemails or hardcopies of your physical mail. My legal team will be contacting you shortly." Dan jabbed the End button and tossed his phone on the desk. "Bull. Shit."

Mel terminated the call and sat back in her chair.

"Well, that sounded interesting." Randolph sipped his tea and placed the cup back in its saucer. "Your half, anyway. Tell me."

Mel wrinkled her nose and pushed back from the table. "It's probably best you don't get involved." She stood and grabbed her phone off the conference room table.

Randolph pointed at her chair. "Sit. And I get involved in everything."

"You need legal distance, boss."

"Talk."

Mel sighed and walked to the bar in the corner. She poured herself a healthy amount of bourbon. She held up the bottle. "You want?"

He waved her off. "It's a little early. The tea will do me for now. I've never known you to need Dutch courage."

She grabbed a coaster from the bar and tossed it on the table. She took a large mouthful of drink and sat, both hands around the glass. "You're not fond of coincidences, Randolph. Neither am I. We don't believe in coincidences. But there's been a rather unfortunate coincidence."

Rand rubbed his eye with the heel of his hand. "Spit it out."

"You know that guy investigating Jeremy's death?"

He looked at Mel and nodded. "An annoying prat, but nothing overly concerning."

"Tenacious though, wouldn't you say?" Mel toyed with the glass, then took another sip.

He frowned in thought for a moment. "I don't recall you ever being in a meeting with me and Mr McGinnis. When did you meet him?"

"Well, I saw him leaving your office after one of your meetings with him." She grimaced. "He didn't seem too pleased."

"I was less. He left three recording devices in my office." Rand shook his head. "I have no idea how he expected to get them back."

Mel looked around the room. "Where are they now?"

"They've been destroyed."

"He'll be sending you an invoice for those."

Rand leaned back in his chair and examined Mel's face. "I'm confused. How is it you seem to know the characteristics of this two-bit detective from a casual, in-passing observation?"

"Yeah. Sure you don't want a drink?" Mel finished hers and headed back to the bar. "I'm topping mine up."

"Fine. Rocks."

"Of course. " Mel filled a tumbler with ice and splashed bourbon over it. She refilled her glass and took them both back to the table.

"So, *now* will you tell me?"

"So what are the odds? I go far outside of town, near Callum's place, to find someone to set up that kid. An hour south. Found a little PI in Campbelltown."

The light came on. "No. McGinnis?"

Mel nods. "Honest, boss, a total coincidence."

"So what was that call about?"

Mel plucked a copy of the latest paper off a small table by the window. She tossed it on the conference table in front of Rand. Callum Ryan, in bold black and white, graced the cover, snorting cocaine. "This."

Rand smiled. "He didn't pay, he gets front page treatment."

"That photo was the result of me telling that McGinnis guy that I wanted to void a prenup with the Callum kid and needed evidence."

Rand rubbed the back of his neck. "Has he connected you with my organisation?"

"No. I only talked to him with burner phones."

Rand swirled the ice in his glass. "I still don't see a problem."

"Well, there's that tenacity problem. I didn't pay for his work. I used the argument that there was nothing in what he delivered that would void the prenup. He's gotten a bit stroppy after seeing the latest issue."

Rand sipped and smiled. "I imagine he would. You've gotten yourself into a bit of a pickle. But, as usual, I have full confidence that you'll find a resolution to your problem." He took another sip. "Or am I mistaken?"

"No. It's all good, boss."

The smile slipped off his face. "Good. It doesn't come back to me or this company. Under any circumstances."

"Understood." Mel tipped back the rest of her drink. "I'll handle it."

"And pull the trigger on Cassie Johnson. She's not responding."

Gerald and Robert sat on a park bench under trees in St Leonards Park in North Sydney. Cassie was on the far side of the park, jogging with her dog.

Gerald pointed. "See? Every day, like clockwork."

Robert stood. "Let's get this over with."

Gerald grabbed him by the arm and pulled. "Sit down, idiot. There are a dozen witnesses. She'll be looping around and passing in front of us in a couple of minutes."

He slowly sat. "And then?"

Gerald jerked his thumb behind him. "Music shell is right behind us."

"So what?"

Gerald smiled. "Follow my lead."

They watched her jog. Her pace was steady and relaxed and the dog, a small terrier, ran beside her, tongue lolling out of the side of its mouth looking like it was having the time of its life.

"Cute."

"She's gorgeous."

"I meant the dog."

Gerald scowled. "Don't get attached."

Robert grunted and crossed his arms. He watched her complete the length of the park on the far side and loop back their side.

They stood as she came closer and blocked her path. They shifted to keep her from passing.

She slowed to a stop, but kept jogging in place. "Excuse me guys. I don't want to cool down."

Robert reached for the dog's leash and Cassie pulled it away, jerking the dog. "You're from Rand."

"You were warned. Pay or the dog goes. Don't make us hurt you, too."

"Tell Rand he can go blow himself." She scooped up her dog, tucked him under her arm and started sprinting.

"Jesus Christ, Robert. We were supposed to get her out of sight first. Go. Get her."

"Me?"

"Never mind. You'll never catch her." He jabbed his index finger in Robert's chest. "You need to explain this to Rand."

CHAPTER 16

Beryl poked her nose in Dan's office. "Boss, there's a young man here who would like to hire you."

"Want me to stay?" asked Stew.

"Sure." Dan nodded at Beryl. "Send him in."

Beryl stood to one side and escorted Callum Ryan into Dan's office.

Dan looked at Stew and raised his eyebrows. He stood and extended his hand. "You're Callum Ryan, right? I've seen you in some stuff. Sit. Tell me what I can do for you."

Callum was slight, his hair tousled with a few days of patchy beard hung around his chin. He sat in the chair across from Dan. "Um, yeah." He pointed at the *Oz Express* on Dan's desk, then reached across the desk and grabbed it.

"This. I want to hire you to find out how in the FUCK they got this picture of me. In my house."

Dan took the paper and furrowed his brow, looking at the picture with his head cocked. "That's you?" He looked at the paper, then at Callum's face and nodded. "Huh. It is. You say you don't know when this was taken?"

Callum stood and paced. He finger combed his hair, to no effect, and shook his head. "No. I absolutely know *when* this picture was taken. I need to know HOW it was taken. Dammit."

Stew raised a finger. "That's a fair pile of blow, kid. You're not afraid of legal problems?"

Callum dismissed him with a wave of his hand. "No. My place is clean." He jabbed a finger at the picture. "Nothing in that picture says that's coke. But my property has been violated. My *privacy* has been violated. I want you to find out who did it." He clenched his fists. "And find whatever other devices are in my house. I can't go back in until all those things are gone."

Dan nodded. "Yeah, we can do that. Right, Stew?"

"Sounds like something right up our alley, boss. We're free this afternoon."

Callum stopped pacing. "Today? Could you? I'll pay you double your daily rate."

"Beryl will get your details and we'll follow you to your house."

Stew cleared his throat. "So, where do you live?"

"Just outside Camden. Kirkham. Maybe a fifteen minute drive from here." He grabbed a pen off Dan's desk. "Got a piece of paper?"

Dan slid a notepad across his desk.

"Thanks." He scribbled details on the pad and handed it back to Dan. "Give this to the nice lady out front. My accountant's details."

"Where are you parked?" asked Dan.

"Out front. Gull wing Mercedes."

"Okay. Wait there. Stew and I will be coming around in his car."

"An old Mazda 3. Blue."

Callum nodded and smiled for the first time. "Solid. I'll see you out front. I really appreciate this, guys."

Callum shook Dan and Stew's hands and ran down the front stairs.

Dan waited until he heard the front door close and exhaled. "Well." He picked up the piece of paper. "Can you read this? I can't read this."

"You were wondering how were going to get the electronics back."

"And he wants to pay us for it."

They walked down the back stairs. "So, boss, we going to tell him it was us?"

Dan expelled a burst of air "Hell, no. Not now. That would be a very bad thing." He thought for a second. "Maybe later."

"My thoughts, too. Just checking."

They drove around to the front of the office and Stew tapped his horn as they pulled up near the Mercedes. Callum waved out the window and pulled from the kerb.

"You're going to have to keep up, Stew," said Dan. The Mercedes pulled ahead of them on Queen and turned left on Dumaresq, accelerating into the corner.

Stew pressed the accelerator to the floor. "This is going to be fun."

Stew followed Callum's car up his driveway.

"Looks nice in the daylight."

"Pretend, Stew. Pretend," said Dan.

The Mercedes pulled around the right side of the house and stopped. Stew rolled his Mazda to stop beside it and he and Dan got out of the car.

The house sprawled across the large lot. The lawn was perfectly manicured. A row of small trees lined the drive.

Callum motioned for them to follow. They walked around the back of the house and into the kitchen. He opened the fridge and grabbed a beer. "You want one?"

"I'm good,' said Dan. He looked around and pointed to the living room. "You were in there for that photo, right?"

"For the cover shot, yes. Some of the others in the article were in here, some in the bathroom." Callum waved his hands around. "This whole place is wired. I want you to find *all* of them, and who planted them."

"Yeah, sure, we can find them. Stew will start. The 'who' might be a bit more of a challenge. You and I need to chat."

"I'll get the detector from the car, boss."

Dan sat at the dining table and motioned for Callum to sit across from him. "Have you talked to the rag?"

"Who, the *Oz Express*? No. Not yet. Not about where the pics came from, anyway."

"You've contacted them about something else?"

Callum scrubbed his scalp with his fingertips. "Ah, this is awkward."

"The more you tell me, the more I can help."

Callum leaned his forehead on his hands and sighed a particularly deep sigh. "Okay, so, they warned me this would happen."

"What, the photos? When?"

"A couple of weeks ago."

Dan nodded at Stew as he walked through the kitchen into the living room. "A warning implies a proposed deal."

"Not really a deal. More like blackmail. Or extortion. Or whatever you call it. If I didn't pay them an ridiculously large amount of money they'd ruin my career."

"How ridiculous?"

"A million. I thought they were full of shit. I mean, how would they get pictures, right? Ridiculous."

"Yeah, well they did," said Stew. He dropped seven pinhole cameras on the table in front of Dan. "I'll keep looking."

Callum pointed at the cameras. "You know people who would use these?"

"They're pretty common in our line of work. We use cameras just like this." He slipped them in a small plastic bag. "But go back to what you were saying. They came right out and demanded catch and kill money?"

"Brassy bitch. She wasn't subtle. Nothing in writing, but she was clear on the phone."

"So, nothing in writing. That's not good."

"I've got a recording of one of the calls," said Callum. "That help anything?"

"Yeah, of course."

Stew walked into the kitchen and dropped three more cameras and four listening devices on the table. "This place is wired like a concert."

Callum picked up one of the listening devices. "Man, I hope you find the bastards who placed these."

"We'll do our best. Like I said, though, it's pretty common equipment. The recording?"

"Right. Half a sec."

Callum retrieved an older mobile phone from a drawer and turned it on. "I put the call on speaker and used this old phone to record the call." He unlocked the phone. "This was the last call. Three days ago." He pressed PLAY.

"Callum Ryan speaking. Who is this?"

"This is your final opportunity to buy your way out of an embarrassing, and most definitely career ending, exposé. And because you've been delaying, the price has increased to two million dollars."

"Listen, bitch, there's no fuckin' way I'm giving you or your shithouse rag a penny. Publish whatever the hell it is you think you have and leave me the fuck alone."

Callum closed the app. "So there's that."

"Audio's not that clear," said Dan. "And it sounds like you hadn't seen what they were threatening you with."

"They offered. I didn't care because I didn't think they had anything worth worrying about."

"Send me that recording, will you?" He handed Callum a card. "Email is on the back."

"Sure thing." He typed a couple of commands on his phone and they heard the *whoosh* sound of a sent email.

Dan wrote a note in his phone. "When did she first approach you?"

Callum opened the calendar on his phone and tapped the screen while thinking. "Ten days ago. Always by phone."

"Ten? You sure?"

"Positive. Why? What does that mean?"

Dan frowned and shook his head. "Nothing. Just confirming details."

Stew stood on a stool and pulled a small video recording device from above the stove vent. "I think I've got all of them."

"You guys are fast. I expected a full day of this."

Stew dropped the video recorder on the table with the rest and swept all of the devices into a plastic bag. "Experience. I know these types of devices. Limited places you can conceal them."

Callum grabbed one before it got swept into the bag. "So these must be wireless, right?"

Stew nodded and plucked the device from Callum's hand and dropped in the bag. "Wireless everything these days."

"What kind of range?"

Stew looked at Dan, who nodded. "Forty, maybe fifty metres, depending on construction materials."

Callum looked out the kitchen window toward the back of his property. "That means someone would have had to be sitting out there, just beyond the property line."

"Could have been a neighbour," said Dan.

Callum laughed. "Those guys? No. Never. Seventy-year-old retirees on one side and left-wing, granola-crunching trust fund babies on the other. Parking in my drive would be a little conspicuous, so it would have had to have been back there." He crossed his arms. "No security video out that way. I'll have to add some cameras."

Stew stood behind Callum and caught Dan's eyes, raising his eyebrows.

"So, mate, you've got security videos?"

"No, not yet, Dan. Getting them put in because of that damned magazine cover."

"You should put some in the back. Definitely. Maybe put an alarm system in, too." Dan took the bag from Stew and held it up. "We've got all the devices. Your place is clear. Will that be all?"

"Thanks heaps, guys. Find out who bugged me."

"Clearly it was that magazine."

Callum shook his head and grabbed another beer out of the fridge. "Those wankers couldn't arrange a root in a brothel. They hired someone."

Dan made another note in his phone. "Can you give me the number of this woman who called you? And her name."

"Yeah, sure. She called herself Helen, but it's probably not her real name." He scribbled a number on a piece of paper. "Her mobile. Always goes to voicemail when I call."

"Thanks. Probably a burner." Dan locked his phone and stuffed it in his shirt pocket. "We'll see what we can find out. No guarantees, though."

"Your best is good enough."

Callum saw Dan and Stew to their car. "Call me any time."

"Will do."

Stew waited until Dan closed his door. He started the engine. "The definition of awkward, boss. Are we really going to take the case to find out who planted the bugs? Seems kind of unethical."

"It is. Very unethical." Dan rubbed the top of his head. "And it's more awkward than you know."

"How's that?"

Dan unfolded the paper Callum had given him. "Different number, but I recognise the voice. This is the woman who called me to set up the bogus pre-nup surveillance. Said her name was Melanie."

Stew turned left onto Camden Valley Road. "And she was extorting that kid almost a week before she called you."

"A bluff. He called her on it, so she had to get something." Dan slammed his fist on the dash.

"Hey, mate. Take it easy on the wheels."

"I really hate being conned." Dan rubbed his temples with his thumb and middle finger. "This Helen or Melanie or whatever her name is must be fairly high up in the *Oz Express* organisation."

"So what do we do now?"

Dan leaned his head against the headrest and closed his eyes. "Too many moving pieces. The paying case is Jeremy Brookes' death. Let's focus on that. We don't have to worry about getting our equipment back, anyway."

"You're still going to invoice that Melanie lady for the electronic bits though, right?"

Dan smiled and looked across at Stew. "Hell, yeah. I'd be stupid not to. And she's no lady."

CHAPTER 17

Dan and Stew entered the office to Kat and Beryl in the middle of an argument.

"I'm not covering up my ink. They are works of art. I designed most of them myself." Kat slid her sleeves up her arms to accentuate her point.

Beryl crossed her arms. "I don't care about ink, generally. I've got some myself. And no, I'm not showing you where they are. I don't know you well enough." She pointed to a figure on the inside of Kat's left arm. "That's a little too risqué for an office environment."

Kat turned her arm so she could see what Beryl was pointing at, then started laughing. "Oh, that. The mermaid. She's not topless. There are shells on her titties." She held her arm closer to Beryl's face. "Maybe you need new bifocals, grannie."

Dan interrupted. "Great to see you two are getting along. Beryl, you find something for her?"

"Well, she's *really* good at graphic design. Fake IDs, websites, signage for our stakeout vehicles -- she's head and shoulders better than anyone else in the office. She's also really good at coding. Surprisingly good. Gets a thumb's up from me. Screw the internship. Hire her on for real." She cocked her head and looked at Kat. "As long as she doesn't call me grannie again, because that'll get her arse kicked."

Kat smiled and tugged her sleeves down. "Thanks for the vote of confidence. What do you want me to do?"

Dan looked at his watch. "Do the paperwork for permanent employment this afternoon. You start tomorrow. Beryl knows where it all is. She'll set you up with a place to sit. And a machine. Go through every piece of graphics we've got and make it better, to start with." He held out his hand. "Welcome aboard."

Kat smiled and shook his hand. "What do you pay?"

Beryl took her by the arm and walked her to the door. "He pays well. We'll sort it out this afternoon."

Dan stopped her and handed her the take from Callum's house. "We recovered these. I'll explain later."

She looked at the bag of recording devices. "I'll cancel the invoice."

Dan smiled. "No, don't."

Beryl smiled and dropped the bag on her desk as she walked past it. Dan watched them leave then headed to his office. Stew followed.

"Where are we, boss?"

"We're stalled. Doesn't look like a mugging, but I can't find anything that leads us to Rand as the killer."

He computer 'dinged' within an incoming mail. "Hang on." It was from Doctor Woods. There was an attachment. He opened the file and skimmed it, then printed two copies. They slid out of the printer on the table in the corner of his office. He took one copy and handed it to Stew.

"I asked the medical examiner to run a full tox screen on Jeremy."

Stew took the pages. "Why?"

"There's no such thing as too much information. Scan through it and see if anything jumps out at you."

"Like I'd know what to look for."

Dan shrugged. "Anything that looks strange."

Stew scanned the top page. "He was older than I thought he was."

Dan nodded and flipped to the second page. He leaned forward. "Second page. A third of the way down. Traces of an acetylcholinesterase inhibitor in the liver. What in the hell is an acetylcholinesterase inhibitor?"

Stew typed slowly on his phone, repeatedly referring to the spelling in the tox report. "Hang on. It says, and I quote, *An acetylcholinesterase inhibitor (often abbreviated AChEI) or anti-cholinesterase is a chemical or a drug that inhibits the acetylcholinesterase enzyme from breaking down acetylcholine, thereby increasing both the level and duration of action of the neurotransmitter acetylcholine.*"

Stew looked at Dan, who looked back.

"Well," said Dan. "That clears absolutely nothing up. Do some digging and see if you can find what that means, will you?" He flipped a couple of more pages then tossed the paper on his desk. "Tell you what, go see your doctor friend and get her to interpret this. I don't have a clue what most of it says, other than his blood type and that he wasn't HIV positive. I couldn't even tell you if these cholesterol levels are good or not."

"They're not. He was a heart attack waiting to happen." Stew folded the report lengthwise. "I'll see what I can find out, boss." Stew stood to leave.

"Thanks." Dan laced his fingers behind his head. "So how do we handle the Callum conundrum?" There was a half-smile on his face.

Stew grimaced and sat back down. "There's a first for everything. For me, anyway. You ever have this kind of problem?"

"Oh, no. No, no, no. Nothing like this. Bug Subject B for Client A, then have Subject B hire you to find out who bugged them."

"And Client A turns out to be a low-life, skeeving piece of shit."

Dan threw his hands up in the air. "All new." He smiled at Stew. "What a wonderful time to be alive."

Stew grunted as he stood. "It's just special." He held up the tox report. "I'll get on this."

"Thanks. Ring when you've got something."

"Will do, boss." Stew waved as he walked out of the office. Beryl nudged him as she walked in. She held the bag of surveillance devices pinched between her thumb and forefinger. "I feel a little bit dirty about this. I'm going to regret asking, but why are we invoicing someone for something we've retrieved? Very unlike you, Danny."

Dan took a deep breath and let it out slowly. "It is. We're going to be invoicing the *Oz Express*."

Beryl nodded. "Fifty percent mark-up, then?"

"More, if you're feeling it."

"Noted." She stopped at the door. "Don't stay here too late. You're looking tired."

"Have a seat for a sec. I need your opinion." He handed her a glass of whiskey

"What moral dilemma do you need my advice on now?"

Dan reached across his desk and picked up the paper. He held it with two hands in front of his face. "You obviously recognise this picture."

"I brought it to your attention."

"Exactly."

"So what's the moral dilemma? We're charging her for the equipment we recovered, plus a healthy margin, for purely punitive reasons. That bothers you?"

"Fifty percent?"

Beryl smiled and winked. "Seventy-five."

"Nice. No, I've got no problem with that." He pointed at the picture on the cover. "This is Callum Ryan."

"Yeah, loved him in that bank heist movie."

"And Callum called us today, to hire us, to find out -"

"Who bugged him. Oh, damn." She swallowed her drink and refilled, a bit more than the first one. "What did you tell him?"

Dan held up a finger. "That's not all. It gets way better."

Beryl narrowed her eyes. "What?"

"The magazine was extorting him, or trying to extort him, to keep the pics out of the rag."

"Not surprising, and full credit to the young man for resisting. He's young. He'll be able to weather this."

"The woman extorting him is the same woman who hired us to bug his place."

Beryl stopped her glass half way to her mouth. She looked at it and took a mouthful, coughing as it burned down her throat. "I haven't sent the invoice yet. I'll double the amount I was going to charge."

"I like your style. My dilemma is, as you guessed, how much do I tell Callum? He's caught in the middle of this and I can't really take money from him to investigate what we've done."

Beryl nodded and sat back in her chair, thinking.

Dan sat quietly, waiting. He sipped his drink and held the bottle up, asking if she wanted more. She placed her hand over the glass and shook her head.

"Get him on our side. I'm not sure how. You're clever that way, but use him. He'll be especially pissed off and we need to harness that before he turns it on us."

Dan nodded. "My thoughts, too. I'll need to think of an approach, but it'll work. Thanks."

Beryl dropped back the rest of her drink and gave the glass back to Dan. "Make sure you wash these. See you in the morning." She walked out as Terry entered, a stack of papers in his hand and a laptop case hanging from his shoulder.

He dropped the papers on Dan's desk. "Print outs from Jeremy's laptop. Summary on the top page. I'm running late or I'd go over it with you."

"Thanks, kid. This is fast work," said Dan. "Maybe you need to get smacked on the head more often. It's getting late. We'll go over it all in the morning." Dan slid the papers to the edge of his desk and butted the edges together. He slid them into his top desk drawer and locked it. "Get out of here. See you in the morning."

CHAPTER 18

Kat was waiting at the back door when Dan arrived the next morning, large bag over her shoulder, hair in a high ponytail and a big smile on her face.

"Nice bike."

Dan looked back at it and nodded. "It is." He entered a six digit code on the panel by the door. It clicked and Dan pushed it open. "Not buying you breakfast this morning. There's a good coffee machine in the kitchenette, though." He looked at his watch. "Beryl will be here in about thirty minutes. Familiarise yourself with the office. I'll have a meeting at 9:30 and introduce you to the team." He held the door open for her. "Door code is 853211."

"Reverse Fibonacci. Cute."

Dan smiled. "You'll fit in well."

He followed her up the stairs, pointed her in the direction of the kitchenette and headed to his office. He had the file Terry had dropped off the day before -- the contents of Jeremy's laptop -- spread across his desk when Kat deposited a cup of black coffee on his desk.

"Thanks for this, Dan."

Dan sipped the coffee and smiled. "I should be thanking you."

"Thanks for the job."

Dan looked up at her. "Thank Beryl. You convinced her, and she's not an easy mark. Thanks for the coffee." He turned his focus back to the papers on his desk.

"Okay. I get the message. We'll chat later, I guess."

He nodded and turned over a page. "That we will."

He grabbed a pen and started making notes on the papers. The top few pages contained email summaries for the past three months. Plenty with staff within the *Oz Express*. He marked off any sent to or received from Randolph specifically.

Terry knocked on the door frame. "How's it look, Dan?"

"Good summary." He fanned the pages. "You printed out all the emails?"

"And the calendar and any documents he'd been working on."

Dan looked sideways at the stack of paper. "All of it?"

"Documents for the past three months. Calendar for the past three months and out a month from his death."

Dan nodded. "Cool. Have a chance to look at any of it?"

Terry sat across from him. "Nah. Really needed a hot shower and sleep last night. Happy to go through it with you now, though. What are you looking for?"

Dan looked up. "You should know it when you see it. Something that doesn't feel right. Something out of character."

"Yeah, but, we don't know the guy. We wouldn't know what's not in character."

Dan hefted the stack of paper. "Read this and by the end of it you'll get a feeling for the guy. In here, somewhere, will be a few grains of something off. Our job is to find it." He peeled the top half of the stack off and handed the bottom half to Terry. "Dig in."

Terry pulled a pen from his shirt pocket. "Fantastic." He started reading through the first document.

"This is part of the job, too, kiddo It's not all electronics and gadgets. Sometimes ya gotta slog."

"Slog. Right." Terry half smiled and went back to reading.

Terry was about a quarter of the way through the documents, no happier than when he started, when he flipped through the calendar pages and tapped on the desk. "Dan?"

"What?"

"Calendar drops off quick a week and a half after his murder."

"Not surprised, actually."

Beryl knocked on the doorframe. "Team meeting, Dan."

"Thank God." Terry dropped the pen on the pages and stood. "See you in the room, Boss."

Dan sighed and neatly stacked the pages. He slid the pile Terry was working on to the edge of his desk and butted the edges together into a neat stack.

Terry, Andy, Beryl and Kat were in the meeting room when Dan entered. He sat at the head of the table. Kat and Beryl were on his left and Terry and Andrew, his right. Terry couldn't keep his eyes of Kat.

"So, like, you're working here now?" asked Terry.

Kat turned away from her conversation with Beryl. "*So, like*, why don't you wait for the boss to talk, Tommy."

"It-it's Terry."

"Yup." Kat turned back to Beryl. "What's the fastest you've set up a backstopped website?"

"Later, Kat," said Dan. "Okay, quick meeting today." He looked around the table. "Where's Stew?"

"He said something about seeing a doctor," said Beryl. "He sounded healthy enough."

"Right. That's for me. He's getting help interpreting the post mortem report we received. It's all Greek to me."

"Probably more like Latin," said Beryl

Dan laughed. "Not good with that, either." He cleared his throat and nodded at Kat. "You've all bumped into Kat over the past couple of days. Kat Brady. Kat is joining our little family. She has skills that should help us create more convincing back stories in the event we need to be somebody else." He held up his hand. "No fault with what Beryl's been doing. Kat's skillset will allow the backgrounds to be deeper."

"And better, and I'm glad for it, " said Beryl.

"Kat, you've met Beryl and I hope she hasn't scared you too much." Dan pointed at Andy. "Andy Smith and I go way back. We played footie together in school. He claims he was better than me and I'm more than happy to have that discussion with anyone in the office. He spent a few years in the Australian Defence Force in places he's not allowed to talk about before joining me here. He's our surveillance lead."

"Good to meet you, Kat. Welcome aboard. And in case you were wondering, it's not Smithee. It's Andy."

Kat smiled. "Got it, *Andy.*"

"The young man to his left is Terry Graves. Just finished near top of his class at ACAP where he got his criminology degree."

"Not near top, boss. Top top." He smiled at Kat. "Anything you need, just let me know."

"Down, boy," said Kat.

Dan cocked an ear. Heavy footsteps came up the front of the building.

Dan raised an eyebrow. "And the old fart who isn't here is Stewart Williams."

Stew entered the room and dropped a folder on the table in front of Dan. "Stew is good enough. Stewart sounds like something a judge would call me." He walked to the end of the table and sat. "And if you call me Stewie, you're dead to me."

"A long, long time ago Stew used to be a cop. For half a dozen years or so, and then he left and did manual labour on the north shore, throwing rocks around for dumb rich folks," he paused, "for reason's he'll be more than happy to tell you over a couple of expensive drinks. Stew can find anybody, anywhere. Doesn't matter how well they think they've hidden."

"Nice to meet ya, Kat." Stew nodded at the folder. "Dan-o, we've got to talk."

"Kat, this is Stew on a good day. Don't let him intimidate you. Stew, be nice to Kat. She's going to be helping Beryl set up our covers, when we need them." He picked up the folder and stood. "You can talk among yourselves, get Kat up to speed within anything we've got open. Terry, behave yourself."

Stew followed him into his office. Dan opened the folder as he sat. "What did the fine doctor say?"

Stew smiled and sat. "She *is* fine. Almost broke her down. I'll be licking whipped cream off her body before the month is over."

"What does Doctor Jane see in an old fart like you?"

Stew shrugged. "Her ex- is a PI up on the Central Coast. She's got form. She likes a more mature man."

"Yet she hangs out with you. What's the short version?"

"There's two copies in there. Hand me one."

Dan lifted the top copy off and slid it across his desk. "Speak, old man."

"If you're lucky, you'll be old one day, too."

Dan scanned the top sheet. "The man wasn't healthy. Bad cholesterol. You got that one right. Heart disease, that doesn't look good. Arthritis in his hands." Dan looked up. "The punchline?"

"The acetylcholinesterase inhibitor found in the liver. That's the punchline. The guy was terminal. Based on the levels found, Jane figures he was at maximum dosage. She called the morgue and asked a few questions. Notes on the last page."

"You could have led with that." Dan read the doctor's notes. "*Terminal, terminal. Like, months at most. Early onset dementia, Lewy's Body disease. That would suck.*"

Stew nodded. "Kinda puts a different twist on the whole murder thing."

Dan blew out a breath. "What are you thinking? Planned suicide?"

"Well," Stew shrugged. "The guy was a brain. Losing all that -- who'd want to invite that into their life if there was a way out?"

"Do you think Sally knows?"

"That her husband was terminal? I would hope so. She doesn't strike me as someone who doesn't know what's going on. Plus, she's a brain doctor."

Dan placed his phone on his desk and dialled Sally Brookes. He put it in speaker mode.

"Sally Brookes speaking."

"Hi there, Sally. It's Dan McGinnis. I've got you on speakerphone with Stew Williams, one of my investigators. Do you have a couple of minutes?"

"You have an update?"

"I was hoping you might have one."

"I don't understand," said Sally. "An update about what?"

"I asked the medical examiner's office to run a full tox screen on your husband."

"Why would you think -"

"And we found some interesting results."

Stew leaned forward and spoke into the phone. "You knew your husband was terminal, right?"

Silence on the phone.

"Sally, are you still there?" asked Dan.

"Yes. Yes I knew. It's not relevant. He was murdered. A more instant type of terminal. Have you made any progress on *that*?"

Stew looked at Dan and raised his eyebrows.

"We're still working it. This is a significant piece of information though, I would think. No?"

"It has no bearing on his murder. Have you linked Randolph and his thugs to my husband's death yet?"

"We're still working on it, like Dan said." Stew looked at Dan, then continued. "How long did you and your husband know that he was suffering from a rapidly developing terminal disease?"

"Gentlemen, I hired you to find his murderer, not question his medical background. If there's nothing else, I need to go. Please do call when you find out who killed him."

The call ended. Dan picked up his phone. "Nothing at all strange about that."

"You thinking he took a hit out on himself?"

"He's wealthy enough. And from what I've heard so far, more than stubborn enough." Dan placed his hand on the stack of notes on his desk. "What's in this pile might be more important than anything else we've done so far. I think arranged suicide trumps anything to do with Rand and the *Oz Express* at this point."

"We're back to square one." Stew fell back in his chair.

Dan nodded. "We're back to square one." He gathered the papers. "Get everyone together in the conference room."

"Everyone?"

"Yeah, Kat, too."

CHAPTER 19

Kat slowly sat in the last chair. "You want me here, too?"

"You're part of the team, right? Beryl hasn't fired you?"

"Yes, I mean, no. I mean -"

Beryl rested her hand on Kat's arm. "Don't worry about Dan, dear. He's like this when the pressure hits."

Dan looked at Beryl for a beat and turned to the whiteboard. "Okay. Back to square one. Our client's husband was terminal. He had rapid, early onset Alzheimer's with LBDs. We need to confirm a couple of things." He wrote on the board while he talked. "First, did our client know her husband was terminal?"

"She would, wouldn't she?" Kat looked around the table. "Shouldn't she?"

"She said she did when we talked to her earlier today. But that doesn't mean she was telling the truth. She could have been covering for the fact she *didn't* know and was embarrassed we *did* know." Dan shrugged. "We need to know if the wife knew prior to his death."

"First rule, dear, never assume anything. Find out. Be sure." Beryl scribbled a note on her pad.

Dan nodded. "Right. Second, we need to scour the info Terry's pulled from Jeremy's laptop and look for any evidence he set this thing up. Contacts with people that look sideways, abnormal, out of the ordinary compared to the regular correspondence he has."

"Do you really think he'd use his laptop to -" Kat stopped. "Right. Never assume."

Dan nodded. "As I was saying. I'm going to need a couple of you to go through the stuff on the laptop. Terry and," he pointed at Kat, "new girl."

Kat narrowed her eyes. "Thanks."

"Not a problem. *He* knew he was terminal. How terminal, we still need to find out. If he arranged to be killed, maybe he had a life insurance policy that wouldn't pay out for suicide. Look for anything related to that. You don't find someone to kill you in the phone book."

Kat put her hand up.

"You don't have to do that. Just talk."

"I can find data a lot faster *not* combing through paper. Do we still have the laptop?"

Terry nodded. "You're right. Paper is too slow if we're starting from scratch."

"Fine. Glad you're here to do that." Dan turned back to the whiteboard. "Third, there's got to be surveillance video of that stretch of Harris street. There are dozens of businesses either side of that lane, and across the road. We're going back and pounding the pavement until we find something." He looked at his team. "Andy, that'll be you and I, Stew and Beryl. Dress nice. I don't want you scaring anyone.

"Stew, we're going to need Jeremy's full medical profile. I need you to convince your doctor friend to convince the medical examiner to do a full brain workup." He looked at his watch. "And you're going to have to get a move on while the remains are still accessible. I'll need you in Pyrmont, too. See if you can get your doctor friend on board fast."

Stew winced. "That's going to be a bit tough."

"Do your best. We need to know how terminal he was."

Stew stood and opened his phone and started dialling as he left the room.

Beryl watched him leave then raised her hand, laughing at the look at Dan's face. "And me?"

"Don't raise your bloody hand. But I do have a special task for you. We need to know the relationship between the victim and Randolph."

Beryl smiled. "Subterfuge. I like it." She leaned forward, elbows on the table. "This building where he works -- is there a coffee shop downstairs?"

Dan smiled. "You've got the idea."

Kat looked between Dan and Beryl. "Hang on, you really expect the head of a media conglomerate to pop downstairs for a coffee? And even if he does, Beryl, you think you'll get a peep out of him?"

"Oh, no, dear. That's what the subterfuge and wiring's about. The people who work for him *do* go down there for coffee. And lunch. And if they're like everybody else in this world, they like to gossip. I'll be a worker in a different department than whomever I'm talking to. My improv skills will once again be put to good use." She beat a drum cadence on the table with her open hands. "When do I start?"

"Come with Andy and me. We'll prep after the meeting. What else am I missing?"

"Financial activities," said Beryl. "Who he paid to kill him, if that's what he did."

Dan wrote it on the board. "We're going to have to get that second hand, though. We're not going to get direct access to his banking details."

"From the wife then."

Dan shook his head. "She's not going to give it to us willingly."

Beryl puffed out her cheeks while she exhaled. "So, if it turns out we need them, we'll have to trick her."

Dan scrubbed the back of his head with his fingertips. "Yeah, if we have to. If it comes to that." His phone, face down on the table, buzzed. He flipped it over and looked. It was a number he didn't recognise. He flipped it back over. "Terry, set up a remote access to the laptop so both you and Kat can access it at the same time. Andy, get Beryl wired up. Doesn't need broadcast. Just record." He clapped his hands. "Let's go. It's an hour's drive. I want to leave in the next thirty minutes."

He picked up his phone and dialled the missed call.

"Callum speaking. This is Dan, right?"

Dan walked into his office and closed the door. "Yeah. Callum Ryan?"

"The thing you're working on for me? Any progress?"

He sat back in his chair. "We're looking into the source of the bugs. Fairly standard equipment. Could be a few more days."

"Well, I wanted to talk to you about something else. Can I stop by?"

Dan shook his head. "It'll have to be tomorrow. Heading out for some surveillance. Need to leave in the next ten. Pop by tomorrow morning, if you want. Around 9:00 work for you?"

Callum sighed down the phone line. "No can do. Today or not at all. It's that critical."

Dan tapped his finger on his desk in thought.

"You still there?"

Dan grunted. "How fast can you get here?"

"Fifteen minutes. Tops."

Callum cleared the call, dropped the phone on his coffee table and looked across at Cassie. "Let's go."

Cassie was sitting on the edge of her chair, elbows on her knees, nervously playing with her fingers. "You think he'll help?"

"He and his pal found pretty much every bug in this place in about an hour. They're good."

Cassie nodded. "Yeah, that's what they normally do. Stuff like that. Will he help us with *this*?"

"He's got this White Hat aura about him. All for justice and shit. He hears your story, I'm sure he'll help."

"I hope so. Maybe with some of the others, too. This is bullshit." She stood and grabbed her phone. "I'm driving."

Kat walked into the small meeting room as Beryl opened wide her unbuttoned blouse to expose her bra.

"What in the hell is going on?" asked Kat.

"Knock if the door's closed, dear. Always." She held her blouse open while Andy threaded a wire behind the front clasp of her bra, between her breasts. "Andy, dear, I'm married. Be careful what you do. I can be led into temptation, and you're a very handsome man."

"Oh, give me a break," said Kat. "Wrong room. Where is Terry?"

"His electronics lab is down the hall to the right." Beryl adjusted her shoulders. "I can feel it, Andy. Loosen it up a bit."

Kat shook her head and walked out as Dan walked in.

"Almost finished, boss. We'd be finished already if Beryl didn't keep flirting with me."

"It takes two, sonny." Beryl flapped the tails of her blouse and lined the buttons up with the holes. "No more perving, gentlemen."

"Get over yourself," said Andy. "We're ready to go, Dan."

"Take your time. No rush. Callum just called in a panic. Needs to see me now. He'll be here shortly. We'll crack on in an hour."

"Time for a cuppa. Good."

Dan narrowed his eyes. "I won't be stopping for piss breaks on the way in, Beryl."

"I'll bring a bottle," said Beryl. She laughed as she walked into the kitchenette.

"I want to raise the stakes," said Randolph. He and Mel sat at a small table in the coffee shop in their building lobby.

Mel took a quick glance around. "This would be better in the office, I think."

Rand shook his head and made minute adjustments to the sugar packets, lining them up. "Too many ears."

"We've got quiet rooms upstairs. We're in the open here."

"That PI has got me paranoid. There's no telling what ears might be in my office. Or yours. Or any of them, for that matter."

Mel rubbed her forehead with the palm of her hand. "Fine. But keep your voice low. What do you mean, raise the stakes?"

"We can get more out of that Ryan kid. And probably Cassie. Different picture, this time."

Mel flipped open her book and scribbled a note. "I'll arrange for a PI to get more photos."

"No. Put the pen down. No more PIs. We've got all we need. We can digitally manipulate the pictures, photoshop anything we want in them."

CHAPTER 20

Cassie stopped on Queen street in front of Dan's office. Sitting, she was half a head taller than Callum. Her hair was a little longer than Callum's but held in a bun with a pencil. Callum sat in the passenger seat, typing something on his phone.

"You sure?" asked Cassie

Callum nodded, then shrugged. "Up to you, really. I'm not going to, like, force you or anything, but he seems like a good guy. I'm sure, for a fee, he'll help us out."

She snorted as she turned off the ignition. "*Any*one will help for a fee." She gently closed the car door. "We'll see."

Dan escorted Callum and Cassie into the conference room. Callum immediately took a seat. Cassie walked around the table, standing tall, looking at the posters on the walls.

"You were an athlete." Cassie's American accent had a soft, southern cadence. She pulled out a chair and sat across from Callum. "My friend thinks you can help."

Dan stood at the head of the table. He looked at Callum and raised an eyebrow. "Callum hasn't explained what it is you need help with. Do you want us to check your place for recording devices, too?"

She laced her fingers and settled into the chair. "No. My place is clean."

"How do you know?"

"Every picture of me in that rag is from when I'm out of my apartment." She took a breath. "Well, not exactly. They published a series of pictures of me getting into and out of my shower. I'd left my curtain open. But I'm on the twenty-seventh floor. They would have had to have used a drone."

"Or a long lens," suggested Dan.

Cassie shook her head. "The pictures were too good." She smiled. "If I do say so myself. Not grainy at all."

"I'm really sorry to hear that," said Dan. "Still not sure what you want me to do."

Cassie placed her phone on her table and opened the voice memo app. "I received a call this morning. I recorded it."

She pressed play.

"Cassie Johnson. Who's this?"

"Good morning, Cassie Johnson. Love what you do. Do you love what you do?" It was Mel's voice..

"Who is this? You fucking around, Stevie?"

"We've just started, Cassie. You should have paid. It's going to get worse. Monumentally worse."

"Go fuck yourself. There's nothing worse *in my life. What, you going to*

photoshop some bullshit?"

"Oh, you'd be amazed at what video mimicking technology can do now."

There was a pause. Dan went to speak and Cassie held up a finger, stopping him.

"What do you want?"

"You've got the bank details. The same details we gave you the last two times. Except it's $2 million now. You've got forty-eight hours. Or we'll do your dog."

"Do your dog?"

"They said they were going to kill her. Two apes tried grabbing her yesterday. You've got to help me -"

"- us," said Callum.

Dan nodded. "Any idea who it is?"

"The fucking *Oz Express*, obviously." Cassie slammed her phone on the table. "Jesus."

Dan held up his hands in surrender. "Yeah, yeah. I got that. You ever get a name?"

Cassie shrugged. "We never had tea together, if that's what you mean."

"It's the same woman who called me," said Callum.

Dan opened his phone and scrolled through to his voicemails. He put his phone on speaker.

"Mr McGinnis, I'm afraid the information you've gathered is useless. There was -- never mind. I'll call you back."

Callum squeezed his eyes shut and concentrated on the voice. He started nodding half way through the recording.

"Yeah. That's her." He looked up at Dan. "How -- what -- why is she calling you?"

"We've both been played." He leaned back in his chair and scrubbed his face. "Jesus." He took a long, slow breath. "Okay. Callum, we -- my agency -- got those pictures for the rag."

"Hang on. What?" He looked at Cassie. "I had no -- wait, what?"

Dan pointed at his phone. "That woman claimed she was married to you and wanted evidence to void a prenup."

Realisation dawned on Callum's face. "Wait a second. *You* planted those bugs in my place?" He kicked his chair back as he stood, fists clenched. He was a head shorter than Dan and a good twenty kilos lighter. "You son of a bitch. Were you going to charge me for *finding* those things? And when in the hell did you plant them?"

"Sit down, Callum. I apologise. It's what we do, and this came across as legit."

"Well it wasn't."

Cassie pushed her chair back and stood. "Let's go, Callum. Waste of time."

Dan held his hands up. "Hang on. Wait a minute. We've got a common enemy here. Mel or Helen or whatever her name is has screwed all of us."

Cassie set her face. "She screwed you out of a payment, but she, with your help, has probably screwed Callum out of any future work for a few years, until this dies down."

"Or millions of dollars, Cass."

"I'm not fucking paying a cent. I don't care what they come up with. I've got enough money stashed to live off forever. I don't care for this bullshit industry."

Dan nodded. "Sit back down, please. Both of you."

Cassie slowly sat. Callum stayed standing. "Why?"

Dan looked at his watch. "You can help us take her down. She doesn't know that we know each other. We can use that." He pointed at Callum. "And we're not going to charge you for finding the bugs."

Cassie snorted. "Of course you aren't."

"Look, I apologised. I take full responsibility for the pictures. They *were* legit pictures though. There was no doctoring. We opened the door for them, but you actually did what they say you did."

"IN THE PRIVACY OF MY HOME, YOU RATFUCK!"

Stew poked his head in the door. "You okay, boss?"

"It's fine, Stew."

"The little guy sounded kinda angry. It would be really embarrassing for us if he were to hurt you."

"We're good."

"Sorry. A bit pissed," said Callum.

"I think I'll hang around anyway." Stew stepped into the room, nodded at Callum and stepped toward Cassie. "You're Cassie Johnson. I love the work you're doing."

"Which movie is your favourite?"

He shook his head. "Your activism work on immigration. It's nice to see someone standing up to the fucknut in Kirribilli."

She smiled and stood to shake Stew's hand. "Stewart, right?"

"Stew is fine."

She looked at Dan. "If we help, Stew needs to be involved."

"Help with what, boss?"

"We have a common enemy. The woman who hired us to bug young Callum's place -- young, angry, Callum -- was extorting them to keep the pictures private."

Stew looked at Callum. "So, does he -"

"I know. Yes. Fuck you, too," spat Callum.

Dan nodded. "Yeah." He slapped his hands on the table and stood beside Stew. "Sorry, Callum, I know you're pissed. I would be pissed. Anyone would be pissed. We had -- I had no idea that the information we gathered would be used for what it was. And we'll put the full force of our agency behind bringing her down. Whoever she is."

"She's obviously connected to the rag." Cassie has sat back down. "Go after them."

"Could be. Could also be she's freelancing. Pretty clever freelancing, if you ask me."

"Okay. So where do we start," asked Callum.

Dan looked at his watch again. "Tomorrow. My team needs to get into the city this afternoon. Come back tomorrow morning and we'll map out a plan."

"Is what you're doing in the city related at all to our problem?"

Stew and Dan looked at each other. "Not directly, no," said Dan.

"Not directly?"

"Tangentially. A separate case related, loosely, with the *Oz Express*."

"You don't think that's too much of a coincidence?"

"Cassie, I don't believe in coincidences at all. If there's a link, we'll find it. But tomorrow, okay?"

"I want to go with you."

"No. Not a chance. Tomorrow morning. Both of you can drop by at 9:00 and we'll start working out how we find this woman and take her down. It'll be my pleasure." He opened the door. "Stew, can you show our guests out?"

CHAPTER 21

Dan, Stew, Andy and Beryl sat an outside table at a cafe at the bottom of Harris Street. Between them and Sydney harbour was a park with a playground, barbecue stands, and, closer to the water, picnic tables.

Dan pointed at the park. "That's where Jeremy was heading, to meet Sally."

They looked in silence for a minute.

"Kinda makes you think." Dan looked up the street at the shop entrances. "Should be lots of cameras."

Andy pointed at the office building across from the scene of the murder. "Might be some cameras in that place, too."

"Harder to get."

Andy smiled and scratched his chin. "Leave them to me."

"I'll walk to the *Oz Express* office. It's a beautiful day." Beryl was dressed in a smart pantsuit and flat shoes. She pressed under her arm on the left side, then tapped her chest. "Picking this up?"

"Hang on." Andy opened an app on his phone. "Do it again."

She tapped her chest and a line wiggled on his smartphone's display.

"Yeah, you're good."

"But we won't be listening, Beryl," said Dan. "So no smart-arsed stuff, okay? Passive collection. Only."

"Listen, kid, I've been around longer than any two of you put together." She winked at Dan. "I'm not an idiot."

"Didn't say you were." Dan checked the time. "There's a pub at the top of the hill. Back there when we're finished, okay?"

"Guaranteed." Beryl entered the *Oz Express* address in her phone and started the navigation. "Five-minute walk. Too easy."

"Andy are you hitting the office building?"

"I'll see what I can get from them."

"Good luck. Stew and I'll work the shoe leather, see what we see."

The four dispersed, Beryl heading west to the *Oz Express* offices and Andy to the office across the street.

Dan paid at the register and he and Stew started up the hill. "Leapfrog? I'll take the bottle shop, you hit the Japanese restaurant and we'll work it all the way up to the pub on the top of the hill. ANY video from an hour before to an hour after the killing. You got a thumb drive?"

Stew held his up. "Want me to pick up some sushi?"

Dan chuckled and entered the liquor store. "I'm good."

The shop was on the small side. A cooler on the left, just beyond the register, contained beer and alcho-pop drinks. Both sides of a rack down the middle of the shop displayed wines, reds on the right and white and rose on the left. Spirits spanned the right and back walls.

Dan checked the tops of the walls, near the ceiling. There were two CCTV cameras at the far corners, one behind the register and one above the door, looking out to the street.

A young man stood at behind the counter at the register, leafing through a football magazine. He watched Dan for a sec before speaking. "Yo, mate. What are you looking for?"

Dan pointed at the cameras. "Those." He reached into his back pocket and chuckled when the man behind the register tensed.

"Relax, mate." Dan held up his ID. "I'm a private investigator. Looking into the shooting just up the road." He pointed at the camera above the door. "Any chance I can copy some footage off that? A couple of hours either side of this date and time." He placed a piece of paper on the counter. "What do I call you?"

"Alex." He picked up the paper. "Shouldn't be a problem. A file is stored every hour, a week's worth, then the newest overwrites the oldest." He held up the paper. "This was well under a week ago. Do you want to watch it?"

Dan shook his head. "Thanks, Alex. I'm Dan McGinnis. Copies for now. We'll collect now and look later." He fished the thumb drive out of his pocket. "Can you put it on this?"

Alex uncapped the thumb drive and slid it the front of the computer below the counter. He checked the paper and looked at Dan. "This happened at 8:20. You want 8:00 to 9:00 and 9:00 to 10:00 or 7:00 to 8:00 and 8:00 to 9:00?"

"Seven to ten. Play it safe. Thanks."

Alex typed a couple of commands on the computer, waited a second, the ejected the drive. He handed it to Dan. "Good luck. I thought the cops said it was a mugging gone bad."

"Widow thought it was maybe something more. Just crossing some Ts and dotting some Is. Thanks again."

"Sure you don't want something?"

"I'm good."

"All right. Good luck."

Dan walked past the Japanese restaurant. Stew was having an animated discussion with an older Japanese woman at the counter. There seemed to be a serious language issue, and Stew looked to be on the losing end of it.

He walked into the Persian restaurant next to it. He stood in the doorway and inhaled the aromas. Lamb was cooking on a grill. Middle-eastern seasonings wafted through the shop.

A middle-aged woman in costume and heavy makeup approached with a menu. "For one?"

"Ah, no. As delicious as it smells, this is business." He showed her his identification. "I'm working for the widow of the woman shot in the alley next to your shop."

"The mugging. Yes. That was so sad. They have been in here in the past for dinner. Such a lovely couple." She shrugged. "But what can I do?"

Dan checked her name tag. "I'm looking for security video, Maryam. I don't think it was just a mugging. Do you have video cameras? Security cameras?"

"You'd have to talk to my son, Qasim. He handles that sort of thing."

"Is he around?"

"In the back. Please, have a seat. I'll make you some tea, if you'd like."

Beryl stood at the counter waiting for the staff from the small cafe to notice her. It was in a small corner of a very large atrium at the base of the media conglomerate that owned *The Oz Express*.

The cluster of tables was mostly all populated, filled with sharp looking upscale media types discussing very important things over $10 cups of coffee. A young man in a sleeveless shirt, sporting a man-bun finally noticed Beryl.

"Ma'am, what can I get for you?"

"I'd like a cup of English tea and a toasted banana bread. I'll be at one of the tables."

The young man smiled and rang up the total. "$17.50."

"Seventee -- right." She produced a card.

"Would you like a receipt?"

"Please." She walked to the far side of the clustered tables and sat at one near the window. She located herself beside a table of three women closer to her age than the building median.

She waited for a break in their conversation, then leaned over to the table. "Ladies, my name is Beryl. I wonder if I could ask you some questions."

"Pull your chair over, Beryl. I'm Anne and this is Lizzie and Lauren. What can we help you with?"

"I've got an interview in half an hour with the *Oz Express* people. Do you work there?"

Anne looked at the other two women. "What job?"

"I'm legal. Did a lot of corporate stuff for the bigger banks. Almost ready to retire -- almost. There's an opening for a part time legal to vet articles, keep the big guy out of the courts.

Lauren laughed. "I hope they're paying a lot of money. Rand is sued on an almost daily basis."

Beryl raised her eyebrows. "You're in legal, too?"'

"No. We're all in accounts payable. Almost as hard a job as legal," said Lizzie.

"I guess."

"No, it is. We're not supposed to pay anyone until they are screaming bloody murder. We get a lot of 'screaming bloody murder'. Who's interviewing?"

Beryl shook her head. "Not sure. Just have a time and a place. Other than the screaming, how's this place to work at? See the big guy very often?"

"Who, Rand?" asked Anne. "A couple of times a week he pops down with Mel for a coffee. Strategising something, no doubt."

"Really? A man of the people and his right-hand man?"

"Woman. Mel is female."

Lizzie snorted. "In form only."

"No judgement. Cool that he'd come down here," said Beryl.

Lauren leaned forward. "I heard he thinks his offices might be bugged, and there's things he wants to talk about in private."

Anne touched Beryl's arm. "Don't look behind Lizzie, but they just sat where you were sitting."

Beryl turned slightly and looked anyway. To her left, almost within earshot, were Rand and Mel.

"Look, ladies, I'm pleased to have met you. Maybe we'll cross paths. Now I've got to pitch myself."

She grabbed her phone and picked up her chair and placed it beside Rand's table. She stood with her hand resting on its back. "Mr Murray. So glad I ran into you. I understand that you've got openings in your legal department. I'd like to pitch myself."

Rand slid his laptop out of its carrying case and lifted the lid. He typed in his password and hovered his hand over the Enter key. "We're busy, Miss..."

"Beryl Swanson." She held out her hand. "And this is Mel?"

Mel squinted at her. "How do you know my name? And what are you doing at my table?"

"I'm good. I do my research." She pointed at Mel while she talked to Rand. "I don't know her last name, though. I'm correct, aren't I? There's an opening in legal?"

"This is Mel Dvorak. If there was an opening in legal, she'd be interviewing. Are you interviewing, Mel?"

"I'm not. You must be mistaken, Mrs Swanson. Now if you'd excuse us, we've got business to discuss. Confidential business."

"Well. I shall be talking to my recruiter about the absolutely appalling professionalism -- or lack of professionalism displayed in this organisation." Her phone chimed. A message from Dan. "Good day."

She tapped Anne's table as she passed. "Find a better job, ladies. This guy is going down."

Beryl was last to arrive at the pub. Stew, Andy and Dan all had a beer. A chilled glass of white wine sat at the empty seat. "Ah, boys, you know me so well." She sat and quaffed half the glass. "It's a warm one today. How'd you guys do?"

"Hard to say," said Dan. "Got video from a couple of store fronts. Stew almost caused an international incident with the Japanese."

Beryl laughed. "What about you, Andy?"

"Security in the office buildings were most unhelpful, except for one young guy. I got an unfiltered load of video spanning the past week, all cameras in the joint. It's going to take hours to go through it. You're awfully chipper. How did your snooping go?"

Beryl unlocked her phone and placed it on the table. She navigated to the videos file, selected one and pressed Play.

"Mr Murray. So glad I ran into you. I understand that you've got openings in your legal department. I'd like to pitch myself to you."

"We're busy, Miss..."

"Beryl Swanson. And this is Mel?"

"How do you know my name? And what are you doing at my table?"

"I'm good. I do my research. I don't know her last name, though. I'm correct, aren't I? There's an opening in legal?"

"This is Mel Dvorak. If there was an opening in legal, she'd be interviewing. Are you interviewing, Mel?"

Beryl tapped the screen and paused the video. "Recognise the voice, Dan?"

"Yeah. That's her. Dvorak? She's tightly linked to Rand. He identified her as his Chief of Staff at the casino. Should have known. Not freelancing after all." He tipped back his beer. "Great work, Beryl. Excellent work. You all want to split a pizza?"

"You missed the best bit." She scrubbed the video to the beginning and pressed play. "That's him entering his password."

"That's going to come in very handy," said Dan. "What kind of pizza?"

"Wait a minute," said Beryl. She opened the map app on her phone. "Sally's statement in the police report. She said her husband picked up a pizza then walked down the hill to meet her." She pinched the screen to zoom out. "This is where he picked it up."

Dan waved at a server and motioned her over. "Okay, first, can we get a large pizza with the works?"

"Order at the counter, hun." She turned to walk away.

"Hang on, one more thing."

"I can't take your order, sorry. At the counter."

Dan showed her a photo of Jeremy Brookes. "This guy comes in and gets a pizza every month. You wouldn't happen to remember him, would you?"

"Jeremy. Nice guy. Really sad what happened. Scary."

"He was in here the night he was shot, right?"

She nodded. "Had a couple extra drinks that night and left without his pizza. Weird night all around."

"So, he didn't leave with a pizza?" asked Beryl.

"That's what I said. I've got the get back to work now. Order at the counter. They'll bring it to your table."

CHAPTER 22

Jane stirred a packet of sweetener into her coffee. She checked the time and smiled as Stew came in the cafe.

He sat in the booth across from her. "You're looking fine this morning, Jane."

"You staying long enough to eat or is this another favour and dash?"

Stew pulled a laminated menu from between the salt and pepper mills. He waved over a server. "Spanish omelette, couple of rashers and a long black. Anything else for you, Jane? My treat."

She lifted her cup. "This is good for me. So what do you want?"

"I'm hurt. Can't I pop by for a bite with a beautiful doctor?"

"Right-o. So it's a doctor thing, then."

The server placed a large mug of coffee in front of Stew.

"Thanks." He slid the cup to one side and pulled a medical file from inside his jacket. "This thing, again."

"No *good morning*? No *how's it going*?"

"Good morning, Jane. How's it going?"

She narrowed her eyes and looked at the file. She reached across the table and touched it with her index finger. "The murdered guy? Interesting, anyway. What more can I tell you? I think I've gleaned all I can from this."

"You gave me a lot of information with the acetylcholinesterase inhibitor found in the liver. We know he was terminal, early onset Alzheimer's, Lewy Bodies disease, but we need to know *how* far advanced he was."

Jane scoffed. "I'm good, but there's no way I could know that from the file."

Stew opened the file. On the top sheet was the name and phone number of the Medical Examiner who had performed the autopsy. It was circled with red ink. He reversed the page and slid it slowly across the table.

"What?"

Stew cocked his head.

"Oh, bugger off with the puppy dog look. You're too old for that. I'm too old to fall for it. You want me to call the Medical Examiner and get more details? Just ask."

The server placed a plate in front of Stew and Jane snagged a rasher.

"Hey." Stew picked up the other one and crunched. "Okay. Can you please do some doctor magic and call the ME and find out how baked this Jeremy guy's brain was."

Jane pulled the file close and started reading it. "Why?"

"Why ask you? Why find out how baked he was? Why what?"

"The second one. The drug levels seem to indicate large doses which in turn would seem to indicate that he was pretty far gone."

"Lot of 'seems' in there." Stew tapped the phone number. "Give the guy a call. Please."

Jane picked up the file. "This isn't going to work just cold calling him." She flipped through the pages. "I need an angle."

Stew dug into his omelette. It was thick and covered the large plate. He was more than half way through it when Jane sighed and unlocked her phone. She entered the number, dialled and placed the call on speakerphone mode and placed it on the centre of the table.

"Hi there, Doctor Tobias Woods, right?"

"Yes. Who is this?"

"I'm Doctor Jane Golding. I'm at Campbelltown Private Hospital. I'm doing a study looking at the reactions of rapid onset Alzheimer's and Lewy Bodies to various drugs." Jane checked a section of the file. "You have the remains of a Jeremy Brookes at your facility."

"For another day, yes."

Jane closed her eyes. "Great. I was talking with his wife, Sally Brookes, and she suggested I talk to you to get some tissue samples. Not a large amount, just enough for analysis. If necessary I can get permission from -"

"Not necessary."

"Not -- what's not necessary?"

"Permission. He's donated his organs to science. Not a complete brain, of course. Cause of death was a chunk of lead entering his forebrain and rattling around a bit. Should still have enough tissue to help you, of course, but..."

Jane leaned forward. "But what?"

"Well, you're the expert. I'm not sure which bits of the brain you're looking for. And if you want something you're going to have to come by today. His organs are going to one of the teaching hospitals overnight. I mean, I'd take the sample and ship it myself, but it's kind of beat up. "

Jane raised an eyebrow and scowled at Stew. "Absolutely. Thank you so much. I'll drive up right now."

"What was your name again?"

"Doctor Jane Golding."

"I'll look out for you, Doctor Golding. Now if you'll excuse me, bodies are piling up here."

Jane ended the call and opened a mapping app on her phone. She typed the morgue address and whistled. "An hour and thirteen minutes?"

"Shitty traffic this time of day."

"Over an hour? Jeeee-sus."

Stew wiped his mouth with a thick paper napkin and belched. "You've got to try this omelette. My treat. But another day, I suppose. I probably shouldn't hold you much longer. You've got a lot of driving to do. I really, really appreciate this. Call me when you've got something, okay?"

Jane flipped the cover closed on the file and stood. "You owe me big time, mister. Huge."

"And huge it will be." Stew smiled as Jane blushed. "Promise."

Stew finished his breakfast, drained his coffee and checked the time. Still hours before Jane would be back with any information. He took a deep breath and his phone rang. He dug it out of his pocket and flipped it open. "What's up, Dan?"

"How'd ya go?"

Stew dropped two twenties on the table and eased out of the booth. "Good. She's on her way now."

"To Pyrmont?"

"Glebe. It was remarkably easy."

"To convince her or for her to convince the doctor?"

Stew snorted. "For her to convince the ME. I'm going to be paying hugely for this."

"That's okay. Expense it."

"I'll be paying for it in ways that Beryl won't want to know about and won't be able to compensate me for."

"Okay, don't need to know."

Stew chuckled and stepped into the sun. "I'm a five minute walk away. Jane's at least two hours from returning, probably another couple for her to do the analysis. What do we do until then?"

"Lots to keep us busy. Terry and Kat have consolidated the laptop info. There's still some surveillance to go through, from the office building."

"You bet, boss." Stew locked his phone and pocketed it. He turned the corner onto Queen, a block from the office, and almost bowled over Billy.

"You. You arsehole. Where's my girl?"

Stew crossed his arms and looked up at him. "You buy her or something?" He looked around. Way too many people on the street to start a fight.

"Huh?"

"You said she's 'your girl'. You buy her? Win her in a poker game? What's the deal? I'm curious."

"She's my old lady. My girl." Billy shook his head in frustration. "Jesus, don't make a deal out of it. Where is she?"

Stew took a step closer. "I'm what, her babysitter? She's not thirteen. And if she doesn't want you to find her, maybe take that as a not very subtle hint, mate." He uncrossed his arms and leaned forward. "You're lucky there's a crowd of civilians around or I'd rearrange your face so much Picasso wouldn't recognise you. You signed on with those arseholes from the city and beat on my mates?" He shook his head. "That time will come." He poked him in the chest and stepped past Billy.

"Hey." He grabbed Stew by the elbow. "Not finished talking with you."

Stew looked down at his elbow, and Billy's strong grip just above it. He grabbed Billy's index finger and folded it in on itself. Billy contorted his body in a vain attempt to relieve the stress on his hand. Stew pressed harder, folding the finger between his thumb and index finger. "Piss off or I'll snap this in half and you'll have to wank with your other hand." He gave it an extra squeeze and let it go. "Grow up."

Billy shook the pain out of his hand. "Get fucked."

"With any luck." Stew chuckled as he opened the main door to the building. "Stay out of my way. I want to hurt you so bad, but not in front of so many witnesses."

The door swung shut behind him, cutting short a bellow from Billy. He smiled as he took the stairs two at a time to the office.

CHAPTER 23

Randolph returned to his office and closed the door. He docked his laptop and poured a healthy glass of bourbon. He sat at his desk and logged in. The display routed to a pair of large monitors sitting just behind the laptop. He navigated to a library of security videos and selected the folder with footage from the downstairs cafe. He double-clicked one of the videos and maximised it on one of the monitors.

He sipped his drink and pressed an intercom button on his desk phone. "Leah. Get Mel in here, would you?" He released the intercom button and sat back, waiting. He turned in his chair as the door opened. "Mel. I need your eyes."

"What's wrong with yours?"

Rand shook his head. "I don't want to make a mistake with this. Pull up a chair."

"And you don't know how to use the computer. What are you looking for?"

"That woman. The legal looking for a job."

Mel sipped some of Rand's drink. "Industrious old bag. But we're not looking to bring anyone on right now. Not actively, anyway. Don't know where she heard we were."

"She didn't. She was fishing for something. Watch with me and help me find out what."

"There's no audio on those files, boss."

Rand clicked a file and expanded the video to fill the monitor. "Body language speaks louder than words." He started playing the security video. A clock ticked through the seconds and minutes on the lower left hand corner of the image. In the middle distance Rand and Mel entered the frame and sat at a two seater by the window. The camera angle was over Mel's left shoulder, showing her ear and a slice of her left cheek. Her right side was beside the window to the office courtyard. Rand's face was shown in full. They placed takeaway coffee cups on the table between them and silently, slowly started talking.

"It was just after this. Give me the keyboard. I need to magnify." With a few keystrokes Mel doubled the size and centred the table in the middle of the monitor. She slid the keyboard back.

Rand used an index finger and pushed it back to her. "Slow it to half speed."

She poked a couple of keys and the video slowed, coffee cups inching toward their mouths, the whole thing looking like a poorly lit, grainy John Woo film. "Better?"

Rand grunted and leaned forward, fingers interlaced on his desk. "She came in over my right shoulder." He jabbed a finger at the monitor. "There."

On screen, Rand opened his laptop in slow motion. Beryl slowly entered the frame with a chair, the camera looking down on her face. She was impeccably dressed, perfect hair. She had her mobile phone in her left hand. She slid her chair up to the side of the table and rested her hand on the back. The camera showed her in right profile from above, silently talking.

Mel leaned over and waited until she was facing slightly toward Mel. She pressed a couple of keys and the screen froze for a second. "I screen-grabbed her face."

The video continued.

 "See anything unusual?" asked Rand

"Her phone. Think she was recording us?"

"Wouldn't matter. We didn't say anything to be concerned about. And she wasn't there long."

Beryl on screen stood, moved her chair away and walked off screen.

"So," said Mel. "It's a nothing."

"He pointed at the screen. "Nothing to chance, Mel. Tell Gerald to drop whatever he's doing. I want her in my office for a chat."

Gerald handed a copy of the screen grab to Robert and sat in front of a wall of monitors.

"What are we supposed to do with this?" asked Robert.

"Find her. Bring her back here. Boss wants to talk to her."

Robert let out a breath. "I thought, for a second there, that he wanted us to end her. She looks like me mum." He cocked his head. "Actually, more like Nan."

"We just have to find her and bring her to talk to him."

Robert nodded. "Who is she?"

"No idea. I've never seen her before. We track her back. Find out where she came from." Gerald logged into the terminal. "Take the cameras on Harris. I'll check the ones between there and here."

"Why Harris?"

"Parking garage is there. Tonnes of coffee shops. I doubt she'd be able to walk farther than that," said Gerald.

"It's smarter to track her backwards from the building though, right?"

"Pincher action. Work both ends against the middle." Gerald froze a frame. "Is that her?"

Robert looked at the face on the paper in front of him and compared it to the image of a woman crossing the street. "Probably. Make it bigger."

Gerald blew up the image. "Yeah, that's her. Back it up. What camera did she come from?"

Robert opened the appropriate file and scrubbed backward to a couple of minutes before the image of Beryl crossing the street. He pressed play, staring intently at the monitor. He jabbed a finger at Beryl coming around a corner. "There. How far out do we have cameras?"

"Maybe another hundred metres up the road. That's coming from Harris street." He smiled. "What did I tell you. A parking garage and a couple of cafes." Gerald closed down the monitors. "Let's go for a walk."

Randolph leaned back in his chair and snapped open his newspaper. He grimaced at the headline. *Government's Plans to Reduce Corporate Taxes Hang In Limbo*. "My arse." He skipped past the story and started reading an opinion piece on the Sydney housing market when his phone rang.

"What do you want, Gerald?"

"I don't like coincidences, boss."

"No smart man does. What did you find out?"

"Backtracked that woman to a cafe on Harris. Showed some photos around and looked at their security video."

"Get to the point," said Randolph.

"Before she came to the office she had coffee with that Dan guy from the Campbelltown detective joint and a couple of his mooks."

"Jesus. Mooks? You've been watching too much television. So, she works for that detective. Not a coincidence. Find her and bring her to me. Something smells." He terminated the call and returned to his paper.

Beryl locked her terminal and threw a ball of crumpled paper at Kat. It bounced off one of her headphones.

She cleared one ear and paused her music. "What's up, Granny?"

"I'm going for lunch. Come with, and I'll show you some of the better places to eat. Call me granny again and I'll choke you out."

Kat smiled, looked at her monitor and the web site she was working on, then pulled the headphones completely off her head. "Sure. I could eat."

"Do you have any preferences? There's a good Chinese place up the road, kebabs, a Persian place with the most incredible lamb -- you're not a vegetarian, are you?"

Kat laughed. "I like meat. Any Indian places? I feel like tandoori."

"You walked right past it coming in this morning. They have a nice lunch menu. My treat."

"That's good. You guys haven't paid me yet."

Beryl leaned in Dan's office. "You want me to get you something?"

"I'm good." Dan patted his belly. "My trousers are getting a little tight."

"You need more time on the treadmill."

"Yeah, yeah. Those days are long gone. Expense it, okay? Make it an orientation lunch."

Beryl tapped the doorframe and left down the front stairs with Kat.

"So how long have you been working here?" asked Kat.

"With Dan? Four years now."

"You're like, what, his girl Friday?"

Beryl shook her head. "Accountant and legal support, when required. Used to be web and graphic support, but now we've got you."

"Legal?"

"Not often required. We run a tight ship." She shoulder bumped Kat. "And let's keep it that way." She pointed across the street. "Right there."

The fine calligraphy of the Indian Restaurant, gold lettering on black paint, was obvious when you saw it. "That's been there all the time?"

"Years, now. You're going to have to be a bit more observant if you're working here." She stepped off the curb and a large black sedan braked in front of them. Two men stepped out and stood in front of Beryl.

"You're in my way, boys."

A man a head and a half taller than Beryl blocked her way. "My name is Gerald. This is my colleague Robert." He smiled. "My boss would like to have a chat with you."

"Your boss?"

Gerald nodded. "Into the car." He moved to one side and opened the back door.

"You're having a laugh, mate. I'm getting lunch."

Gerald looked at Robert with a half-smile on his face then turned back to Beryl with a condescending smile. "Ma'am, I could pick you up with one hand and deposit you in the back seat and not even break a sweat. I don't want to have to resort to that."

Kat watched the interchange and took her phone out of her bag. She gripped it tightly. "Mate, we're going to lunch. Get the hell out of our way."

"We've got no interest in you," said Robert. "Don't make us have an interest in you. Keep your face out of this. We just want the old lady."

"Boys, you want to have a scene on the street, go right ahead." Beryl crossed her arms. "There's no way in hell I'm getting in that car."

Gerald sighed and reached for Beryl's arm. Kat lunged forward and pressed the base of her phone case against Gerald's arm and pressed a button on the top. The taser built into the phone case jolted Gerald in time with Beryl's swift kick to his crotch.

He staggered back. "Jesus." His back bounced off the back door, slamming it shut. "Good GOD, what the hell was that?" He slid to the ground cradling his groin.

Robert's head whipped back and forth between Kat and Gerald like he was at the Australian Open. He scrambled forward to grab Beryl and met Stew's fist to his chest, stopping him, driving him backwards.

"Lads, piss off back to Randolph and tell him to fuck off." He shoved Robert back toward his car and cocked a fist. "Or I'll hit you again. I owe you a couple of hits. Sorry I missed the party last time."

Robert rolled his shoulders and turned his stance sideways. "Come on, old man."

Beryl stepped between them. "You heard him. Tell that pompous piece of shit to stay out of my town."

Stew gently moved Beryl to one side. "You do your stuff, doll. Let me do mine."

Kat took her by the arm and moved her out of the way. "He'll cream you."

Beryl looked at Kat's phone. "Where in the blazes did you get that? They're illegal."

Kat slid her phone back in her bag. "Don't know what you're talking about." She stepped toward Gerald and kicked at him, just missing his head. "Who are these arseholes?"

"They work for Rand. He's mad at us."

Gerald pulled himself up with his car. "Robert, let's go. There'll be more opportunities." He got behind the wheel and as soon as Robert was in the car, left in a cloud of rubber smoke.

Stew breathed off the adrenaline and faced Kat. "What the hell was that?"

"I was going to ask you. Thanks for stopping by. Could have probably handled it without you, but whatever."

Stew laughed. "Right. Where are we having lunch?"

"You're coming?"

"Yeah. I'd hate myself if those boys showed up again and I wasn't there."

Kat took Stew's arm. "You still hungry, Beryl?"

Beryl took a deep breath and adjusted her sleeves. "Just give me a second. That doesn't happen every day."

"I hope not. Is this because of what you guys did yesterday?"

Beryl shrugged. "I'm assuming so. Not sure I like this. They don't seem to be the type of people who scare off easily." She checked for traffic. "Okay. Let's get some food."

CHAPTER 24

Dan stepped back from the window and looked at the photo on his phone. "Andy. Terry, where are you?"

"Lab, boss," said Andy. "What's up?"

Dan entered the lab. Half a dozen monitors played CCTV video from the night Jeremy was shot, black and white grainy images of the streets and shops around the crime scene playing out in the half-darkened room. "Got anything?"

Andy shook his head. "We'd have told you, Dan. This is going to take a while."

"We did find something strange, though," said Terry.

"Tell me."

"About half of the cameras in and around Pyrmont are owned by Randolph. Not just in and outside his building, but about three or four blocks around his building. Suspicious little shit."

"Interesting." Dan held out his phone. An image of Gerald and Robert, taken from above, was on the screen. "You guys remember these two?"

"How could I forget them? When'd you take this?" asked Terry.

"A minute or so ago. Out the window." He mirrored the phone to one of the monitors and walked up to it. "They're really starting to get on my nerves."

Andy paused the unspooling CCTV videos and looked at the monitor. "Yeah. I still hurt." He re-started the CCTV and resumed scanning the images. "Why were they here? What were they doing?"

"Trying to grab Beryl." Dan continued staring at the pictures. He gently brushed the back of his head. "I still hurt, too. That's them."

Andy paused the CCTV again. "Hang on a sec. What? Beryl?"

"She's fine. Stew was there, though from what I saw, she wasn't doing too bad herself."

"Well, fuck that, where are they?"

"Getting lunch. Kat's with her and Stew tagged along."

Andy unbuttoned his cuffs and rolled up his sleeves. "No. Those two." He pointed at the monitor. "They still down there? We have accounts to settle with them. Seriously big accounts."

Dan gently steered Andy back to his seat. "They took off. They may be back, so keep your eyes open."

Terry rubbed his hands on his trousers. "I don't like that."

"Me either, but it does tell us something."

Andy returned to scanning the monitors. He nodded. "We're worrying him."

"If you figure out what we're worrying him about, let me know, will ya? I'm back in my office."

He unlinked his phone from the monitor and tapped on the door frame.

"Take a break and get some lunch, guys. You're going to wreck your eyes."

"Don't go anywhere." Andy paused one of the screens. Two figures stood on the street. "Jesus. Isn't that the same two?"

Dan squinted at the monitor. "Put it on the bigger screen."

He stood closer to the larger flat screen. "Kinda grainy, but," he opened the image on his phone and held it up to the screen, "looks like them. Where was this? And when?"

And checked his logs. "Harris Street, from the vantage point of the Persian restaurant, facing away from the alley where Jeremy was found." He checked the timestamp. "About the same time he was killed. What did the ME have a time of death?"

"Between 8:30 and 9:00 that night."

Andy nodded. "Timestamped at 8:47. They were there. Implicated?"

"Back it up a few minutes and let it play out. Is there an angle on the alley?"

Andy typed a command and the video back up three minutes. "Haven't seen anything facing the alley yet. Unfortunately." He pointed at the monitor. "Play?"

"Play."

The video showed Rand's two men show up from left of frame, walking down the hill. About mid screen Gerald stopped and looked across the street, facing the camera almost dead on. He put out his hand and stopped Robert. They both looked across the street for a minute, then Robert jumped, like something startled him. Gerald made to step off the curb and cross the street and Robert stopped him. They waited for a second. An out of focus shadow flitted across the monitor and the two men continued walking down the hill.

"We need to get video from the other side of the street. Even if it's at an angle."

"There's no shops there," said Andy. "Just the office building. I've got a terabyte of video from there. It's going to take a while to sift through it.

There's no time stamps except the file name, and each file is twelve hours of video."

"Back up the vid of those two. I want to watch it again. Slo-mo."

The two stepped through the video in half time. When they stopped and turned, looking across the street, Dan interrupted. "Slower. As slow as you can make it."

"One-eighth speed."

"Fine."

Gerald and Robert stopped on screen and stared just to the right of the camera. The image looked frozen, except for the frame count spooling up on the lower right corner. The video progressed at three frames a second, dark and grainy. The light capturing capabilities of the digital 'film' was poor.

As Robert jerked, the darkness brightened slightly for a couple of frames.

Andy pointed at the screen. "Gunshot?"

"Probably.

"Start sifting through the video from the office building." Dan stared at the screen as a shadow flitted across the screen in two frames. "We need to see what happened in there. For now, Rand is involved until we know differently."

"They seemed to be surprised about it."

"So it's just a coincidence that those two are witnesses to Jeremy's murder, but weren't involved? Not bloody likely." He tapped the doorframe on the way out. "Sift."

Gerald and Robert drove in silence, Robert behind the wheel of the black sedan and Gerald in the passenger's seat, looking out the side window at the bush along the highway.

They were passing the exit to the airport when Gerald cleared his throat.

Robert glanced over. "What?"

"I didn't say anything."

"You're thinking something."

"Ah, shit. We've got to go back."

Robert changed lanes and slowed to exit. "I was thinking the same thing. We can't go back without her. We need to isolate her."

"If we have to bruise her, we bruise her."

"She's like my Nan, though," said Robert. He exited the freeway, made two right hand turns and entered again, this time heading south, back toward Campbelltown.

"She's a threat to our existence." Gerald flexed his fists. "And I want to get my hands on that bitch who had the taser."

Robert rubbed his chest and laughed. "They double teamed you good."

"I wasn't expecting it. You, you got flattened by an old man."

"He hit like a sledgehammer." He was quiet for a minute. "I guess we were both surprised."

CHAPTER 25

Stew held the door as Kat and Beryl entered the office.

"What in the hell was all that about?" asked Dan.

"You saw?" Beryl placed her bag on her desk.

"Out the window."

"And you didn't come down to help?"

"You guys had it well in hand," said Dan. "Did they say what Rand wanted?"

Beryl shook her head and sat at her desk.

"Jesus. What in the hell did you do to piss him off?" asked Kat.

"A bit of this and a bit of that," said Dan. "So, you two are okay?"

Kat dropped into her seat and tossed her phone on the desk. "Thanks to this."

Dan picked up the phone and examined the oversized case. There were two holes in the base. He flipped it over. In the centre of the other end was a flat button. "Huh." He pressed the button and two small spikes popped out of the holes in the base. "I don't suppose I want to touch those."

Kat grimaced. "Probably need a charge up, but they'll still jolt you."

"I'm 99% positive this is illegal," said Dan.

"I'm 100% positive," said Beryl. "But given the circumstances, I'm willing to overlook that pesky little fact. Just keep it out of sight."

Dan tapped his fingertips on Kat's desk. "What did they want?"

"Beryl. A grab and go, by the look of it. Thank goodness Stew was there," said Kat.

Stew stroked his moustache. "They left too easy. You better keep an eye open. I'll take you home tonight. Keep an eye on your place."

"That's not necessary, Stew."

Dan sat on the corner of Beryl's desk. "Listen to him. We'll rotate for a couple of days. Better safe than sorry."

"Come on. I can take care of myself."

"You don't have a choice." Dan smiled.

Andy exhaled through his nose. "And it'll stay that way until that fuck Rand is under a bus."

Beryl put a hand on Dan's arm. "Calm down. Stew chased them off. I'm sure Mr Murray is regretting whatever hasty decision led him to attempting to grab me."

"Rand? Regret something?" Stew laughed. "No. His only regret will be sending two people who couldn't do the job. We'll keep an eye on you. Either they'll be back or he'll send someone else." He headed to the audio lab. "So don't leave here without one of us, okay?"

Beryl muttered under her breath and turned back to her computer. Dan leaned down and caught her eye. "What he said, okay?"

"Fine."

"*Fine*. A scarier word never heard by man on this earth. Listen to him."

Kat watched, a small smile on her face. She watched Dan follow Stew into the audio lab and waited until the door was closed. She leaned over in her seat to get closer to Beryl. "It's like you're their mother. Is it always like this?"

"The testosterone-driven urge to protect. It can get annoying at times." She smiled. "But they mean well."

Kat took a deep breath. "Yeah. So what's this Rand guy got against us, anyway?"

Dan grabbed a chair in the corner of the audio/video lab. Andy and Terry watched security video shot from the building across the road from the crime scene for the twelve hours spanning the murder at double speed. Most of the images were of the office interior, with small slices of the street outside through windows. They would stop the video every time there was a flicker of movement, rewind it and play it back at half speed.

"This is taking forever," said Terry.

"Keep it up. There'll be something there."

Stew glanced at the videos and pulled on a set of headphones. "It's kinda cramped in here, boss. You don't need to be here."

"What are you listening to?"

Stew flipped one of the cans behind his ear. "Audio."

"No shit."

Stew smiled. "Those bugs you dropped in Rand's office. The ones his meatheads busted and returned to us." He pointed out the door. "Same meatheads that tried grabbing Beryl."

"Waste of time though, right? We got them back in pieces."

"They were recording the whole time they were in there."

"Still. Probably a waste of time."

"Someone once said, and I think I've got the words right, 'Keep it up.

There'll be something there'."

"Fair enough," said Dan. "There's no audio on the security vids, and these guys look like their eyes could use a break. Pull the headphones."

"Sure." He unplugged the headphones and put them on a shelf. "It's only a few minutes anyway." He pressed 'play'. Rand's voice resonated through the speakers.

"Mrs Brookes. So sorry to hear about Jeremy's death. I thought everything had been sorted. How can I help you?"

"Sally has hired me to look into her husband's murder."

"Murder? I thought it was a-- Mr McMaster, or whoever you are. What the fuck are you doing here?"

"Who's McMaster?" asked Terry.

"Name I used at that awards ceremony at The Star. He's got a good memory. Better than yours."

"It's Dan McGinnis. And it's like I said. Sally retained my agency to investigate her husband's death."

"Skip ahead a bit. I know this part. I was there."

Stew pressed the fast forward button . A high pitched warble squirted from the speakers until he released it.

"-ry, Sally. No, fuck it, actually I'm not. Stop chasing delusions. Jeremy is dead and there's nothing you can say or do about it."

"Agree to disagree. Sally's convinced me it's not simple mugging. I'm investigating. Where's the harm in me investigating? It's not your money."

"A little further. He's more of a windbag than I remembered."

"-ready told you. Sum total of his role. Keep my arse our of legal jeopardy. Keeps my company out of legal jeopardy. I'm protected."

"How?"

"I could publish an article that says you eat live kittens and kick puppies and fiddle three-year old girls on the Opera House steps and the lawsuit wouldn't touch me. A construct put together many years ago."

"More."

Stew pressed the button, the speakers warbled, then Rand spoke again.

"He was the legal obstacle to almost every story I wanted to run. So no, not entirely amicable. But he was doing his job."

"Doesn't really answer my question. Would you buy him a flat white if you bumped into him at a coffee shop?"

"No. I don't drink coffee."

"Again, not what I asked. You like it straight, no bullshit. How much did he piss you off? Enough to have him killed?"

"Oh, my. You're serious. I don't have to kill anyone. I can drive them to suicide. I can ruin anybody's life, given the right motivation and a little time. Information is everywhere. And manufactured information is limited only by my imagination. So don't piss me off too much, Mr McGinnis. I'm sure I could have you on the ropes in a matter of weeks."

"Okay," said Dan. "Enough of that. Skip forward to where I was leaving."

"How many minutes, boss?" Stew held a finger of the FF button. "Roughly."

"Another minute. Maybe less, if I remember right."

"-eople I target can afford it and believe me, they are not that clean.

Anything else? I've got a phone call to make."

The sound of footsteps across the office faded and the door closed. There was a grunting noise as Rand sat at his desk and then silence.

"I think that's it."

"Pretty much a waste of time, then," said Terry. "I should get back to sifting, right boss?"

"Well, *sometimes* there'll be something there."

Stew chuckled and was reaching for the stop button when Rand cleared his throat.

"Mr Prime Minister."

"Ssshh."

"No shit."

"You ready for the election? Wilson's not a good choice for business here in Australia, and I can guarantee you a win, if you agree to my terms."

Silence, while Randolph listened to the Prime Minister.

"Mr Prime Minister, that's a hard line to take. And I'm sure that you will change your mind on corporate tax rates once you review the contents of the file that is being dropped off with your driver right about now. Pictures, files, videos, the sorts of things that the average man on the street wouldn't want to be made public, and the sort of things a Prime Minister would do almost anything to prevent their publication. Review the files. I'll call you tomorrow."

The sound of a mobile phone dropping on the desk was followed a second later by the scratchy sound of ripping tape.

"Gerald. Get the hell in here. What's this?"

"Where'd you find it?"

"Under the edge of my desk. That McGinnis prick. Check for others."

The audio was interrupted by a gravelly static, then the audio returned at a lower level.

"That's two, boss. Think there's any others?"

"Those two destroyed?"

"Pieces."

"Take this place apart. I'll be back in an hour. Get rid of all of them."

Dan waved at Stew. "That's good enough. Damn."

There was silence for minute, Terry looking at Stew looking at Dan.

"You heard that, right?" asked Terry.

Stew nodded. "Boss's voice sounds funny on tape."

"No, no. He was blackmailing the Prime Minister."

Dan grimaced. "Not really blackmail. Extortion, maybe?"

"An arrangement of some sort." Stew stroked his moustache. "Not cool."

"So," said Terry. "Is that enough to take him down?"

"What, the call with the Prime Minister?"

"Yeah. That *was* incriminating."

Dan shook his head. "Only one side of the phone call, illegal bugging. He'd say he saw the surveillance devices and was geeing us up. It's not enough, but man, it pisses me off even more."

"And we're no closer to determining if Rand had anything to do with Jeremy's murder."

"No, we're not. Keep sifting."

CHAPTER 26

"Okay, what do we do this time?" Robert slowed and took the Campbelltown exit off the highway. "Pretty sure barging into the PI's office and grabbing her is out of the question."

"Get closer. We'll think of something."

"Yeah, it's just a little out of my comfort zone, you know?"

Gerald grunted.

"It's like, I've got no problem taking someone apart. Smashing them to within an inch of their lives, or just enough to put them in a hospital for whatever number of days you want me to put them there." He turned off the main road onto Queen Street. "Or kill them and dispose of them as required. It pays well, and I'm pretty good at it, if I do say so myself."

"So what's the problem?"

"We're supposed to scoop up some old lady, without hurting her, and bring her back to the boss. How do you even do that?" He looked up at the office windows as he rolled past.

"Turn here."

"Why?"

"Just fucking turn. There's timed parking in the front of this place. They park somewhere out back. Let's find it."

Robert turned right, then right again through a parking lot behind a restaurant, and stopped in front of row of cars sitting behind the office building.

Gerald pointed at a white van. "That's them."

Kat burped discretely. "That was good tandoori. Two hours and I'm still getting repeats."

"You had enough. Surprised you're not having a nap."

"We can do that?"

Beryl laughed. "I don't think it's official company policy, no. And while this is a wonderful country, we haven't achieved peak Spain, yet. A siesta would be nice some days."

"Maybe we can propose it at the next staff meeting."

"By 'we', you mean 'me', right?" asked Beryl.

"If by 'me' you mean 'you', then yes." Kat took a breath. "Dan kinda scares me."

"He's like a big teddy bear married King Arthur and had Dan as a baby. Honourable to a fault, a big softie when you get to know him and will fight to the death for what he believes in."

"Huh. Really?"

"Known him for fifteen years, back when he played footie."

"Yeah, I saw the pictures. Rabbitohs. Why did he stop?"

"Shattered his knee. Bad tackle."

"Tough break." Kat moved her keyboard and picked up something that looked like a small black button. "You think King Arthur was real?"

"With the Round Table, and Merlin and Excalibur? Probably not. Read a great book about it though. A series of books. Historical fiction."

"Old Britain, and the Roman Invasion?"

Beryl stopped what she was doing. "Exactly. A series by Jack Whyte. With a 'y'. *The Camulod Chronicles*. Have you heard of it? The first book is *The Skystone*. The conceit is that Excalibur was forged from a meteorite found at the bottom of a lake caused by the its impact. It's really good."

Kat took out her phone and searched online. "Must be old. There's no eBook versions."

"You interested?"

"Sounds cool, yeah. I'll order a copy when I get paid." She handed the button to Beryl. "Any idea what this is?"

"One of our GPS trackers. Where exactly did you find this?"

"It was under my keyboard. I was wondering why it wasn't sitting flat."

Beryl shook her head. "Terry needs to pull his head out of his arse." She locked her computer and stood, pocketing the button. "Don't buy the book. I've got a copy in my car."

"You're sure?"

"I'll be right back."

Dan leaned against the wall in the lab. Stew had taken a copy of the file and was helping Terry and Andy scrub through the clips. "Are we wasting our time, boys?"

"Well, it does seem like a lot of work for what will at best be marginally useful. There's nothing really visible out the window on these clips," said Terry.

Andy looked at his young colleague. "It's what we do. Tedium is better than getting shot at."

"Barely."

Stew laughed. "You haven't been shot at yet, kiddo. It's much better. And this isn't going to a court of law. We're looking for a glimpse, shadows, fragments that help us stick the story together."

"The old guy's getting all poetic on us. Things going well with Jane?"

"I think I've got something." Stew stopped his video and backed it up a couple of seconds.

The image was out the second floor window of the office building across the street from the Persian Restaurant. Only the right third of the screen showed the outside; the other two thirds were office, dark and uninhabited.

Andy wheeled his chair over to Stew's work station. "How in the hell can you tell? It's grainy. And dark."

"Squint." Stew pressed play and slowed the speed by half.

A shadow inside the restaurant slowly transited one of the windows, then stepped out of the front door and went left, from the camera's point of view, down the hill. Light from the restaurant spilled onto the street. Up the hill, just passed a dark spot, thin light pooled out from lights inside a closed shop.

Stew tapped his finger at the screen. "Here."

A figure walked passed the closed shop, silhouetted against the light. His form disappeared as it passed in front of the dark spot in front of the alley.

"If his walking speed didn't change he should have passed by that by then. Be in front of the restaurant. He didn't."

"He?" asked Terry

"Walks like a dude."

Andy and Dan nodded in agreement.

"And then there's this." He pointed at the screen in the middle of the dark patch. "Wait for it." A flash lit up the alley for a frame. He paused the video and stepped it back to the lit frame. He hit a couple of keys and zoomed in on the two figures visible in the light.

A figure had a revolver pressed up against the man's head. Detail wasn't good, but it was clear it was Jeremy on the receiving end. The shooter was only visible from the back, and wore a hoodie and gloves.

"No way to tell who did the shooting."

"Well, it wasn't one of the two we met today," said Stew. "Too small."

"Grab and print that. And step it forward. Which way did the shooter go?"

Stew snipped the screen, then played it forward at half speed. Shortly after the flash the shooter stepped out of the alley, flipped off their hoodie and removed their gloves.

"Is that a woman?"

She appeared to wipe her eyes then shove her hands in her pocket and run down the hill. A couple of seconds later someone stepped out of the restaurant looked up and down the street, then stepped back in.

"That's all the response a gunshot gets in Pyrmont? I thought it was a nice neighbourhood," said Terry.

"Small calibre, low powered round, pressed up against the head. It probably didn't sound much louder than a cork popping." Dan stepped closer to the screen. "Frame by frame of the woman walking past the restaurant, Stew. Need the best shot."

Stew backed it up to the flash and moved it forward a frame at a time.

"Speed up through the black parts, mate."

Stew smiled and rapidly progressed through until the first frame the woman stepped into the light.

Andy tapped Dan on the arm. "Hey, that woman with Rand in the pictures Beryl took."

"Mel Dvorak. Yeah. Thinking the same thing. Make it bigger."

"That's what she said." Terry laughed. "Sorry, boss."

Stew zoomed and advanced a frame at a time. The hood pulled off frame by frame.

"Dark hair. Mel has dark hair. About the same length. Keep it going."

The woman slowly moved to the left on the screen, a frame at a time. Just before she disappeared off the left side of the screen she turned her head left, facing the camera.

"Snip that. Is there any way to improve that picture? Difficult to make out features."

Stew looked back at Dan. "That's as good as it gets. If you want to enhance it, step back and squint."

Dan pulled the door open. "Kat, you got a minute?" He held the door while she came in. "It's a bit cosy in here. Dan, give her your chair. What can you do with that?"

"It's pretty grainy."

"My eyes work too, Kat. Can you make it better?"

Kat checked the folders on the computer. "What software do you have on this?" Her fingers flew across the keyboard. "Good. This might work."

She opened an application and dragged the image in. "There's not a lot I can do. It's not like there are extra pixels hidden in the background. I laugh when they 'enhance' photos on those cop shows. It's not possible. Or if it is, they're using a piece of software I've never heard of. They take an out of focus picture of a licence plate and like voila, it's clear. I'm talking too much, aren't I?"

"You can do something with it?" asked Dan.

"Sharpen the edges, push the gamma a bit…"

The image came into a slightly better focus. Dan took a step back and squinted. "You're right, Stew. This works too. And it's not Mel." He unlocked his phone. "Thanks a tonne, Kat. Save that and print it for me, please."

He put the phone to his head. "Sally, Dan here. How fast can you get to my office? It's pretty urgent."

CHAPTER 27

Dan terminated the call and pulled the copies of Sally's face off the printer. "She'll be here in forty-five minutes." He clenched his jaw. "Have I told you guys how much I *hate* being played? All of us in the conference room. Full court press."

"Including me?" asked Kat.

"Hell, yes." He held up the photos. "Definitely. You and Beryl. Stew, set up the video on the big screen in the conference room."

He left and Kat turned to Stew. "He seemed pissed."

"It really looks like the woman who hired us to find her husband's killer is her husband's killer."

Kat looked at the screen. "Her?"

"Uh-huh. This is going to be ugly. You've never seen Dan pissed, have you? This'll be a treat." Stew copied the video and the screen grab to a thumb drive. "Take notes. It doesn't happen very often."

Kat followed them out of the room and into the conference room.

Dan sat at the head of the table, the copies of the screen grabs upside down in front of him. "Let Beryl know to send Sally Brookes in as soon as she arrives. And to come in with her."

"Beryl's not out there," said Terry. "Maybe she's in the loo."

"No, she went to grab a book for me from her car." Kat looked at her watch. "But that was like fifteen minutes ago."

"Dammit. Stew, Andy, come with me. Kat, wait for Mrs Brookes and bring her in here. Don't tell her why, and don't show her the pictures."

Terry stood. "And what about me?"

"You come too."

Kat gathered the photos and took them to her desk. She slid them in a large envelope and placed it in her top desk drawer. She ran down the back stairs and caught up to Dan and the rest of the team in the parking lot. They were standing around Beryl's Toyota. The passenger door was open and the key fob was on the ground beside it. Her mobile phone was on the driver's seat.

"Did you find her?"

"What the hell does it look like?" Dan looked past her at the open back door. "Why aren't you waiting for our guest?"

"Beryl came out here for me. She was getting a book."

Dan reached in the back seat and picked up *Skystone*. "This?" He slapped the book against her chest.

Kat took it. "Yes. Where is she?"

Stew picked her keys up off the ground. "Someone grabbed her."

"Someone. Great."

Terry picked up Beryl's phone and unlocked it. "She's got dash cams, guys." He opened an app. "They operate if there is any motion in front or back." He held the phone up sideways and played the video. The left half showed video from the back-facing camera and the right side, the front. Beryl walked past the back and moved out of view. The picture jiggled slightly and they heard the sound of the car door opening.

"There." Terry pointed at the screen. A black sedan blocked in her Toyota. Gerald and Robert got out and walked to the driver's side of Beryl's car.

"Jesus Christ, not you guys again," said Beryl on the video.

They heard another car door open. And the car shook more.

"Come on, old lady."

"Piss off."

They heard an impact and a male groan. *"Bitch."* Followed by a slap. *"Dump her phone."*

Beryl, blouse ripped and struggling between Gerald and Robert came into view on the back camera. She fought as Robert tried forcing her into the back of the black sedan. She was yelling, but they couldn't make out what she was saying. There was blood on her upper lip, dripping onto her chin.

"Shit. Shit, shit, shit." Dan looked back at the office. "Kat, head back in and intercept Mrs Brookes. Get her into the conference room." He checked the time. "She's maybe five minutes out. Stew, Andy head into the city and find Beryl. Keep in touch. Terry, with me."

"Find her? How are we supposed to find her? It's a big-arsed city."

"You know where his office is." Dan looked at Kat. "Why are you still here? Get in the office."

"Um, she has one of those black buttony tracker things. Does that help?"

Terry gave Beryl's phone to Andy and opened a tracker app on his. A map opened and a pinwheel resolved to a blue pulsating dot. "Genius. Thanks. She's heading north on the Hume Highway, toward Sydney."

Andy opened the same app. "Got her."

"Go get her," said Dan. "I'll be right behind you as soon as I deal with Sally." He followed Kat into the building.

She grabbed the envelope out of her desk drawer and handed it to Dan. "You'll want these." She sat at Beryl's desk while Dan and Terry entered the conference room. She fanned the book pages and dropped it on the desk. She leaned her head in her hands. "Fuck."

"Where is everybody?"

Kat looked up. She clenched her fists. "Mrs Brookes, right? This way." She made her way to the conference room without waiting to see if the guest followed. She held open the door. "Take a seat. We need to discuss something with you."

Sally slowly walked in and sat halfway down the table. "What's this about?"

Dan stuck the USB drive in the side of his laptop and opened the video clip. "We have some information about your husband's murder we'd like to corroborate." He pressed a couple of keys and the movie was mirrored on the large plasma TV bolted on the wall. "We have video from a security camera showing the murder and the killer. You should brace yourself. This contains some shocking footage."

"I don't understand. How did you find this? The police said there were no CCTV cameras facing the alley."

"From inside the building across the street. Video only, no audio. And the quality isn't great." Dan pressed the space bar and the video started playing on the large screen. Sally stared at it intently and flinched at the flash from the alley. Dan paused the video and backed it up, frame by frame, until the image of the shooter holding the gun against Jeremy's head was frozen on the monitor.

Sally held a hand in front of her mouth. "Oh, my God."

"Sorry, but that is your husband, correct?"

Sally nodded. "Were you able to tell who pulled the trigger? Is it one of

Rand's people?"

Dan pressed the space bar again and held his hand over the keyboard. When the shooter stepped into the light he tapped it again, freezing the video. "She isn't one of Rand's people."

"She?"

Dan looked at her for a minute, sad, then opened the zoomed, enhanced image of the killer's head.

Sally shook her head and started quietly crying. "No."

"You're telling me that isn't you?"

"It wasn't supposed to go this way."

"Can you tell me why in the hell you'd hire me to find your husband's killer when it was you who killed him?"

"I only advanced the timeline by a couple of weeks, at most. He was terminal and dropping fast."

"Lewy's Bodies. Yeah. We figured that out. What were you trying to do?"

Sally sighed. "I thought there was enough circumstantial evidence to pin this on Rand, or at least one of his stooges."

Dan slid the screen grab of Sally's face across the table. "Walk me through it."

"I don't understand."

"Who's idea was it? Who came up with the idea to shoot your husband in the head? What did you hope to gain by it? Who was your alibi? Where did you get the gun? Where is it now?" He stood and leaned forward. "What on earth justifies you doing this and why in *hell* did you drag my company into this? My investigation, on your behalf, has resulted in my oldest and longest employee being grabbed by Rand. He's pissed off because of what I did on your behalf. And he's taking it out on a fifty-eight year old woman who wouldn't hurt a fly."

Dan held his gaze on Sally. The silence in the room had weight, like a heavy blanket.

Sally sniffed, exhaled slowly and nodded to herself. "Yeah, it probably wasn't a good idea. Do you know what the end stages of Lewy's Bodies Dementia brings? Mental *and* physical degeneration. And it is fast. Very aggressive. We had agreed early on that I'd help him take his life near the end. He was such a smart, fit man and he swore he wouldn't be a burden on me." She sniffed. "Not that he ever would be."

"Why the complicated plot to drag Rand, and me, into this?"

"We had planned something more placid. An overdose of an opiate. Jeremy would just go to sleep one last time. Then, for the past month or so, Jeremy started talking about k-killing two birds with one stone, to make sure that his death wouldn't be in vain. You, you weren't supposed to get as tied up as you were. Rand, well, that's self-explanatory, right? Jeremy has -- had -- been pushing back against him for almost a year. It's been getting worse. The extortion, bribery, general sliminess has escalated. Jeremy had the idea to stage a killing and frame Randolph. Cassie on the cover was the trigger. He was nearing the end. He'd been undecided, but this was a bridge too far."

"You know her?"

A sad smile flitted across her face. "Jeremy did some legal work for her years ago, when she first started working in Australia. Made sure her contracts in Australia weren't screwing her over. She became a very close friend." She wiped her nose with a wad of tissue. "That doesn't matter now, though. It didn't work. I guess this is over now."

Terry cleared his throat. "You maybe haven't thought this through. If the cops decide to look harder into your husband's murder, it doesn't matter how careful you think you were, they'll find something."

Dan nodded. "He's not wrong. And once they figure out it wasn't a mugging gone bad, you're going to be their first suspect. Your alibi, whoever she is, will cave and you'll be out in the cold."

"Which is entirely accurate," said Kat. "You're a psycho, you bitch."

Dan ignored her. "And we're going to appear to be accomplices in a cover up." He dropped back in his chair. "What in the hell are we supposed to do now, Sally?"

"I don't know. I'm really sorry, Dan. I didn't mean -"

"I'm in a bad situation. But not as bad a situation you're in. There's an open homicide case in Pyrmont and I've got the evidence to prove you were the killer."

Sally shut her mouth and the colour drained from her face. "You…but I told you why we…oh, shit."

Dan clenched his jaw muscles a couple of times. "Right." He unlocked his phone, dialled a number and placed the call on speaker.

Stew's voice cut through the tension. "Boss."

"Sit-rep."

"They're about fifteen minutes ahead of us, almost to Sydney."

"Any chance of heading them off?"

"Not really. We're pretty sure we know where they're going, but failing a massive speed increase, he's going to get there first."

"Yeah, don't get pulled over. We don't need any attention right now." He scratched his jaw. "Keep on their tail and let me know where they've stopped." He terminated the call and pointed at Sally. "Go home. Don't call the police. If the police contact you, get an attorney first and call me second. I need to figure this out." He stood. "Kat, show her out."

"Anything you want me to do, boss?"

Dan looked at Terry for a second. "See if you can get me Rand's mobile number."

"Easy as. I'll text you with it when I get it."

Dan headed to the parking lot, stuck earbuds in and placed a call before he pulled his helmet on.

"Boss?"

"Where are you, Stew? I'm on my way."

"Parked outside his office. Andy is at a coffee shop watching the back.

Only two ways in and out of this place, that we can tell."

He started his bike and accelerated out of the parking lot. "Hang there. I'll be forty-five minutes. Less if there are no cops."

"What are we going to do when you get here?"

"What the fuck do you think? Get Beryl and bring her home."

"Might need an army."

Dan accelerated onto the highway. "Let Andy know we're in for a fight tonight."

Beryl stood in Rand's office, arms crossed, Gerald on one side and Robert on the other. Robert had a black eye.

Beryl's hair was a mess and the sleeve on her blouse was torn. She had a bruise on her forearm that was slowly turning an angry purple and blood was caking on a split upper lip.

She glared at Gerald. "How long are we going to wait for the arsehole?"

The door behind her opened and Rand walked in. "That's not very nice. And I apologise for the delay. It's been an interesting day. Tell me, exactly what were you doing in my cafe?"

Beryl stepped up to him, a head and a half shorter and ten years older. "Tell these incompetent apes to drive me home. I've got nothing to say to you."

Rand looked at Gerald and Robert and laughed. "Robert. Did she do that to you?"

Robert touched his face and stood. "Caught me by surprise."

"And you, what, tore her blouse in retaliation? And a bruise? Fat lip? Not very gentlemanly."

Robert opened his mouth to respond and Rand held up a finger. "No. Don't speak." He pressed gently on Beryl's shoulder. "Sit."

"Drop dead."

"One day, I'm sure. Not today." He leaned forward. "Sit down before I let Robert sit you down."

Beryl looked at the chair behind her. It was an old, spartan wooden chair, a cushion on the seat and high wooden arms. She clenched her fists and sat. "I don't know what you want from me, but you're wasting your time." She looked at her watch.

"Expecting someone?"

"You're dead."

"We went over that already. Tell me what you were doing in the cafe. You're not in the legal profession and you're not looking for a job. You work for that McGinnis guy."

"I'm his legal representation, personal and for the company. So you're wrong on that count, I am legal. But you're right on the second: I'd never work for you."

Rand's mobile phone rang. He took it from his inside suit pocket and squinted at the display before answering. "Who's this?"

"Grabbing Beryl was possibly one of the stupidest things you've done. Let me speak to her."

"Is that Mr McGinnis? How did you get this number." He shook his head. "Never mind. Beryl is indisposed right now. And until she tells me what she was doing in the cafe, accosting me and my colleague, she will stay indisposed."

"You've got less than thirty minutes to pack her in a cab and send her home."

Beryl leaned forward and yelled. "There's only three of them, Dan!"

Randolph terminated the call. "That wasn't very smart. Beryl." He moved to backhand her. She stared at him, unflinching. He stared back for a second, then dropped his hand and sighed. "I need to know what you were up to."

"Twenty-five minutes."

"You're dead in twenty if you don't start talking."

Beryl sighed and shook her head. "Right." She motioned him over.

"Come here. I'll tell you. I don't want your goons to overhear."

Rand took a deep breath. "What?" He leaned down, face to face with Beryl and smiled at her.

She leaned forward and motioned him closer and as his face came closer to hers she placed her hands on the back of his head and kicked his nuts with all of her strength. His head instinctively dropped and she shoved it sideways to connect with the chair arm. There was a loud cracking noise and he fell to the floor, groaning.

Beryl stood and was ready to kick him when Gerald lunged forward and pressed his hand against her chest. "You okay, Mr Murray?"

Randolph rolled to his knees, held his hand over his face and slowly stood. He pulled a handkerchief from his inside pocket and held it over his bleeding nose. "You got blood on my carpet. Sit down before you get shot in the head."

Beryl batted Gerald's hand away. "Get off, you creep." She sat, slowly. "Bunch of weak-tea arseholes. I've tagged every one of you. There's nothing to tell you. Let me go and I won't damage pretty boy Gerald again."

"You're not leaving until I say you're leaving."

Dan stopped his bike behind Stew's car. He removed his helmet and knocked on the driver's window.

"You made good time."

"Light traffic. What's the situation?"

Stew pointed at the tall office building. "She's in there somewhere. Can't tell what floor the GPS button's on. How'd it go with the Brookes woman?"

"Long story. Right now we're accomplices after the fact. We need to sort this out first."

"There's what, thirty floors? Security isn't that bad, a few armed guards and dozens of cameras watching us. What's your plan?"

"His office is on the top floor. We walk in and ask for her. See what happens." Dan tapped the car roof. "Where's Andy?"

"Round back."

"Give him a call." He pulled his phone from his jacket pocket and pressed *redial*.

"Mr McGinnis. You're outside, I take it?"

"You're not a very smart guy, Randy."

"It's. Randolph." He took a second. "Your Girl Friday -- Beryl -- is not cooperating. And if she doesn't tell me what I want to know, now, she's going to step off my balcony. It's a big drop. I don't think she can fly."

Dan gripped his phone. "Send her downstairs now and I'll make sure you live long enough to stand trial. Make me wait and I'll throw you off your balcony myself."

Rand laughed. "She's got fifteen minutes. If she isn't forthcoming, I'll find someone else in your organisation and I won't stop until you're the only one left."

CHAPTER 28

Stew leaned against his car. "What's on your mind?"

"We need free reign of that building. What have you seen so far?"

"Nobody is patrolling the outside, but there are three at the front desk -- one goes on patrol every fifteen for five minutes." Stew pointed at a column of windows up the narrow side of the building. "Stairwell. There's stair patrol every fifteen. Not the whole span, of course, but what looks like a random couple of floors checked each time. It's always one of the uniforms from the front desk. That's probably all the security this building has."

Dan nodded. "Beryl's in there. We're not leaving without her. This is a commercial building, so security shouldn't be too high tech. Pass cards, no thumbprints or retinal . We need a card from one of the faces at the front.

Beryl's on 30."

Andy nodded. "We go in with three, or wait until one starts his walk?"

"Three," said Stew. "Don't want one wandering around and us not knowing where he is."

"Sounds good to me." Dan walked to the front of the building and into the lobby, Andy and Stew coming up the rear.

One security sat behind a curved reception desk and the other two stood on either side. The guard on the left held a clipboard in front of him.

Stew walked in behind Dan. He slid a small knife out of his pocket and flicked the blade open.

Dan walked up to the desk and leaned on the counter. "You guys see Randolph Murray leave yet?"

"I'm not at liberty to say. Who are you?"

Stew stood close to the security guard on the left and sliced the pass card off his belt with one hand and tapped on the clipboard with the other. "We're not on there, are we?"

The guard lifted the clipboard and moved it out of Stew's reach. "Security protocol. You guys need to leave."

Stew held up the pass card. "I work here. Left something on my desk. Let's go guys." Stew headed toward the lifts and as soon as he was past the guard he swung his elbow back and hit him on the back of the neck. Andy hit the one in front of him on the throat as Dan launched over the desk and landed on top of the man behind the desk. Two sharp punches and he was out.

Dan pushed himself up and slapped the unconscious guard. "Drag them behind the counter."

Stew grabbed his guy by the arm and dragged him across the floor. Andy stacked his guy with the other two and adjusted his collar. "Thirtieth floor, right? Let's go get her."

"We're just going to walk in and escort her out?" Dan smiled. "Don't think so. These guys were bush league. Rand's got some muscle around him."

He took a deep breath. "We need a plan."

"You got a plan?"

"I've got a plan, Andy."

Beryl looked at her watch. "Your fifteen minutes are almost up. You going to throw me off your balcony?" She looked around the office. "Do you even have a balcony?" She remained sitting on the wooden chair with her hands clasped in her lap. She glanced at the smear of Rand's blood on one of the arms and smiled. "I *should* be leaving. You *should* be letting me leave before my boys show. You won't like it when my boys show."

Rand dabbed at his nose with a piece of tissue. His sodden handkerchief sat on a pad of paper on his desk. "You *should* keep your mouth shut."

A loud crash echoed through the empty building.

Randolph nodded at Gerald. "Find out what in the hell that was."

"But -"

"Now!"

Beryl watched Gerald leave. "Only two of you now. I could probably take you both myself."

Rand snapped his index and middle fingers down on his thumb. "Shut it."

"I'm still unclear what you expect from me." She held up her hand. "And don't say 'I expect you to die.' I didn't like that line in the original movie. And you're not pretty enough to be a Bond villain."

Rand stood. "You know what I want? I want to know what the *fuck* you were doing in the cafe downstairs, pretending you were looking for a job. You weren't, and you targeted me, so I can only assume that you and your boss were trying to pull something on me. And you're not leaving until I know what that is."

"Oh, my God, you're stupid."

His desk phone rang. He jabbed the speaker button. "Gerald, what's taking you so long?"

"Gerald is a bit indisposed right now," said Dan. "Send Beryl out. I'm just getting warmed up." The call dropped.

Robert stood. "Boss?"

Rand shook his head. "Oh, for fuck's sake. Why are you asking me? Find him. Kill him if you have to. I'll take care of her."

"Right, right, right." He reached for the door handle and the door swung open, hard, hitting him on the head. He fell backward and Andy dropped a knee on his chest.

"I owe you, arsehole." Andy lifted his knee a couple of inches and dropped it back down on his chest. "Stay. We've done this before, remember?"

Stew rounded on Rand, who was holding his hands up. "Sit down. I'll sit you down if you don't." He looked closer at Rand's face. "What happened to your nose?"

"That was me." Beryl stood and hugged Dan. "Cutting it close, boys. He was going to throw me out of his balcony." She leaned close and spoke with a conspiratorial whisper. "I don't think he has a balcony up here."

Dan extricated himself from the hug. "*You* did that? I'm going to have to put you in the field more often." He looked closer. "Who hit you?"

Beryl pointed at Robert. "Big guy backhanded me. I got him with an elbow to his eye, though. So we're almost even."

"Nowhere near even." Dan clenched his teeth. "Let's get the hell out of here."

Stew stared at Rand's nose. "A little old lady did that to your face?" He could barely contain the smile. "Damn." He swung his fist toward the broken nose and pulled short, laughing when Rand flinched. He put his hand on Rand's chest. "Stay here until we leave. Your other guy is in the lady's room. He'll be conscious in an hour or so."

Beryl steadied herself on Dan's arm. "Is there going to be blow back?"

"On him? Oh, hell yeah." He looked at Rand as they left. "We're not finished. Not even close."

Rand stood and brushed Stew's hand away. "You have started a war you have no hope of winning. I will *ruin* you. Your company will be bankrupt and you will be homeless before I'm finished with you."

Dan stared at him a minute. He nodded. "Right-o. Let's go, Beryl."

Beryl got in the back of Stew's car and yawned. She winced and gently touched her upper lip. "You're going to end this guy, right, boss?"

"If we do, it has to be for good. He's got the ethics of a used car salesman and unlimited digital ink. But I'm getting an idea."

"Spill."

"Not yet, Beryl. I've got to work out a few angles."

"So, tomorrow then."

"For you. Stew will take you home." He leaned down and looked in the car. "Contact Cassie and Callum and tell them we need them in the office. Tonight. Sally, too. Don't take any shit from them."

"Stew won't be taking me home. I need to be part of this."

"No."

"Don't make me hit you. You saw what I did to Rand."

Dan smiled and pulled on his helmet. "Okay. See you guys at the office."

Rand kicked the bottom of Robert's shoe. "Wake up, you useless piece of shite."

Robert wheezed and grabbed at his chest. He rolled to one side and tried taking a breath. "Ohhh. Cracked my sternum, I think."

"Christ. Get up and walk it off, Nancy. Find Gerald." He watched while Robert pulled himself up using Rand's desk.

Robert held one hand to his chest. "What the hell." He looked at Rand. "We're going to kill him, right?"

Rand nodded. "You can go first. But we all get a turn. Find Gerald. We need to put a plan of attack together."

Dan rolled into the parking lot at the back of the office. It was just after 10 pm and the lot was full. He smiled and walked up the back stairs and directly into the conference room. Kat was talking with Cassie, having an animated conversation about something. Beryl was telling Stew and Andy about her altercation with Rand, and Callum and Terry were talking cars.

Sally sat by herself, quiet, listening.

Dan stood at the head of the table and knocked on its surface. "Thanks. It's late, and I appreciate your attendance."

"What's this about, mate?" asked Callum. "Stew said it was urgent. Looking at who you've called in, I'd say it's got something to do with Randy." He hesitated, then pointed at Sally. "Who's this?"

"I'm Sally Brookes. My husband used to work for Rand and…" she trailed off. "Let's just say Rand is a horrible, vile piece of dog shit who doesn't deserve to breathe the same air we do."

"We're going to do some things that might be a little bit close to the edge of the law, but I think it's imperative that we get rid of Rand." Dan looked at the faces around the table. "Any objections?"

"Hell no," said Cassie. "What do we need to do? Because he's like vibranium Teflon. Absorbs all attacks without anything sticking."

Dan clasped his hand together in front of him. "Systematic unravelling. He's at the apex and we'll need to get everyone below and around him out of the picture first."

"So that means we start with Mel," said Cassie. "I'll stab her if you want me to."

"Ground rules from the drop: We get to the *edge*, but I'm not going to put you at risk of jail to do this." He looked at each of them in the eye. "I agree with Cassie that Mel needs to be first. She is what keeps him running. But we're not going to stab her. There's a smarter way to do it. I'm going to need all of you to be involved in one way or another. I've only got broad strokes right now, but we'll nail it down tonight and tomorrow."

He sat in the chair at the head of the table. "Okay. Mel. Rand's slavish loyal right hand. Does whatever he wants her to do."

Cassie nodded. "She's cold. And very avaricious. Money is her status symbol, where power is Rand's."

Dan nodded. "You know her so well."

"Multiple interactions."

"Okay. Rand will respond to money threats, also. Power is his prime, but his money comes a close second." He yawned. "I won't keep you long, but I'm going to need your commitment over the next couple of days." He looked at each of them, one at a time, making eye contact with each of them . "Every one of you. Deal?" He pointed at Sally. "I'm going to need your revolver."

"Are you sure?"

"Final act stuff. Definitely need it."

She took a deep breath. "Okay."

"I don't know how I can help," said Kat.

"You're the most important. Can you all be back here tomorrow morning at 10? We've got to rob a bank account."

He stood and waited for the others to leave the room. He held out his hand and stopped Beryl from leaving. "Hang on a second. Want a quick word."

"I'm tired, Danny."

"It'll only be a minute." He waited until the remainder of the team left. "So, how are you doing?"

She let out a shuddering breath. "I'm tired, I told you."

Dan smiled. "Rand has a busted nose and one of his thugs had a black eye and you've got a split lip and a nasty bruise. How old are you again?"

"Fifty-eight." She sighed. "And I kicked Gerald in the Easter eggs earlier. I had a few lucky shots, and I look like their mother. Nobody wants to hit their mother. I took advantage of that." She patted him on the chest. "Don't worry, big guy. I'm not going to take your job as team muscle."

Dan hugged her and kissed her on the top of the head. "I'm worried about your mental health. Andy and Stew are the muscle. I'm the brains. Grab some sleep. Get in tomorrow when you get in. I'll lock up here tonight."

Kat was waiting for her at the door and they walked out together.

He locked the door behind them and returned to his office. He dragged a pad of paper out of his top drawer, grabbed a pen and started writing a list.

CHAPTER 29

Callum looked freshly scrubbed. He sat on the corner of the conference table. "She's not an idiot. She'll know if I'm wired."

"You've got an iPhone, right?" asked Terry.

"Yeah."

"Air Pods?

"Yeah, so what?"

"We'll have a call set up between us. Pretend you're listening to music when she shows up. Pull one pod out and leave it on the table. We'll catch it all. Stew will be a couple of tables over taking photos and video."

Callum's foot bounced.

"You nervous?" Terry took Callum's phone and sent himself a text.

"Dawning on me that this isn't a role. This is real. No re-takes if it doesn't work." He chewed a hangnail on his thumb. "You don't think she's armed, do you?"

"What, like a gun?" Terry absently shook his head while he typed something into his phone. "Not likely. This isn't America. Don't worry about it. We'll have you blanketed."

Callum looked out of the conference room door. "What a team. You, an ex-Army muscle man, an overweight former footie player and an old guy? I feel safer already."

"Sarcasm is the refuge of the witless."

"Shallow mind."

"What's that?"

"The expression is *sarcasm is the refuge of a shallow mind*," said Callum. He checked his watch. "Got to be on the waterfront in two hours. One of those coffee places on Circular Quay."

Terry clapped him on the shoulder. "So go. Meet her. We'll be there. I'll call you a few minutes before the meet."

"You'll be there?"

"I don't actually have to be. I can do it from here. But I'd rather be closer to the target. Get going. Stew, Dan and Andy left fifteen minutes ago."

Kat came in with a cup of takeaway coffee for Beryl. "You fine?"

"Thanks. Never better."

"You sure? Yesterday was a bit wild, especially for you."

Beryl looked away for a second. "I'm fine."

"Okay, but I've seen that look on others before. Let me know if you want to talk."

Callum left, purpose in his stride with Terry close on his heels, kit bag in his hand. "See you there, Ter. Got to pick something up from home."

"They get all the fun," said Kat. She flopped into her chair. "Anything we can do to help?"

Beryl connected her phone to her computer and copied files. "More than you would think. Sending you some photos and videos. Study them carefully. I'll be right back. I need to buy a laptop."

Stew and Andy sat at one table, Dan at another. Terry walked into the open air cafe and sat across from Dan.

The boardwalk between the cafe and the water was thick with tourists and tourist traps. A man pretending to be a silver statue received coins and bills in his hat for doing literally nothing. An indigenous man played a didgeridoo for sad money. At the other end of the boardwalk, near the Manly Fast Ferry, a couple busked, him with a guitar, both of them singing.

Callum was sat at a table in the adjacent cafe nursing a large long black. He looked at his watch and his phone rang.

He popped in his Air Pods. "This is Callum."

"Mate, relax," said Terry. "You can literally see us. Open the music app on your phone and without being too obvious, make sure she sees it."

"What song?"

Terry sighed. "Doesn't matter what song. She'll see it and think you were listening to music when she arrives."

"Cool. Supertramp."

'Who? Shit, how old are you?"

"I like their stuff. Okay, here she comes."

"Deep breaths. Pretend you don't notice her until she sits, then pull one Air Pod out and place it on the table."

"Which one?"

Terry took a deep breath. "It doesn't really matter, Callum. Either one."

"Right." He looked up as Mel approached and sat at the table.

She placed her handbag on the table and looked pointedly at Callum.

"What? Oh." He removed an Air Pod and left it on the table. "Supertramp. Love them." He cleared his throat. "This needs to end."

"Why did you call me, Callum? Why are we meeting?" She waved at a server. "English breakfast tea, soy milk."

Callum looked at his phone. He flipped it over, Supertramp's 'Breakfast in America' on the screen. "This needs to end."

"Are you wired?"

"I've had a couple of cups of coffee, so, yeah. Vibrating."

Mel closed her eyes for a second. "Wired for sound. Bugged. Recording this conversation."

Callum stood and lifted his shirt. "Give me a break."

Mel looked at his abs for a second then waved at him to sit down. "What do you mean that it has to end?"

"This bullshit extortion scheme. Fuck. I give you money now, what guarantee is there that you don't come back at me in month for more, with the same dirt?"

Mel crossed her legs and sat back. "Who says I wouldn't have new dirt?"

Callum shook his head. "Clean and sober. There's nothing more for you to get."

Mel choked back a laugh. "What, all of three days?"

"Serious. How much to get the originals? Pictures, videos, the lot."

The server arrived with a pot of tea and a cup on a tray. She placed it in front of Mel and left.

Callum waited while she poured out a cup. "Well?"

"What?"

"All of it. I'll pay a premium. But I want the originals."

Terry spoke into Callum's ear. "We need her to make some definitive statements about extorting you. Nothing yet."

Callum pressed his finger against the Air Pod in his left ear. "Um, yeah."

Mel looked at the Air Pod on the table and the finger pressed in Callum's ear. "Oh, you shit." She grabbed his phone and terminated the call. "Who was on the other end?"

Callum held out his hand. "Give me my phone back."

Mel tossed it at him and stood. "I'm gone. Money by sunset or we go to print with another pile of photos."

"Sit down." He grabbed the phone, closed the music app and flipped it face down. "Why do you do this?"

"I like money."

"You like hurting people."

Mel smiled and shook her head. "Nah, that's bullshit. You've got more money than you'll ever spend, and I don't release the photos if you give me a tiny fraction of your net worth."

"Give you? I thought it was the magazine."

Mel shrugged. "I get a healthy cut." She sipped her tea. "So, no, I won't give you the originals. How is that even possible? Everything is digital now. In the cloud. Well and truly out of your reach. It's not like I've got a reel of celluloid locked up in a vault somewhere. And you've got maybe eight hours to pay up." She leaned forward. "And it doesn't matter how clean or sober you now are. I can create you in any scenario I want you to be in. Snorting coke off a hooker? That's PG compared to what I can do. Do you like donkeys? Young Asian boys? Maybe at the same time? This gravy train can go on forever for me. Just know that anything you can think of, I can do worse. Go to the cops and the vilest video you can imagine appears on the internet within twenty-four hours."

Callum raised one hand and signalled the others. He took his old phone out of his shirt pocket and placed it on the table. The voice recorder was active. He pressed the end button. "Gone to the cloud. Digital. Well and truly out of your reach. How much do you think *that's* worth?"

Dan, Stew and Andy grabbed chairs and sat around the small table.

Terry picked up the mobile phone and played back the recording, pressing the phone hard to his head. The didgeridoo started up and he stuck a finger in the opposite ear to block it.

Dan looked closely at Mel. "You hired me to bug his place, which I did. Unfortunately. Unfortunate for you, mostly."

Terry smiled, nodding while he listened. "She's fucked, boss," he said, a little too loud.

"There's nothing." Mel crossed her arms and sat back in her seat. "It'll never hold up in court."

Terry sat between Dan and Mel. "Boss, I've got her straight up threatening to dump falsified dirt on the internet if he even thinks about going to the cops."

Mel swallowed and looked at Terry, then at the phone. "Jesus Christ."

Dan leaned on his elbows. He played with a sugar packet. "Remember that woman who Tweeted a bad joke just before she got on a flight to Africa, something about being safe from AIDS because she was white? And remember the total meltdown of her career, without her even knowing, while she was in the air?" He smiled. "Like that, if we release this. Your boss will immediately distance himself from you — you're a rogue, he had no idea the lengths you went to get stories, yada, yada, yada."

"So, what, you've turned the tables and want money? How much?"

"No money. Except for the invoice for bugging young Callum. My accountant will send you that and you'll pay it and be glad you did. But no, I'm not extorting you. Or blackmailing you. I want you to go away."

She looked between Dan and Stew. "What?"

"Leave."

"Just leave?" she asked. She shook her head. "What do you mean?"

"Piss off. Get the fuck out of town. Stay out of our way for a week. Maybe two. Go to Hong Kong and go shopping. Watch the Tour de France up close. Hit Disneyland. I really don't care, just get out of the country. Today. In the next hour." Dan tossed the sugar packet on the table. "If you're not on a flight this afternoon, the recording gets sent to every media outlet in the western world. You'll be identified as Rand's chief counsel -- I don't care if you are or not -- and you will be buried."

"The Tour de France is in July."

"I don't fucking care. Get off this continent."

"Why?"

"You don't get to ask that." Dan stood. "And you might want to update your LinkedIn page, because when you come back you're not going to have a job." He took the phone from Terry and handed it to Stew. "My young associate will escort you to your apartment. Throw a few things in a bag and make sure you get to the airport today. Fuck with him and it gets released. Try to throw his tail and it gets released. Don't make an international flight this afternoon and it gets released."

"Yeah, yeah, yeah. I get it."

"And don't call Rand and tell him you're leaving."

"Right. It'll get released." She chewed the inside of her cheek. "What are you going to do with him?"

"Read about it in the papers. Terry, you're on her like white on the Liberal Party. Check in with Stew every fifteen minutes." He placed a finger on Mel's chest. "Stew pulls the trigger if he doesn't hear from Terry every fifteen."

Mel's lips were a pair of thin straight lines. The colour had washed from her face, except for a flush of red in her cheeks. She smacked Dan's hand away. "You fuckers."

"You're getting off easy. Enjoy your vacation."

Dan watched Terry follow a Mel, her steps short and sharp. He smiled and sat back at the table. Stew was listening to the recording. "What do you think, boys?"

Callum's grin split his face. "Damn. You toasted her."

"Let's not get ahead of ourselves. We can't take the next step until she's out of the country. Tonnes of places for this to still fall apart."

"Yeah, but still. She's sidelined permanently." Callum bounced one heel off the ground. "You guys are good."

"I wish I still had your youthful enthusiasm, kid. It'll hold her for a little while. Long enough to finish the job." Dan looked at the menu on the table. "Not much more than that, though. We've got a couple of hours. You guys feel like lunch? It's a beautiful day."

CHAPTER 30

"You don't trust me?"

Terry slowly shook his head. "Doesn't matter if I do or if I don't. I was told to make sure you got on the flight. I'm going to the gate with you."

Mel placed her handbag, coins, magazine, book and mobile phone in one X-ray tray and her jacket in another. "I just spent a stupid amount of money for a last minute business class ticket to Singapore. You think I'm actually not going to take it?" She walked through the magnometer without setting it off.

Terry placed his wallet and mobile phone in a tray and followed her through. "Doesn't matter." He waited by the conveyor for the trays, took Mel's phone and wallet and pocketed them and placed his phone in her handbag and handed it to her with her jacket. He looked at the departures board. "Better hustle. The flight's boarding now."

"I'm going to the lounge and getting a drink."

"You miss the flight and that recording is on the news tonight."

"Fuck."

Terry watched Mel board the Singapore Airlines flight, waited until the gate closed, then placed the call.

"She's off to Singapore, boss. Wheels up in about twenty minutes, then well and truly out of touch for at least seven hours."

"In-flight phones. But I'm banking on her not wanting to have that recording in the wild."

"She won't call him from the plane."

"I envy your confidence."

"I've got her wallet.. And I'm calling you on her mobile."

There was a brief bit of silence. "Oh. Well done. Head back here as fast as you can. Need your electronics skills for the next phase."

"No problem. Got to stop by the phone shop to get a new SIM. She's got my phone. Wiping it remotely as soon as I hang up."

"Right. Okay. Don't take too long. And ditch her phone. Someone will be looking for it before too long."

Dan hung up his desk phone and chuckled. "Damned good job."

Stew stood in the doorway. "Terry?"

"Yeah. Mel's on a flight to Singapore and he's got her wallet and mobile phone." He laughed again. "Better than I expected."

"So what's next"

"Standard bad guy take down. Get rid of his close associates and work our way in to the middle. Mel's out of the picture for now. Those two fucks -- Gerald and Robert -- we need them next."

"You got a plan for Rand?"

Dan nodded. "It'll take all of us and a healthy amount of luck."

"The more prepared we are, the luckier we get."

Dan stood and clapped Stew on the shoulder as they walked out of his office. "Exactly. Where's Andy?"

"Grabbing a coffee."

Andy walked in the door with a tray of coffee and a bag of pastries. "A bunch of coffee. What's going on?"

Dan nodded toward the conference room. "Quick catch up."

Beryl and Kat were already in there. New laptop packaging was stacked on the table and Beryl was dirtying up the case. An image of Rand's laptop was on the monitor. It was a screen grab from the video made during her contact.

Kat was creating a web page. Dan stood behind her and watched. "Looks good. How deep are you going?"

She looked over her shoulder. "All the way. He's got to think it's real."

"Fantastic. This is going down tomorrow. Will you be ready? We can put it off a day if we need to, but it means we'd have to string him along an extra day."

"Tomorrow's fine. I should be finished with this in a couple of hours. Then it's just a matter of adding the keylogger and duplicating the laptop profile." She looked up at Dan. "That part will be thin." She pointed at the monitor. "Just the icons on the screen. You're going to have to get him to act fast."

"Noted. We'll set him up for tomorrow, then."

Kat pushed back from the laptop. "I know what you're trying to do, and I'm pretty sure I know why, but I don't get the how."

Beryl put down a small dirty cloth. "That's not our problem to solve, Kat. Division of labour. Dan will figure it out of he hasn't already."

"Dan has, and you, Kat, are inextricably involved," said Dan. "But that's for tomorrow. You will play a small part. But don't worry about that. Keep on with the laptop work."

"No, no. Wait. What do you mean? I'm a background worker. I can't -"

"Don't worry. It'll be easy. And I'm pretty sure you'll enjoy it." Dan took a coffee from the tray. "Andy and Stew, tonight's the night. Go get some rest and meet me back here at 6:00."

Randolph sat at the head of the table, trying to look professional with a splint on his nose and two black eyes. The editorial board filled the other chairs in the conference room. One chair, to his immediate left, was empty. The low murmur of gossip and personal chat stopped when Randolph slapped his folder on the table. "Where is Miss Dvorak?"

Nobody answered.

"For fuck's sake, where is she? She is punctual to a fault."

"I'll try calling her?" One of the team held up his phone.

"You're asking me? Call her. Put it on speaker."

The guy dialled the number, put the call on speaker and placed it on the table. It went immediately to voice mail. *"Leave a message. I'll get back to you when I can."*

He terminated the call. "You want me to try again?"

"To what end? Reschedule this meeting to a time when she is available."

The man with the phone held up a finger. "The issue is meant to go out tonight. We're running it tight to the wire."

Rand looked at his watch. He sighed and drummed his fingers on the table. "Is there anything in this issue that will get me sued?"

The man grimaced. He held his hand out, palm down and waggled it.

Rand waved his hand dismissively. "Anything more contentious than any other issue we've put out?"

"No, not really."

"Then send it." He stood. "If anyone hears from Mel, tell her I need to talk to her immediately."

He made his way to the security offices. Gerald and Robert were having a coffee. CCTV monitors covered the far wall.

Gerald stood when Rand entered. "Boss. How's the nose?"

"Where's Mel?"

"Don't know. She left to meet the actor kid this morning. Something about a payment." Gerald smiled. "Congratulations."

"She hasn't returned. Find her phone."

Robert spun his chair to a terminal and entered her phone number. A map appeared and a green dot flashed for a second, then turned orange. "It's off." He zoomed the map back to get a broader view. "But it was last on at the International Terminal at the airport."

"She didn't mention any travel plans to me. You?"

Gerald shook his head. "She told me she was pissed she had to go to the waterfront for the meet. Was worried she'd miss the editorial meeting this afternoon."

"She missed it. Shit. Can you check her phone calls?"

"Yeah, just a second." Andy logged into the carrier's website and selected her phone. "That call at the top of the list. Three and a bit hours ago. I don't recognise it."

"So fucking call it."

Andy poked the numbers into the desk phone and called on speaker.

"McGinnis Investigations, Beryl speaking. How may I -"

Randolph reached over and terminated the call. "The damn PI. Find out what happened to her. Start at the waterfront. See what happened that would cause her to skip. It's not like her. Find out what they've done to her."

Gerald shrugged. "Maybe she's got enough money now. Took it and ran."

"She doesn't know the meaning of 'enough' money. And why would she be calling McGinnis? Find out what's going on."

"If she's gone overseas do you want us to follow her?"

"No. Just let me know, one way or another."

Terry entered the office to empty desks. "Hello?"

Dan stuck his head out of the conference room. "Mate, come on in. There's pizza. Good job, by the way."

Terry tossed Mel's wallet at Dan. "Might be something useful in there."

Dan hefted it. "I'm sure there is." He looked at his watch. "She's in the air a couple more hours, right?"

"Six more. And even when she lands, without a phone or wallet she's going to be at a disadvantage." He nodded at Beryl and sat beside Kat. He grabbed a slice and looked at what she was doing. "That's excellent. Looks exactly like the website. I bank there and it would fool me."

She glanced at him. "Thanks. Kinda busy. Leave me alone."

"Right, right." He took a bite of double pepperoni. "So what electronics work do you need me to do, Dan?"

"I've got the phone number of one of Rand's meatheads. Pretty sure they are trying to find out what happened to Miss Dvorak." He smiled at the confused look on Terry's face. "Mel."

"Right. This isn't NCIS. I can't track a phone with just it's number."

"Yeah, I know. But there's that find my phone thing, right? Can you hack it?"

"That's done with an email address not the mobile number." He stood and reached in his pocket. "Instead of find them, maybe they can find us." He handed Mel's mobile to Dan.

"Thought you were going to ditch it."

"Thought maybe it would come in handy."

Dan powered up the mobile. It asked for a passcode. He held it up. "Any ideas?"

Terry took the phone. His thumbs flew over the keypad and he handed it back. "I've reset it to 1-2-3-4-5-6." He smiled at the look on Dan's face. "There's a hack that gets you into any of the phones with the latest iOS. Apple has an upgrade coming that fixes it."

"So let's lay a trail."

"What's the goal?"

Dan tapped the edge of the phone on his chin. He powered it down. "We need to be able to find them on our terms.. They don't need to find us. Yet." He handed the phone back to Terry. "Hang on to this. We're going to need it later."

He checked his watch. "Stew and Andy will be here soon." He thought for a second. "Come up with a way to find Gerald and Robert."

"Assuming they're looking for Mel, they'll be at the waterfront and the airport. Probably now. We can find them there, I'm positive of it."

Dan shook his head. "Want to get them individually and alone. I was banking on you being able to track their phones."

Terry smiled. "So, I've got an idea. When are Stew and Andy getting here? I need to get some electronics ready."

CHAPTER 31

"You think she skipped town with the money?"

Gerald shook his head. "Boss would have checked the accounts by now. If she had, he would have let us know."

"Maybe. He's got a warped sense of right and wrong. He'd more than likely have us on a wild goose chase just for the hell of it."

Gerald parked at the kerb in front of her apartment building in Darling Point. "Nice place."

"She's on a much better packet than we are, mate."

"Yeah, no shit." Gerald fished a folded piece of paper from his shirt pocket. He entered a code at the gate and pushed it open. "She's not going to be here."

"You're probably right. But if we don't check, we'll be constantly wondering."

"Constantly?" Gerald entered a different code at the main door. "Maybe you. I wouldn't give it another thought. I know she's not here."

"So why'd you come?"

Gerald looked at him. "Boss says check it, we check it. Even if it's a waste of time."

A third keypad at the apartment door later and Gerald and Robert were inside.

They stood in the alcove taking in the white and stainless steel furniture. A glass coffee table reflected the low light coming in the window.

"Nice," said Robert.

"She's not here. Let's go."

Robert wandered into the kitchen. It was spotless. He pulled the dishwasher open. "She even live here? You could eat off the floor."

Gerald called him from the bedroom. "Check this out."

A row of suitcases lined the back of the deep walk-in closet, arranged by size. There was a gap near the big end. "She's left town." Robert tipped his head sideways and studied the gap. "Too big for carry-on."

Gerald pressed a speed dial on his phone. "Boss, have you checked the accounts?"

"Nothing unusual financially. You find Mel?"

"There's a suitcase missing. Looks like she flew the coop."

"Damn. Keep digging."

Gerald grunted as he parked the car. "Pay the meter."

The walked along the waterfront, in front of the ferry terminals, leading to the Opera house. Robert was looking at the map on his phone. "Up ahead, in front of Wharf 3. Looks like the phone was there."

Robert stopped at the entrance to the restaurant and checked his phone.

"This is the one." He looked up at his surroundings. The Manly Fast Ferry was just coming in. Crowds were gathering for dinner.

Gerald walked into the wait station holding up a picture of Mel on his phone.

A waiter with a tattooed sleeve and a manbun glanced up at him. "Do you have a booking? There's no tables without a booking."

Gerald tapped on the phone screen. "Look. This woman. Have you seen her here today?"

"So you don't have a booking? No tables until 11:30 if you don't have a booking."

"Jesus, man. Look. At. The. Picture. What she in here just before lunch?"

The waiter focused on the picture. "I don't recognise her."

"So she wasn't here?"

"My shift started like twenty minutes ago. I have no idea."

Robert stepped in. "I need to talk to someone who was working tables this morning. And we need to see whatever type of security video you might have."

The waiter blinked and moved back a step. "Way above my pay grade, man. Let me get the boss."

A middle-aged, severe looking woman showed up a couple of minutes later. "Lewis says you want a table but you don't have a booking. I'm sorry, but we're fully booked out until late."

Gerald held the phone at arm's length, the photo in the woman's face. "We don't want to eat at this shithole. We're looking for this woman. Her life may be in danger."

"Shithole? Goodbye."

"Wait, wait." Robert held out his hand. "This is his wife. He's very concerned. I apologise on his behalf. Are there any staff still here who worked this morning?"

"None. Rotated everyone through between 3:00 and 5:00. Sorry to hear about your wife. Can't help you."

Robert persisted. "Do you have security footage?"

The manager hesitated. "We do. I don't have time to go over it with you. Our dinner rush is starting."

"Then let us have a look. We don't need a copy. We're just looking."

She crossed her arms. "So who are you guys anyway?"

Gerald leaned forward. "I'm her husband. She's in danger. I need to find her."

"So, call the cops."

He sighed. "Don't you think I've already done that? She needs to be missing for forty-eight hours. It's only been eight. And I'm really, really worried for her."

Patrons lines up behind them. The manager looked at the lengthening line and sighed. "Okay. Follow me. Leave a drivers licence. I'll give it back when you leave."

Gerald nudged Robert. "Give her your licence. Where do we go? We'll just take pictures with our phone. I really appreciate it."

Unmanned consoles played live feeds from cameras at the entrance, two behind the register and a couple on the outside part of the restaurant.

The manager pointed at three consoles. "These are live. Don't touch them. Use the one over here to dig through the archives. They're filed by date and time. Hope you find her. Don't break anything." She paused at the door. "And don't be long, okay? I really shouldn't be doing this."

Robert found the video file for the two hours between 9:00 am and 11:00 am and played it at double speed.

"Faster."

Robert looked up at his partner. "It doesn't go faster."

"Then jump ahead in five minute increments. She had to be sitting here longer than five minutes."

Robert nodded and jumped the video forward, pausing for a few seconds at each jump. A couple of minutes in and Gerald jabbed his finger at the screen.

"There."

Robert paused the video. Mel was at a table on the left half of the screen, clearly visible.

"She looks pissed," said Robert.

Gerald tapped on the screen. "You recognise the kid with her?"

"That actor dude she said she was going to meet." He hit the play button at normal speed. "No audio."

"Speed it up."

Jerky hand motions, Mel's anger evident from her face, then three more people sit at the table.

Gerald jabbed his finger against the screen. "Those PI arseholes. Again. If they took her out I'm going to kill them."

"Hang on. She's going on her own. No, with that young kid from the PI mob," said Robert. "Doesn't seem to be under duress."

"Look at the way she's walking. She wants to stab somebody."

"Want me to back it up, get some pictures?"

Gerald shook his head. "No need. So she went from here to her flat to the airport." He looked at the timestamp on the video. "She really had to hustle to get to the airport when she did."

"Wonder why."

"We go to the airport and maybe we find out. Get your licence from the nice lady and meet me at the car."

"You're positive they're going to go to the airport?" Andy leaned between the car seats. "Seems kind of obvious."

"I placed a call from her phone just outside the terminal. They would have tracked it," said Terry, squashed in beside him.

"Like finding needles in a haystack." Andy sat back. He was behind Stew, who was driving. Dan was in the front passenger seat.

"We know where they're going to be. As long as we get there before them," said Dan.

Terry took the small plastic container out of his shirt pocket and looked at the four small disks, about the size of five cent coins. "So, we're not going to scuffle with them in front of the airport, are we? Federal Cops won't like that."

"We'll follow them into the parking structure. And only a bit of shoving, okay? Just enough to get hands on them." Dan pointed to an exit. "Park in there, Stew. We split up. Two at arrivals and two at departures. Terry, you come with me."

Terry handed two disks to Stew. "Peel the back off before you stick them."

"I know, kid. Used these plenty of times."

Andy and Stew headed upstairs to the departures terminal and Terry followed Dan down to arrivals.

"They should be looking for her upstairs, right? She was departing."

Dan trotted down the escalator. "Never underestimate the stupidity of your enemy." He found a seat in the waiting area with a view of the sidewalk outside. An empty baggage carousel behind them came to life and started moving. "And we don't engage until they're back in the parking garage."

Terry held up the case with the remaining two disks. "We've just got to get these on them somehow."

"You definitely got it." He tapped Terry on the arm. "There's one of them."

Robert was standing on the sidewalk looking at his phone. He pointed to his left and Gerald walked into view.

Dan made a quick call. "Andy, they're down here. Arrivals. Head into the parking garage now. I'll let you know which way they go."

He hung up and pushed Terry down in his seat. "Stay out of their eye line.

I don't want them to notice us yet." He held out his hand. "Give me one of those bugs."

He moved from pillar to pillar, subtly, staying behind Robert and Gerald's line of sight. A swarm of arrivals lined up at the carousel and waited for their baggage.

"Blend in with these guys. And keep an eye on our friends."

Robert and Gerald engaged in an animated discussion about something, then Robert shoved his phone in his pocket and crossed the street toward the parking garage.

Dan jammed his phone to his head. "Heading to the P7 parking lot, Andy. Pick them up. Wait until they get near their car."

He hung up. "Let's go, kid."

Dan and Terry walked behind Rand's two security heads, leaving a wide gap. The two targets entered a lift and pressed a button. Dan held an arm out and stopped Terry. "Hang on. Let them go."

"We'll lose them."

"It's only five floors. And it's open air. We'll be able to see them leave the lift. Back up a bit." He redialled. "Andy, they're on their way up. Give me a sec and I'll tell you what floor. Don't hang up."

Dan and Terry back up and watched pedestrian traffic either side of the lift column. Gerald and Robert appeared moving left. "Third floor, Andy. Heading north. Slow them. We'll be right there."

Terry and Dan ran to the lift and repeatedly pressed the "Up" button. The indicator showed it was stopped on the fifth floor.

"Stairs, kid."

They ran them, two at a time, and exited onto the third floor of the parking garage. Andy and Stew had Gerald and Robert against a car, finger pointing and yelling at each other. Stew gave Gerald a shove in the chest.

"What do you mean, what did we do with Mel? We didn't do anything with Mel. Who's Mel?"

"I've got video of you with her on the Quay this morning. Don't bullshit me."

Dan ran up. "Hey, hey. What the hell's going on. You guys? Stew, how did you run into these arseholes? Come on. We've got shit to do."

Robert stuck out his chest. "Arseholes? What in the hell did you do with -" He looked at Terry. "You. You left the cafe with her this morning." He pushed past Dan. "Where in the hell is she?"

Dan grabbed him by the neck and pulled him back. He slid a disk in Robert's back pocket and pushed him against a car. "Hands off, dickwad."

Gerald rushed in to defend his partner and Stew grabbed him from behind. He looped an arm around Gerald's neck and tightened it. "Ease up, kiddo. Nothing to see. We good?"

He peeled the backing off a disk and stuck it under Gerald's shirt collar and pushed him away. "We don't know where Mel went. She said something about a shopping trip. My bet is Hong Kong, Bangkok or Singapore."

"We saw you talking with her this morning."

"You were there, too? You should have joined us." Dan smiled and pushed Gerald back toward Robert. "Now calm the fuck down. There's two of you and four of us. You wouldn't have a chance. And I'd welcome a re-match if not for the fact that there are dozens of cameras around here and the Federal Police are bored out of their mind what with the no terrorist activity lately. A brawl on the third floor of a parking garage would draw at least half the AFP based at the airport."

He crossed his arms. "So piss off, go home, and relax. Tell Rand she's on a shoe shopping trip."

Gerald and Robert backed toward their vehicle. "We see you again, we're taking you apart. Even if there are four of you."

Dan waved him away. "That's flattering. Enjoy your trip."

The car pulled away and started the circular route down to the exit. As soon as they left the floor Dan, Terry, Andy and Stew took out their phones.

The tracking software showed three blips.

"Three?" asked Dan. "I thought it was only two."

"I've been practicing," said Stew. "Dropped one in Gerald's shirt pocket when I shoved him." He smiled. "Then stuck one under his shirt collar. I could make a good living as a pickpocket."

Terry closed the app. "Come on. When do we hit them?"

"At 3:00 a.m. In their homes," said Dan. "We don't know where they live, and this is as central a place as any, so I've booked rooms here at the airport. Let's get dinner, then we all should get some sleep. 3:00 isn't that far away."

CHAPTER 32

Dan leaned back and made room for the server. "Thanks."

"Salad? You're getting old, mate." Stew cut into his steak. "Need meat."

"You must have a stainless steel colon. And you're at least fifteen years older than me."

Terry laughed and necked a beer. He waved at the server and held up the bottle. "How long have you two known each other?"

Andy waved the server away. "Enough, Ter. Need your wits about you."

"Fine. Whatever." He opened the app on his phone. He placed the phone beside his plate and waited for the map to resolve while he picked at his barramundi. "Why is coverage so shitty at the airport?"

"Coverage is fine. Flight must have just landed. Everyone and their kid just took their phone off airplane mode. Sites are swamped." Andy finished his linguini and pushed his plate back. "We're charging all of this back to that Mel bitch, right?"

Dan nodded. "I'm hitting the sack. Meeting at the front door at 3:00." He pointed at Terry's phone. "Make sure that thing is charged up."

"Yeah, I will. They're still together. In Darlinghurst."

Gerald and Robert sat in the car in front of Mel's flat. "When do you think she's coming back?" Robert picket his teeth with a fingernail. "She's coming back, right?"

"Who knows. Not looking forward to being around Rand if she skipped town, maybe for good." Gerald shifted in his seat. "So what in the hell was that with those PI guys at the airport?"

"How do you mean?"

"They show up out of nowhere. Got the drop on us. Could have put up a really good fight if they wanted to, and if I was them, I probably would have." He jacked open the door. "Doesn't make sense. Let's go."

"Where we going?"

Gerald looked at Robert. "Where do you think. We're in front of her apartment. We're going to pull it apart until we figure out what's going on."

"Cool."

They passed through the gates and the main door and Gerald was entering the code into the keypad beside the door to the flat when it was yanked open. Gerald looked down at the short, tanned, impossibly blonde woman in front of him. "Danni. Hey. How's it going?"

"What the fuck are you doing, Gerry?"

Gerald leaned on the door frame. "Ah, checking in on Mel. Haven't heard from her. I -- we -- thought you were out of town. Match in Perth or something."

"Yeah. I'm back. You ever think about knocking?"

Gerald looked past Danni into the flat. "You win?"

"You don't follow the sport?"

He shrugged. "Kinda busy. Can we come in and have a look around? Concerned about Mel. Have you heard from her?"

"No, you can't. And no, I haven't."

"You're not concerned?"

Danni crossed her arms. "No. Take off, Gerry, and take your puppy with you." Danni stepped back and slammed the door shut.

"Well that's a dead end." Robert returned to Gerald's car. "Puppy? Fuck her." He jerked on the car door handle. "Unlock it."

"I'll drop you at your place. We'll pick this up again tomorrow morning."

Dan left the lift and entered the hotel lobby. The noise curfew made the airport unnaturally quiet. The lobby was empty save Dan's crew sitting around a table near the floor-to-ceiling windows.

"You're early boss." Terry looked at his watch. "It's 2:30."

"We all are." He sat beside Terry. "You got them?"

Terry placed his phone on the table. Three blue dots blinked, one just north of Sydney and two to the north-west.

Dan scrubbed his face. "Okay. We go together. Hit them one at a time. There is nothing legal in what we're doing, you need to understand that. They need to be out of commission for at least a week. Clear?"

The other three nodded.

"North first, then northwest. Easier run home after that. Do you know if those are houses or apartments?"

Terry changed the map background to satellite imagery and zoomed on each one. "Houses. Both of them."

"Damn." Dan thought for a couple of seconds. "You still have Mel's phone?"

"Yeah." Terry handed it to Dan.

"Okay. We'll use it to get them out of their houses. Let's go."

Terry's people-carrier van rolled to a stop outside the house to the north. "So who's is this?"

"One tracker, it's Robert," said Stew. "Gerald has two."

Dan grabbed Mel's phone, unlocked it and spun through the contacts. He found Robert's number. "Where do we do this?"

Stew looked in the sideview mirror. "There's a train station a block south of here."

"Too well lit. Cameras," said Andy.

"He won't get that far." Dan thought for a second, then sent a message to Robert.

Robert, this is Mel. Are you up?

Dan stared at the phone for a minute before he received a response: *Mel? Where are you? Overseas? It's late.*

He smiled.

Sorry. I was. I'm at the Roseville station. That fucking PI took my cards. Can I get a couple of bucks from you until I get my shit sorted out tomorrow?

Sure, come by my place. I'll make you a coffee.

"No, that won't work," said Dan. He thought for a second and typed. *I can't. I don't feel safe walking through the dark. It's bright at the station. There's cameras. Please.*

There was a long pause.

I'll be there in a couple of minutes.

"That's that, then." Dan flipped the dome light off so it wouldn't come on when the doors were opened. "He'll be passing be here in a minute. Bundle and we take him to the bush."

Andy and Stew hopped out of the van and stood behind it. Andy unfolded a black pillow case and Stew held a shot-filled length of hose.

Dan slumped down in the driver's seat. He rolled down his window a crack. "The front porch light just came on. Get ready."

The front door opened inward, then the fly screen door pushed open and Robert stepped onto his porch, pulling on a windbreaker. He walked hunched over, face in his phone.

"Ten seconds," said Dan. Mel's phone chimed on his lap. *Walking there. Two minutes. I'll walk you back for that coffee.*

Dan switched the phone to silent and flipped it on its face. He waited until Robert had passed the passenger's side of the van then quietly opened the door and walked around to the back. He heard a scuffle just before he turned the corner. Stew had Robert under the armpits and Andy had the legs. His hands were secured by a cable tie and the black pillow case was pulled over his head.

"You haven't lost your touch."

Stew grunted. "Not as young as I used to be. Get the door, will you?"

He slid it open and Terry flipped one of the bench seats forward, creating a small flat space.

Stew lifted the unconscious body unto the van. Terry grabbed an arm and helped drag Robert in.

"We set?" Dan started the van.

Andy was the last in and slid the door closed. "We're just going to dump him?"

Dan sat in silence for a minute, the put the van in gear. "More. I've had enough of these pricks. A fair good pounding, then we'll dump him in Middle Harbour."

"Where's that?"

"Ten minutes down the road, Andy. I used to go fishing there when I lived up here." Stew scratched his jaw. "Don't recall ever dumping a body there."

Dan glanced in the rear-view mirror and caught Stew sharing a look with Andy. "What?"

"A little bit out of your comfort zone."

"I'll be fucked if he threatens anyone again."

Dan pulled the van off the main road onto the park access road. Robert's still unconscious body rolled around in the gap, banging his head off one of the supports as the van trundled over the joint between paved and gravel road.

He drove on a few hundred metres and pulled under an overhanging tree by the edge of Middle Harbour. He turned off the engine and, other than the pinging noise of the cooling engine block, all he heard was frogs croaking on the river bank and the quiet hum of distant traffic. "Okay, lads. Drag this piece of shit out and wake him up."

Andy pushed Robert up against the van, sliced through the tie-wrap restraints with a boxcutter and pulled the pillowcase off his head.

Dan stepped close and slapped Robert's face. "You awake, big guy?" He smacked him again. Robert snapped his head away and lifted his hands.

"What the fuck?" Robert squinted into the darkness around him. "What's going on? Where's Mel?" He looked closer at Dan. "You?" he pushed at Dan and Stew and Andy grabbed his arms.

"You grabbed an old woman?" Dan punched Robert in the gut, doubling him over. He grabbed him by the hair and lifted him upright. "An old woman." He punched his gut again and brought his knee up under his face when he doubled over. A loud crack was accompanied by a spray of blood and Robert slumped to the ground. His nose was bent to one side and blood pooled in the dirt.

Dan stepped to one side. "Son of a bitch. He got blood on me." He rubbed some dirt on it. "Make sure when they find him he's barely alive." He crawled back into van and closed the door. He looked at Terry and laughed. "You okay?"

The sound of kicks and grunts outside the van drowned out the frogs. Terry swallowed. "A bit more violent than I'm used to."

"He fucked with Beryl. Big mistake." Dan looked out the window at the pounding. "The other guy is bigger. We might need your help. You up for it?"

The van's side door slid open and Any and Stew crawled into their seats. "He's in the water. Most of him," said Stew. "On his front, water up to his armpits. Figured out how we're getting Gerald?"

"Pretty good idea." Dan started the van and drove out of the park with the headlights off. "Cops are going to be all over that place. We've left a shit load of forensics."

Stew thought for a second. "What's on tomorrow morning?"

"Prepping for Randolph's take-down. Why?"

"Do you need Andy and I for that?"

Dan shook his head. "Most of the work is Kat, Terry and Cassie."

"Andy and I will come down here in the morning. Early. Do some fishing. Fuck the scene up completely. Then we'll find the comatose man and make sure he gets the help he needs."

Dan glanced at him in the rear-view mirror. "Not a terrible idea. You sure he'll stay out?" He eased the van up to the entrance to the main motorway. There was no traffic as 4:00 in the morning. He accelerated onto the macadam and headed north.

"Cracked his skull. Legitimately cracked it." Andy shrugged. "He fucked with Beryl."

"See kid? What did I tell you?" Dan smacked Terry on the chest. "You don't do that and get off lightly." He checked his GPS. "Grab a kip. About a forty minute drive to the next one."

Dan checked the tracker on Terry's phone and eased the van to a stop. He turned off the ignition. Terry was asleep beside him, leaning against the passenger side window. He looked in the rear-view mirror.

Andy winked at him and gently elbowed Stew. "Wake up, old man."

Stew blinked and sat up straight. "Plan?"

Dan looked at the house they had stopped in front of. It was a low bungalow on a largish lot. There was no fence around the yard. The streetlight was a few properties down the road and the yard was blanketed in shadows.

"We going to draw him out with that phone again?" Terry looked at the blinking dots. "Might work."

Dan shook his head. "No fence. We don't have to worry about a dog. I say we just go in and do it in there." He tapped Terry on the arm. "You up for this? Or do you want to wait in the van?"

The youngster looked in the back seat. Dan nodded at Andy who leaned forward in his seat. "Come in. Break your duck. We'll take care of you. Make sure you don't get too banged up."

Dan turned the dome light off and opened his door. "Let's go, keep quiet."

He walked along the property line as far from the driveway as possible. The lights were off in the house. It was dark and quiet. Dan held out his hand and stopped the team. He squatted and the other three squatted around him. "We go in the back door. If he's not sleeping in front of the TV, and I don't see light from a TV so he's probably not, then he's in the bedroom. We split up and the first person to find him, drop him and let the rest of us know."

"That's the plan?" Terry looked at Stew and Andy. "The entirety of the plan?"

"It's worked before, kid. Make it too complex and I'm liable to forget it." Stew rested his hand on his shoulder. "Stay behind me." He stood and walked to the back door. Terry scrambled to catch up.

Stew checked the door. It was locked. He took a thin piece of credit card-size metal from his wallet and jimmied the lock. "Idiot. No deadbolt."

The door creaked slightly as Stew pushed it open and stepped into the kitchen.

Gerald stepped out from behind the fridge and swung a cricket bat at Stew's head.

"Bloody hell." Stew ducked and the end of the bat connected with Terry's jaw, driving him sideways, catching his ribs on the counter before he fell to the floor.

Stew let out a growl and launched an upper cut under Gerald's chin that snapped his head back and straightened him out.

Before he hit the ground Stew was kicking him in the ribs. "Dan, Terry's down." He stuck the boot in, kicking him in the head and torso, Gerald unconscious and flopping around like a rag doll. "Caught the tip of the bat to the jaw." Gerald's face was a pulpy mess.

Dan grabbed him by the arm. "Enough. Don't kill him." He kneeled by Terry. "You okay, kid?"

Terry pushed himself up to a sitting position and winced, grabbing his side. "Oh, shit." He wiggled his jaw and spat out a bloody tooth. "I think I've got a broken rib."

Andy helped Terry stand. "I missed all the fun, as usual. He was expecting us."

Terry groaned and handed his phone to Andy. "Lucky you. I need a lie down. Maybe a painkiller or two."

"Stew, we've got to go. Drag the arsehole out into the yard and light up the house."

"What?"

Dan looked around the kitchen. "Turn on the gas and do something with the toaster."

"Boss?"

"Do it or I will, and you can do it without blowing yourself up. I don't think I can." He leaned down and grabbed the back of Gerald's shirt. "Rig the house. Andy, get Terry to the van and start it. We'll be right behind you."

Dan strained with Gerald's dead weight. Blood bubbles formed around the unconscious man's nose. He dragged him over the door frame, bounced him down the back stairs and across the grass to a tree in a far corner of the backyard.

He let him drop and rolled him over on his front and made sure he was still breathing. He stood, stretching his back and catching his breath when

Stew ran by. "Move it, boss. We've got a minute, max."

They ran to the van and Dan jumped in the back with Terry. Stew was in his seat with the door still open when Andy floored it.

"You okay, kid? Blurry vision? Headache?"

"Dan, I'm fine. Other than the ribs." Terry winced. "We can't go to the doctor, can we?"

"Sure we can. You fell off a motorbike. Happens all the time."

Terry sniffed and held his side. "Good. This -"

An explosion a block behind them shook the sides of the van.

Andy kept driving while Stew, Dan and Terry looked behind them at the glow in the sky.

"Damn," said Terry. "You're going to have to teach me that, Stew."

CHAPTER 33

Dan eased himself into the chair at the head of the conference table, wincing as he sat. Beryl was at the other end with Kat on her left and Terry, looking very uncomfortable, to her right. He sighed. "Terry, you okay?"

"Just fine." He wore a large shirt hiding the tape wrapped around his chest. He had a glorious purple bruise on his jaw.

Dan's knuckles on his right hand were raw. He flexed his fist and smiled at Beryl. "What?"

"Nothing."

"You've got that look my mother would throw at me when I came home from a match with a split lip and a torn jersey."

"What in the hell were you guys up to last night?"

"Taking care of the arseholes that grabbed you."

Beryl sat up straighter. "Taking *care* of? Where are Stew and Andy?"

"Rela -" Dan stopped at the look on Beryl's face. "It's all good. It can't come back to us. It won't. No need to worry."

Kat laughed. "He always this dumb?"

"I'm afraid so. What's the damage?"

"Other than Terry's ribs, just knocks and bruises."

"You know that's not what I meant."

Dan chewed the inside of his cheek. "The smaller, Robert, was on the bank of Middle Harbour with at least a concussion. Stew and Andy went 'fishing' there this morning, muddied up any forensics we may have left last night and 'found' him and called emergency services. He's at Mona Vale Hospital. The boys are on the way back. The bigger guy, Gerald, we left in his backyard and blew up his house. He's no doubt in a hospital somewhere."

Beryl leaned her head in her hands. "Jesus. If it *ever* comes back to this office, *I* do the talking. Understand?"

"Yeah. Thanks."

She trained her attention on Terry. "How many ribs and how bad?"

He rested his right hand on his left side, almost without realising he was doing it. "Two ribs, only cracked. Tore some muscle between them. Hurts like a prick."

Beryl returned her glare to Dan.

He held up his hands. "You're right. He shouldn't have come with us." He glanced at Terry and subtly shook his head.

Beryl seemed satisfied. "So now what? Randolph is still in frame."

"Last piece on the board. We need to put him away, for good, and we should be able to do it today."

"Where are they?" Randolph stuck his head into the security room. "Gerald. Robert. Where are they?" He hadn't showered. His thinning hair was plastered to his head and sheen of sweat covered his face and neck. His clothes were wrinkled and looked lived in.

The sole young lady in the room glanced at him, scowled and went back to what she was doing.

"Jesus." He dialled a number, pressed the phone to his head, then hung up with a short, sharp jab of his index finger. "Voice mail. Straight to voicemail. He's hung over again."

He straight-armed his office door open and threw his phone on his desk. "Son of a bitch." He leaned forward and looked out of his office to the woman sitting outside the door. "Hey. Have you heard from Mel yet?"

"She's still not answering her phone. It rings out, when it's on. It's not on very often."

Randolph leaned back and closed his eyes, summoning a memory. He smiled and grabbed his phone and scrolled through emails from Mel until he found the number he was looking for. He was in the middle of entering it on his phone when it rang.

An incoming call from Mel.

"Mel. Where are you? What were you doing in Campbelltown?" He heard breathing on the other end of the call. Light and shallow. "Mel?"

The call terminated.

"Mel?"

He tapped the incoming call log, found her number and dialled out.

Dan looked at Mel's phone, vibrating on his desk. He chuckled and sent the call to voicemail. "He's going to call that number every fifteen minutes. And he knows it's here." He turned the phone off and dropped it in the top drawer of his desk.

Kat, Terry and Beryl were in the office with him, Kat and Beryl in the two chairs across from his desk and Terry leaning up against the door jamb.

"I assume you've got an endgame for this, one we can get out of without getting bashed," said Terry.

"Working on it. Kat, can you spare half an hour?"

She nodded. "I'm pretty much ready but I've got a question about the laptop scam."

"I'll get to that. First, call the hospitals in the city and see if Gerald has shown up.' He slid a slip of paper across his desk. "You know how to do this, right?"

"Kidding me? I'm his little sister, worried because he didn't show up. Leave it to me." She grabbed the paper off Dan's desk and headed to hers.

Terry watched her leave then took the chair she had been sitting in. "So what are you working on?"

"What's Randolph want over anything else?"

"Toss-up between power and money."

"Not a 50:50 tossup though. If had to choose one, I'd put my money on - - well, money," said Dan

"Take the power, he's happy as long as he has money. Take the money, though, power doesn't get him into the nice places."

Dan nodded in reply. "So we take his money."

Terry raised an eyebrow. "Good luck with that."

"Perception is just as important as reality," said Beryl. "We'll have two choices. One, wipe him out, which is the obvious desired option, and two, make him think he's wiped out. Either way, we trigger him."

Terry thought for a minute. "That banking site Kat was working on, right? What if we can do both?"

Randolph finger combed his sweaty hair off his face. A half-full glass of bourbon and ice beaded water on his desk. "Fuck, fuck, fuck." He swallowed a mouthful and leaned back again, getting line of sight with the woman at the desk outside his office. "I need two new security. Now. Their best."

The person at the desk nodded in acknowledgement and placed a call.

Randolph heard her voice, but not the content of the conversation. He slid his phone closer and unlocked it. Mel's contact was open. He rubbed an eye with the heel of his hand, sighed and just before he pressed the handset icon to call her, his phone started ringing.

An incoming call from Mel. He jabbed the phone and put it on speaker. "Where are you?"

There was silence on the phone, then a slight, slow tapping.

"Who in the hell is this? Shit." He leaned back and yelled out the door. "Get someone to trace the location of Mel's phone. It's an emergency."

"Robert used to do that. I don't know where he is."

"Jesus." Randolph pressed the phone against the side of his face. "Look, whoever the hell you are, I will find you and if you've harmed a single hair on Mel's head I will kill you slowly."

Beryl looked at Dan, then back at the phone on the desk. "Slowly. You will regret whatever you've done," said Randolph.

Dan nodded at Beryl. She leaned close, getting her mouth near the microphone. "Thanks for that. A threat. Recorded. This will be useful."

"Who in the hell is—"

Beryl jabbed the 'End' button. "Weirdly satisfying."

"Keep it up. Random intervals for the next couple of hours, and make sure you turn the phone off between calls."

"When do we go?"

"How's Kat going?"

Beryl turned off the phone and dropped it in her purse. "Finished, as near as I can tell."

"Cool. After she's finished we go." Dan held the door for Beryl and followed her out, closing it behind him. "The audio lab?"

"That's where she was the last I checked."

Kat had a screen grab of the video of Randolph's laptop on the wall monitor. It was magnified to the keyboard, full frame.

Dan closed the door behind him and sat beside her. "How's it going?"

"Checking. I think it's close." She increased the magnification until the monitor displayed half of Randolph's laptop screen.

"What are you looking for? It looks identical." Dan picked up the laptop and held it close to his face. "Damn. I wouldn't change anything. This is good."

Kat took the laptop back. "'Good' isn't good enough. He's got to pick it up and think it's his."

"It's just after 11:00. Will it be ready after lunch? 2:00 pm?"

"Yeah." She tipped the laptop on its edge. "Close the door on the way out, please."

Dan chuckled and gently closed the door. "Beryl, can you get me Cassie's number?"

"Johnson?"

"The one and only."

"Mr Randolph, sir?" A balding, over-muscled man leaned his head in the office door. "We're your new security." He walked in followed by a near-clone, with more hair. They walked like their joints were seized, the awkward jerky movement of steroid-abusing gym rats. The sleeves of their golf shirts strained against their biceps. Both of their left arms were covered in ink.

Randolph scratched the stubble on his chin. "It's Mr Murray. Mr Randolph Murray. Not Rand. Definitely not Randy. And for fuck's sake, not Mr Randolph. What are your names?" He held up his hands. "Never mind, I don't care."

"I'm Manny and this is Joe."

"I'm not going to remember your names, so I don't care. We're going to Campbelltown. Now." He threw his car keys in their general direction. They hit Joe in the chest and fell to the floor. "I hope your reflexes are better than that in a pinch." He slid his laptop and tablet into a leather satchel and dropped his phone into his inside suit pocket.

Joe picked the keys off the floor. "Manny will stay with you and I'll bring your car 'round front."

"No. We all stay together and I get in the car in the garage so nobody can see me leaving." He adjusted the cuffs of his shirt and suit jacket. The shirt cuffs were food stained.

"We stopping at your place so you can freshen up first, sir?" asked Manny.

"We're going to Campbelltown."

Joe pushed the lift button. "Of course. What's in Campbelltown? And where in Campbelltown?"

"McGinnis Investigations."

Manny shared a glance with Joe and frowned. He entered the name in his phone, waited for the result and nodded. "On Queen Street. Got it. I'll call them and let them know you're on the way."

Randolph batted the phone out of Manny's hand. "No. We're arriving unannounced."

His eyes narrowed as he squatted and picked up his phone. "Right," said Manny.

The lift doors opened and as they stepped in, Randolph flanked by the two big men, Randolph's phone rang. He clenched his jaw muscles, took a deep breath and looked at the display. He clenched the phone in his fist and answered. "Fuck off. I know this isn't Mel calling. And my security has tracked -"

The lift doors closed and the call dropped.

"Son of a bitch."

"What's this about, Mr Murray?" Manny stood with his hands clasped in front of himself.

"None of your business."

"As part of our remit it benefits us, and more importantly, you, if we are fully aware of the situation we are entering. If there is chance of conflict, we need to know who the other party is or are and under which situations we might engage them. As well as knowing the rules of engagement. Are we defensive only, or do you wish us to be offensive? The best defence is an offence, as they say." Manny looked behind Randolph's head and caught Joe's eye.

"Exactly," said Joe. "Forewarned is forearmed."

Manny nodded. "Right? Are you expecting a dust up? Are we running into battle? What happened to Gerald and Robert? They were with you for years. Were there any actions they did we should be aware of, if only to avoid?"

Rand turned in the lift and faced the two. "Shut up." He jabbed Manny in the chest with his forefinger. "You talk too much. Get me to that address and do what I say when we get there."

CHAPTER 34

"Kat, he doesn't know you. It can't be one of us. Our faces are on the company web page and pretty good odds he's checked," said Dan. "You're up for this, right?"

Kat nodded, flushed. "This is the most fun I've had in a long time."

"It's probably going to get hairy. Back out if you feel the slightest danger."

Kat grinned at him and turned and grinned at Beryl. Both of them wore sombre faces. "What?"

"Back out if you feel the slightest danger, got it?"

Her grin slipped a couple of notches. "Right. Right." She cleared her throat. "Where and when are we doing this?"

Beryl raised her eyebrows. "She's asking good questions, Dan-o. Where and when? Sydney is a big city. We can't spend a week trying to track him down."

Stew stepped into the conference rom. "Track who down? I can find anybody."

"Randolph Murray. Phase one of our plan to completely ruin that arsehole needs us to find him and relieve him of his electronics." He shrugged. "Any ideas where we might find him?"

Stew looked at a message on his phone and smiled. "That's what I was coming in to tell you. He's going to be here in about twenty minutes."

Beryl shook her head and walked out of the room. "How in the hell does he do that?"

Stew held his phone up to her departing form. "Nothing magic. Friend on the inside."

"What? Who?"

Stew looked at his phone, bemused smile on his face. "One of his new security guys. He had to replace the two we took out of commission, yeah? Can't expect him to travel solo. One of them is a guy named Manny. I used to work at his parents place years and years ago. Did a lot of rock work for them. He was, I dunno, 12 back then. Kept him out of jail -- I told you about this, right? That's how I know Chang." He chuckled. "The kid went all roid rage gym rat for a while. Seems like he's got a new job."

Dan chuckled. "He knows you work for me?"

He shook his head. "We don't actually keep in touch that much. He knows I live down this way, is all. I haven't told him where I work. His message didn't seem like he knew. Just said he was heading down here and thought we could catch up for a beer later."

"Okay, okay. A change in plans. You're not involved in this first part. Can't risk it. Get Terry to take your place."

"You sure?"

"Yeah, I'm sure. Tell me about this Manny guy."

Dan, Kat, Terry and Andy sat in Dan's car in the parking lot behind the office. They were at the base of a 'U', where cars entering the lot came in on the left arm of the 'U' and exited on the right.

Kat, sitting in the back seat with Dan, had an article featuring Randolph Murray open on her phone. "This guy is vile. Even if he *didn't* take Beryl I'd want to hurt him, after reading this."

"I've got icing for the cake." Dan pulled the headphones out of his phone and found the file and pressed play.

"Mr Prime Minister, that's a hard line to take. And I'm sure that you will change your mind on corporate tax rates once you review the contents of the file that is being dropped off with your driver right about now. Picture, files, video, the sorts of things that the average man on the street wouldn't want to be made public..."

Dan paused the audio. "On tape, extorting the Prime Minister."

"That's not enough to tank him?"

Dan shook his head. "Not on its own, I don't think. He's got a lot of ink. But I do think it needs to be the final nail in the coffin."

A large, black Chrysler sedan pulled into the parking lot.

"Hey," called Andy from the front seat. "That's them. I recognise the car."

"Bets on whether he gets out or not?" asked Terry.

"Mate, if he doesn't get out, we need to do this somewhere else. He needs to get out."

The front doors opened and Joe and Manny got out. Manny walked to the back door and opened it. He looked in, saying something to the occupant, then stepped back, smiling. Randolph unfolded himself from the back seat and stood, adjusting his suit jacket.

"You're up, Kat. You know what to do. Terry, get the lock jammer ready."

"This is the office?" asked Randolph.

"The back side of it. It fronts on Queen, but there's a lane between the buildings to the front. Right beside the back door to the restaurant." He pressed the key fob to lock the car and he and Joe headed toward the walkway, unaware that Randolph had stopped to check his phone.

He looked up. "Hey, morons. You're supposed to be my security. Not just a ride."

Kat ran from behind a van, yelling. "Baby killer!"

"Excuse me." Randolph tried pushing her to one side and copped a kick in the shin. She was wearing her steel-capped bikie boots. "Jesus." He looked for his security, almost to the door. "Manny, Joe, whatever the fuck your names are, get back here."

Kat pushed him again. "You're letting those babies die in detention and you support it! You bastard."

"What in the hell are you talking about, young lady?" He took a picture of her with his phone. "You stupid bitch."

Kat swung her hand at his phone but was grabbed from behind by Joe before she could connect with it. "No." She struggled against the grip Joe had on her. "No. Let me go. Shit."

Randolph took a step closer to her, phone gripped in his hand and a sneer on his face. "Stupid, stupid bitch." He held up his phone. "I've got your picture. It'll take me less than a day to find out who you are. A week after that you'll be homeless, broke, living on the street sucking dicks for food. I will ruin you."

Kat narrowed her eyes, quickly leaned back and lashed out with her foot. Her steel-capped bike boot connected with Randolph's hand. Fingers bent the wrong way and the phone flew through the air, shattering the glass when it hit a concrete kerb.

"Ah, son of a bitch." Randolph bent over, cradling his hand. Two middle fingers weren't pointing in the right direction.

Manny took him by the arm. "Let's get some ice on that." He led his boss toward the restaurant. He glanced and Joe and shook his head. "Hang on to her." He leaned down and looked Randolph in the eye. "Your pics go right to the cloud, right?"

Randolph gritted his teeth. "Yes. Shit."

Joe struggled with Kat, trying to get her to the car. "Listen, kid. Stop fucking around and get in the car." He let go of one arm to open the back door and Kat kicked back with her boot, her hard rubber heel connecting with his kneecap. She wrenched her other arm free and ran.

Andy and Dan leaned on the open doors and sagged with visible relief when Kat ran back toward their car. She had a massive grin on her face.

"Did you see that? I think I broke a couple of his fingers." She gave Dan a quick hug. "And that other guy." She watch Joe limping into the restaurant. "This is awesome. Now what?"

Terry got out of the back seat with a laptop and tablet tucked under his arm. "Now we keep our fingers crossed he left his electronics in the car."

"I'm going with you. Andy, Kat, stay here."

"I don't need -"

"Shut up, kid. You're staying with Andy." He walked beside Terry. "You sure the jammer worked?"

"One of the muscle pushed the key fob and I didn't see any lights flash on the car."

Dan smiled and trotted across the parking lot with Terry. "Adrenal gland working overtime?"

"Yeah." He reached the car and paused, then tested its back door. It opened. "It worked."

"Had no doubt. Let's do this. He's going to be heading to the hospital very soon."

Terry put the replacement laptop and tablet on the back seat and grabbed the leather satchel on the armrest in the middle. "Take these." He handed a laptop and tablet identical to the ones he brought to Dan. Glancing out the car window toward the restaurant he slid the replacement tablet and laptop in the case, closed it and carefully placed it on the center armrest. He looked at it for a second, both hands up framing the image, adjusted it slightly then smiled. "Got it."

"Let's go."

"Wait, wait, wait. Almost forgot." Terry took a small plastic case from his pocket and extracted the final small tracker. He unzipped an outside pocket on the satchel and dropped the tracker in it. "Now we can find his home."

Dan closed the door and followed Terry back to their car.

"So when that big guy grabbed me I thought I was screwed," Kat said to Andy. "Then he got close and I saw my chance and my high school soccer came out." She looked into the back seat. "Hey, guys, gotta question."

"Yes, Kat, you were great,' said Dan.

"Thanks, but not that. The tablet. I know what I did to the laptop, what did you do with the tablet? You set up a fake banking app on it, too?"

Terry smiled. "No. Didn't change a lick of software on the tablet."

Kat furrowed her brow. "I made a duplicate laptop that effectively makes it look like his bank accounts are empty. If he can get on the real banking app on the tablet, everything I did was a waste of time."

"The tablet is dead. I opened it up and disconnected the battery. He'll never be able to power it up."

Kat's face broke into a massive grin. "That's good. So good." She rubbed her hands together. "Now what?"

"Back to the office." Dan looked at his watch. "He'll need to get those fingers checked out. He'll be back at his place in three or four hours. Plenty of time to prep for the next step."

Randolph left the restaurant with a napkin tied around his middle two fingers of his right hand, a butter knife as a splint. "As security, you guys are shit."

"To be honest, Mr Murray, I didn't expect a young, slight woman to attack you like that."

"Manny, that's your name, right? Manny, no excuses." He cradled his hand. "Get the fucking car door for me. And take me to the hospital."

"Campbelltown Private is just around the corner."

"No." He eased into the back seat and leaned against the headrest. He rested his hand in his lap and closed his eyes. "Royal Prince Alfred. And take it easy on the bumps."

"You sure? Campbelltown Private Hospital is good. Get that pain killer into you and ease the discomfort."

Randolph opened his eyes and glared at Manny in the rear-view mirror. "Royal. Prince. Alfred." He reached into his inside suit pocket with his good hand and sighed. "Where's my phone?"

Joe turned in his seat and held up a mobile phone with a shattered screen. "Don't think it's going to be of any use to you."

Randolph grabbed it and rested it on his leg. He used his thumbprint to unlock it. The display was fragmented into a hundred little slivers. He swiped his index finger to the left and jerked it back. "Shit." A shard of glass was stuck in the ball of his finger. He stuck it in his mouth and picked the piece of glass out with his teeth and spit it on the car floor. "I'm going to need another goddamned phone, too. Pick one up and bring it to the office tomorrow." He stuck the bleeding finger in his mouth then pulled it out and looked at the small bead of blood slowly growing larger.

The car bounced over a speed bump on the way out of the parking lot. Randolph winced and grabbed his wrist. "Jesus Christ you oaf. Watch the bumps. Fucking hell. Get me to that goddamned hospital."

CHAPTER 35

Randolph sat on his balcony looking over Neutral Bay. The view wasn't fantastic -- Sub Base Platypus across the bay to the right and the ferry wharf closer, on the left -- but it was quiet. He'd have enough money, soon, to get that place in Vaucluse. He looked at the middle two fingers on his right hand, splinted and taped together, a beautiful eggplant purple. The pain throbbed through the prescription pain meds chased with bourbon. He rubbed his nose with the edge of one of the finger splints, bumping against his nose split, pushing that pain to an almost unbearable place. "Unghhhh. McGinnis is going to hang for this."

He placed his drink awkwardly on the side table and reached for his mobile. "Shit." He sighed and pushed himself up with one hand and padded sock footed into his den. He sat at his desk and took the handset from the desk phone and stuck it in the crook of his neck. Speed-dial '1' had 'Mel' beside it. He poked the number and grabbed the handset.

It rang three times before being picked up.

Randolph leaned forward. "Mel?"

Silence on the other end of the line. Except maybe a faint street noise.

"I can hear something. Is that you, Mel? Say something."

More silence.

"If you've done something to Mel, I swear to god I will find you and ruin you."

A deep chuckle at the far end of the line ended abruptly as the call was terminated. Randolph slammed the handset into the cradle. "Prick."

He rummaged through the top drawer of his desk for a piece of paper with a phone number on it. He jabbed the speakerphone button and dialled. The number rang three times and it was answered.

"Gerald, where have you been?"

The same deep chuckle was cut short as the call was dropped.

"What in the fuck is going on? I can track the phone. And I'm going to track it to you. You're dead."

"Not yet." The voice was artificially pitched deep.

"Too chickenshit to use your real voice?"

"Want to keep the element of surprise. Never know when we might bump into each other, face-to-face."

"What in the hell do you want?"

There was a pause on the phone, then Randolph heard his voice. "*Mr Prime Minister, that's a hard line to take. And I'm sure that you will change your mind on corporate tax rates once you review the contents of the file that is being dropped off with your driver right about now. Picture, files, video, the sorts of things -*"

"Enough. Where did you get this?"

The deep chuckle rumbled through the lines. "You're not very smart, for all you pretend to be. I'm going to release this to the media in the morning if there isn't an apology for the heinous stories you've written and a confession to the murder of Jeremy Brookes."

Randolph leaned forward. "This is McGinnis, isn't it?"

"Not even close. If I don't see an apology in the morning, and read about your admission of guilt by 9:00, the recording goes to all of your competitors."

Randolph held the phone in front of his face. "Fuck you, McGinnis. You can spread that wherever you want to whomever you want and it will have absolutely no impact. And within a week there'll be video of you abusing a three year old boy. Take that recording and shove it up your arse." He hung up.

Andy terminated the call and turned off the voice changer. "I don't think he likes you, Dan. He's going to track Gerry's phone."

"Back to Campbelltown. Smart to forward it to yours.

The van was in a parking lot next to Anderson Reserve, less than a block from Randolph's house. A directional antenna on the room was pointed at his house. Andy was in the front passenger seat and Stew was behind the wheel. Dan and Cassie sat in the bench seat in the back.

The van's side door slid open and Terry hopped in and squeezed into the back. He was wearing a hi-vis vest with the local telco name on the back. He dropped a bag of tools on the floor. "Found the copper pair to his house. The interrupter is installed and ready to go." He adjusted a dial. "And I'm on his home Wi-Fi. Weak signal, but good enough for what we need to do."

He stole a glance at Cassie and blushed. "Great to have you helping out, Miss Johnson."

"Call me Cassie. Anything I can do to take down that slimy prick."

"Set up for this movie shouldn't take too long. Written and directed by Dan, starring you, and our favourite right-wing psycho."

"My favourite part of the process, actually, setting up."

"Terry has the hardest job, though," said Dan. "The final edit has to be perfect. And very fast."

"Not that hard." Terry hoisted a duffel bag from the back of the van. "Do you watch the set up before you act, or is everything ready when you show up?" He squeezed through the tight gap and hopped out. "It's just trailer time until you're up, right?"

Cassie smiled and jumped out of the van. "For a couple of the big ones, yeah. I spent more time in the trailer than in front of the cameras. And one of them, anyone could have played the part. I was a CG'd forest nymph. Almost all green screen."

"I loved that part. You could tell it was you. Anyone could tell." Terry was rapt, hanging on every word.

"You're too kind. The final two movies I wrote, I directed and I partially funded. Finding locations, setting up cameras, making sure everyone was where they should be, tweaking the script -- that was my life for three months. Each movie. What are you setting up? Not standard movie equipment."

Terry hoisted the bag over his shoulder and headed into the park. "It'll be a low-budget short. I don't hold out any hope for SXSW awards, but it might run locally for a while."

Cassie chuckled. "I'm prepared. Show me what you're doing with the cameras and lights."

"Won't need lights."

Cassie looked up at the sky. "Sun's going to be down within the hour. "

"The lights will be coming on shortly. This park is well lit. Council wants it to be safe for the very affluent residents." Terry stood by the edge of the trees and placed the duffle on the ground. He opened it and he and Cassie squatted beside it.

She grabbed a small case and opened it. "What do you have here?"

"A dozen GoPros, an LTE pocket Wi-Fi box, a bunch of back up batteries.

It's a portable outdoor surveillance set up."

Randolph topped up his glass and settled into his chair on the balcony. He swallowed a mouthful and winced as it burned. The painkillers took the edge off and the booze was getting him to that floaty feeling. The combination wasn't hurting any. He leaned back in his chair, watching a small pleasure craft idle out on the bay, when his phone rang.

"Ah, fuck." He pushed himself out of his chair and half-trotted into the office and grabbed the phone on the fourth ring. "Who's this?"

"Randolph, ya miss me?" asked Mel.

Randolph dropped into his office chair. "Where in the hell have you been?"

"Shanghaied to Singapore. Just got back. I'm at the airport. We need to talk. Why aren't you answering your mobile?"

"Long, boring," he looked at his fingers, "painful story." He tapped his desk. "Why are you calling me and not what's-her-name?"

"Danni? It's training night. She's tied up for a couple of hours. I'd grab a cab, but the arsehole that trucked me to Singapore stole all my cards. A friend in Singapore got me the flight back, but she's not flush with cash. Can you send a car?"

"Hang on and tell me about this trip you took, and who sent you."

"A long, boring and painful story. Send Gerald with the car."

Randolph sighed. "There'll be a car at Arrivals in ten minutes. Different guy. He'll have a sign. He'll take you here. We need to talk. Some stupid shit is happening and I can't quite figure it out." He looked at the phone's display. "You're calling from a blocked number. New mobile?"

"Payphone. Like a fucking peasant. Thanks. I'll watch for the car."

He heard the handset hit the cradle a little harder than it needed to. He leaned forward and gently hung up the phone, deep in thought. He reached in his pocket for his mobile phone, swore and grabbed the handset on his desk phone. He flipped through an old rolodex and dialled.

"Security. This is Leah Kasmerik. Is your call relating to an issue at an *Oz Express* site?"

"This is Randolph Murray. I need you to find the number of one of my security, a Manny something or other. Just started."

"He's your driver and security agent, isn't he? You don't have the number?"

"Would I be bloody calling you if I did?"

There was a moment of silence on the phone. "Certainly. I've got the number. Do you have a pen and paper?"

"I'll remember it. Fire away."

She recited the number and Randolph closed his eyes, memorising it. "Thanks.

He hung up and dialled. "Manny, get to International Arrivals and pick up Mel Dvorak. She's already there, waiting."

"Mr Murray?"

"Who else would be calling?"

"Right-o. Where's she going?"

"She's coming back to my house in Neutral Bay. You have the address?"

"Of course. Dropped you off earlier."

"Hold up a sign. M-E-L D-V-O-R-A-K. She won't know you."

Cassie peered over Terry's shoulder in the back of the van. Two monitors were quartered, a total of eight video feeds from cameras placed liberally around the park. "This is slick. Audio too?"

Terry pulled the headphone jack out of the console and adjusted the volume. Tree frogs, crickets, the crack of a bat from a cricket cage came through the speakers. "Wired for sound."

Dan checked his watch. "It's time, Cassie. You ready?"

She held out her hand. "Phone?"

Dan placed a phone in her hand, number dialled, just waiting for 'Send'. "Everybody quiet." Dan held his finger to his lips and nodded ad Cassie.

She took a deep breath, closed her eyes for a beat and smiled. She pressed send and held the phone to her head.

"Who's this?"

"Good day, Randy."

"It's Randolph. Who is this?"

"You don't recognize my accent? You had my picture on your cover implying I had a dick. And if I *did* have a dick, it would be bigger than yours."

"Cassie Johnson."

"Right in one."

"How did you get this number?"

"I have friends."

"Why are you calling? You finally decided to pay?"

"You tried to grab my dog, man. That's really low. You're lower than snake shit. You're not getting a single dollar from me."

"The price goes up tomorrow."

"Makes sense. You're going to need the money."

"So what is the fucking reason for this call? You're wasting my time. I've got things to do."

"I want you to meet me in Anderson Reserve. In ten minutes."

"Why in the hell would I do that? Put the money in my account by midnight or add 50% to the fee and go looking for another dog."

Cassie laughed. "Check your bank accounts."

Randolph paced the limit of the cord on his phone, back and forth, one fist clenching a handset to his ear, the other clenched in a fist. "Bullshit."

"Check. I'll wait."

He sneered and laid the phone down on his desk and pulled the laptop from its case. He opened the browser, navigated to his bank website and entered his username and password. He clicked through to his account summary page. It showed a combined balance of $0. He logged out, logged back in, and checked again. Same result. "Son of a bitch."

He grabbed the handset. "What in the hell have you done?"

Cassie looked at Dan who nodded. "I've cleaned you out, Randolph. Ten minutes. Anderson Reserve."

Dan pointed at Terry who pressed a button on a small remote. The call dropped.

"How was that?" Cassie handed the phone back to Dan with a smile.

"You were great. Terry, we got him?"

Terry held up the remote in one hand while he typed with the other. "Phone line is cut." He dropped the remote on the small table and kept typing. He threw his hands in the air. "Yes!"

Cassie tucked in behind him, looking at the laptop screen over his shoulder. "That his bank?"

"Yeah." He presented the screen with both hands.

"How did you get his bank password?"

Terry smiled. "Kat installed a keylogger that sends the results to me."

"We cut his internet."

"Camped on his wi-fi until I got it. Hot spotting off my phone now. Anybody have any idea what to do with a little over a million dollars?"

Cassie snorted. "I thought he was rich."

"This is his liquid assets. I expect he's got many millions more in property, stocks, that sort of thing," said Dan. "This needs redistribution." He checked his watch. "But we've got more pressing matters first. Cassie, are you ready for your close up?"

She checked her pocket, gingerly checked her torso and smiled. "I am, Mr DeMille."

CHAPTER 36

Randolph slammed the handset repeatedly on the telephone. He held it to his head -- no dial tone -- and slammed it down again. He balled a fist in rage, picked up his desk phone and threw it across his study. "AARRHHHHHH."

He looked at his watch. "No choice. You fucking bitch. I can't login, I can't call the bank. Ten minute walk to the park. Fuck me."

He grabbed a jacket off a hook and slammed the door behind him.

Cassie adjusted the earpiece and made sure it was covered by her hair. She placed a small duffle on the ground under a bench and sat facing the bay. A couple of catamarans bobbed in reflected lights from the apartment blocks on the hills.

"So you guys can hear me?"

"Loud and clear," said Terry in her ear. "We're keeping an eye out for him. You ready for this?"

"Well, it's a little different than the sets I've usually been on. You guys have my back, right?"

"One hundred percent. We're just across the street. You warm enough?"

"I am." Cassie adjusted herself on the bench and pulled her jacket tighter. She pulled on a pair of thin, kidskin gloves. "You think he's going to show?"

"Give him a couple more minutes."

Manny stopped in front of Randolph's house. "You want I should wait for you?"

Mel pushed open the door. "No. I'll get an Uber."

"It's no problem. Got nothing else to do."

She slammed the car door shut and leaned down to the driver's window. "Go home. Rand and I have a lot to talk about."

She waited until Manny turned in the narrow dead-end street before she walked up the steps and knocked on the door. She peered through the glass panel beside the door. The house felt still. She knocked again and tried the door. It was unlocked.

She stepped into the foyer. "Randolph? You here?" Her voice echoed in the hallway. "Rand. What the hell are you up to?"

She poked her head in his study and saw the phone console on the floor. Items on the desk were out of place and in disarray. She picked up the phone and placed it on the desk. She pressed the speakerphone button. Instead of a dial tone there was silence. She checked the handset. Still dead.

"What is going on, Rand?" she muttered under her breath.

She paced through the house quickly, confirming it was empty. "What the hell." She checked the fridge. There was food and a bottle of white wine chilling. "I'll just hang around here, then."

Cassie slid her hand in her coat pocket and rested her gloved hand on the revolver. She was familiar with the weapon, but only on movie sets, in controlled environments, with a script and weeks of practice with a stunt coordinator.

"Hey, Cass, you still awake?"

"Fat chance of sleeping, Dan. The adrenaline pumping through me will keep me awake for days."

"Well, the arsehole is walking down the hill. He's about a minute out. You're up. Take a couple of deep breaths. If you feel like you're in any danger -"

"I know. Platypus." She took a deep breath and let it out slowly. "I'm good. Is the light okay?"

"It's good. Here he comes. Make sure you hit your marks. We need this to look right."

"That's *my* specialty." Cassie looked to her left. Randolph walked down the steps and across the small footbridge over a fetid canal. He looked around and Cassie stood. "Over here." She stood on the walk, facing him, hands in her coat pockets.

Randolph walked toward her slowly. He wore khakis and deck shoes. The splint on his nose was bracketed by two black eyes. He pushed up the sleeves of his jacket, gingerly avoiding the broken fingers on his left hand. "What in the hell is this all about? Give me my money back or I'll make sure you spend the rest of your pathetic, miserable life in jail." He stopped walking when he was a couple of metres away from Cassie. "You think you'll actually get away with this?"

Cassie looked Randolph in the eye, hands in her coat pockets. "One million, one hundred and twelve thousand, four hundred and thirty-eight dollars and seventeen cents."

"What?"

"One million, one hundred and -"

"I heard you. What is that? Are *you* now trying to extort *me*?"

"That's the amount that was in your account and will be, immediately after this meeting, donated to worthy causes that I support. The receipts will be in your name, of course."

Randolph bared his teeth and took a step toward her. "You stupid bitch."

She stepped back and extracted the revolver from her pocket, levelling it at Randolph's waist.

He pulled up short. "Now, now. Where did you get that?"

"And after one that one million and change is redistributed to worthy causes, I'll take apart your brokerage account and distribute ten percent of that money to every right-winged, Nazi-based scum-filled organisation here and overseas. I'll publicise every single donation, with your name and face and the atrocities these groups stand for. And I'll keep the rest. You will be financially and professionally ruined."

She raised the revolver and pointed it at his head. "You can't believe the self-control it's taking to not just finish you right now. One in the forehead and you're over." She took another step forward, the muzzle centimetres from Randolph's forehead. "You threatened harm to my dog, you useless pile of pig shit."

Her hand trembled and Randolph grabbed the gun from her hand and turned it on her. Cassie held her hands out and took a step back.

"Shoe's on the other foot, bitch."

Cassie smiled. "Except you're a spineless twat who prefers to attack people from behind a trashy rag. You don't have the balls to go face to face. I doubt you're strong enough to even pull the trigger. You're an impotent old man. A joke."

"You don't think I'll do it?"

"I *know* you won't do it. You can't. You're constitutionally unable to. I've never met a weaker man in my life." She nodded in his direction. "That nose. An old woman did that. A little girl broke your fingers. You're useless."

Randolph bared his teeth and squeezed the trigger twice. Two loud pops echoed off the hills and Cassie fell to the ground, red blooming over her chest.

Randolph stepped back and dropped the gun. "Shit." Sirens wailed in the distance. "Shit, shit, shit." He turned and ran out of the park.

Cassie was motionless on the ground, arms splayed, the red stain on her chest slowly spreading.

Dan's voice spoke in Cassie's ear. "You okay?"

She grunted in response.

"That was fantastic. He's gone. You can get up."

She rolled over and pushed herself to her feet. "I keep forgetting how much those squibs hurt. Tell Terry his timing was perfect." She winced and pulled the squib pads from under her blouse. "You guys ready for your part? I see the police lights."

"Yes. Cover up your blouse. And sort the revolver."

She looked down at the corn syrup and red dye stain on her chest. "Right." She pulled the duffel out from under the bench, shed her coat, grabbed a red jumper, and pulled it on. She grabbed four intact cartridges and two fired casings from the bag and replaced the blanks in the revolver and placed it on the ground where Randolph had dropped it. She was putting her coat back on when two marked cars and an unmarked car stopped on the road, their lights flashing.

"Bin the blanks and the earwig. I'll be over in a second," said Dan.

She plucked the small listening device from her ear and walked a few steps over to the water. She leaned over, her hands to her mouth and made a retching sound, dropping the blanks and the earwig in the water. She stood and took a deep breath, her eyes closed and her hands shaking.

"Excuse me, miss. I'm Detective Chang. We received reports of a disturbance in the park. Do you know anything about it?"

Cassie pulled her coat tight around her and crossed her arms. "Randolph

Murray tried to kill me." Her breath shuddered and she turned to face Chang. "He's insane."

Recognition dawned in Chang's face. "Miss Johnson. Small world. Are you okay?"

She pointed to the revolver in the grass with a shaky hand. "He shot at me with that."

Chang unclipped the snap on his holster. "Where is he now? Are you injured in any way?"

"He took off. And no, I'm not injured. You're going to arrest him, aren't you?"

"We'll take a statement from you and see if we can find anything forensic that can corroborate your story."

"Good evening, Detective," said Dan.

Chang turned and squinted in thought. "And you. McGinnis, right? What are you doing up here?"

"Cassie Johnson retained my firm. Mr Murray was extorting her and she wanted a video of the interaction. Cassie -- Miss Johnson -- was aware of the recording, but Mr Murray wasn't."

Chang cocked his head. "Did Miss Johnson believe the recording was reasonably necessary for the protection of her lawful interests?"

Dan smiled. "Yes. I believe that's the legal phrase. It's not a long video and certainly not one of Miss Johnson's best piece of work, but I've got clear video of Mr Murray pointing the weapon -- that weapon on the grass -- at Miss Johnson and him pulling the trigger. I shut it off, called the police and ran over here. The old fool's hand was shaking like a leaf. Not surprised he missed."

"Ran over here from where?"

"We're in the parking lot. I set a camera up. Thank God Cassie's okay."

"Can you show me the video?"

Dan nodded and dialled a number. "Terry, I'm bringing Detective Chang to the van. Queue up the video, okay?"

Randolph trotted up his stairs to the front door, sweat staining his shirt. He wiped at the sheen on his head with little effect. He pushed open the front door to the smell of cooking. "Who's here?"

Mel walked out of the lounge room barefoot with a glass of wine. "Rand. Where in the hell have you been?" She looked at his splints. "I have so many questions."

"I could say the same. Make yourself at home."

"I already have. You don't look so good."

Randolph looked back toward the park. "Yeah. No, I'm not. That Cassie bitch lured me to the park and I think I've killed her."

"What?"

Blue and red lights rolled closer down the street and flashed through the glass panels beside the front door. "Damn it. Get out of here. Upstairs. Out of sight. I'm going to need someone on the outside to help me."

There was a sharp double rap on the door. "Mr Randolph Murray, this is Detective Chang of the Sydney Police. Please open the door."

Randolph shook his head. "Dammit. Go."

Mel ran up the stairs with her wine. Randolph waited until she was out of sight and opened the door. "What do you want?"

CHAPTER 37

Dan sat back in his office chair reading the news on his iPad. Randolph had been remanded for the attempted murder of Cassie and the murder of Jeremy Brookes. The ballistics from the revolver he used in the shooting at Anderson Park matched the revolver used in the Brookes killing. His prints were on it and gunshot residue was found on his hand.

He wandered into the conference room. Cassie was holding court with Kat, Terry and Beryl. "He's behind bars. His prints on the gun and the ballistics from Jeremy's murder did him."

"Am I going to have to testify?" asked Cassie?

"We all might. I'll talk to Chang. You might be able to get by with the statement you made. But he's not going to beat this." He shrugged. "Video of

273

him shooting at you, his prints on the gun. He's not going to be able to mount much of a defence."

"But you'll call him?"

Dan's phone rang. "Yeah, sure." He answered his phone. "McGinnis Investigations."

"Chang here. You got a minute?"

Dan smiled at Cassie and pointed at his phone. He mouthed the word 'Chang' and gave her the thumbs up. "No problem, Detective. What can I do for you?" He walked into his office and closed the door.

Dan heard a long slow breath before Chang started talking. "I find it incredibly curious that your original reason for visiting me so neatly coincided with your subsequent case, helping that young actress Cassandra Johnson."

"Sometimes coincidences happen."

"I'd say so, considering Cassandra was Mrs Brookes alibi on the night her husband was killed. Extremely curious."

Dan sat forward. "Really?"

"Right." Chang sighed. "Randolph Murray has an alibi for that night, but it's weak, and the ballistics are incontrovertible. He's denying it, but we are going to trial."

"Will we need to testify?"

"We?"

"Cassie and Sally. Cassie was asking me that very question earlier today. She's worried about the publicity."

"It's pretty much a slam dunk. The video you gave me is one hundred percent conclusive. He's holding the revolver, she's got her hands out and bang, before it stopped."

"Sorry it wasn't longer. I was more concerned about Cassie's well-being."

"Understood. His prints are on the revolver and there's GSR on his shooting hand. The ballistics tie him to the Brookes killing. I can't put him there, but I can put the gun there and that's enough for conspiracy to murder."

"Oh. It's registered to him?"

"It was registered to Jeremy Brooks. We think he tried defending himself in the alley and it was taken from him. His wife has confirmed it was theirs."

"So, no court time for my client?"

"No. Neither of them."

"That's good news. I'll let them know."

Chang cleared his throat. "There are two other cases, outside of my jurisdiction, that I should tell you about. Two of Randolph's personal security are in critical condition in two different hospitals. Both the same night. Both were beaten to within an inch of their lives. One, a Robert Merrick, was found floating in Middle Harbour. The other one, Gerald Rogers, was dragged out to his back yard and his house blown up."

"I know about the Middle Harbour one, I think. A couple of my boys were fishing there and found who they thought was a dead guy. So is he going to be okay?"

"No idea. Like I said, outside of my jurisdiction. Thought you should know."

"Thanks. I guess. My guys gave a statement to the police about the Middle Harbour one. The two cases are obviously connected."

"I only tell you because I thought you might be interested. Both of them were frequent fliers. Jackets a mile long. The Rogers fella had an outstanding warrant against him. My understanding is that the police will be putting in minimal effort on both of them."

Dan leaned back in his chair and looked at the ceiling. "Interesting. It's been a pleasure doing business with you, Detective."

"Yeah. Stay the fuck out of my jurisdiction and we'll be fine." Chang hung up.

Dan let out a long slow breath, hung up his phone and walked back to the conference room.

Terry and Cassie were standing off on their own in a corner, close and chatty. Cassie had a hand on Terry's arm and he had a blush that would light up a room. Dan sat beside Beryl and nodded toward the pair in the corner. "Really?"

"It would seem so. She breaks his heart and I will end her."

"She doesn't seem to be the bunny boiler type."

Cassie put her hand on Terry's chest and said, "Hang on a second." She leaned on the table between Beryl and Dan. "We good?"

"We are, apparently, good. You knew Sally was behind Jeremy's death all along?"

She shrugged. "What are friends for?"

"What's this?" asked Beryl.

"I'll tell you later," said Dan. "His friend or her friend?"

"Both. Equally."

Dan exhaled slowly. "Right. So, you and Terry?"

She smiled while she shrugged. "He's a nice guy. There aren't many of those around. We'll see how it goes. Thanks, really. I know you didn't have to help me out. And you put yourself at risk doing it." She looked pointedly at Dan. "Send me a bill for my part of your work."

"We will," said Beryl. "Count on it."

Cassie nodded toward Terry and he came over and took her hand. "We're getting a bite. I'll have him back in a couple of hours."

"I'll walk you out." Dan winked at Terry as he walked by and smiled at his deepening blush. He held the door and as Cassie and Terry left, Sally Brookes entered. She gave Cassie's hand a quick squeeze and came up the stairs.

"We're clear," said Sally.

"We are." Dan held the door for her. "My office."

Sally sat across from the desk and waited until Dan sat. "I don't know exactly how you did it, and I probably should never know so I can have full deniability, but Rand is in jail for murdering my husband."

"You were a terrible client."

"Excuse me?"

"Cassie was your alibi?"

"I couldn't tell you that. She stuck her neck out way too much as it was." She cleared her throat and sat up straight. "I don't regret what I did, much. And I don't know how to thank you."

"Beryl will help you find a way."

She waved that away. "Money can't even come close."

"You haven't seen the invoice yet."

"Be that as it may, I'm forever in your debt." She checked her watch. "I'd love to stay, but this was just a quick drop in. I've got a flight to catch."

"Chang's okay with you leaving town?"

"He better be. I'm heading to the Grand Teton Park. Better late than never." She stood and stuck out her hand. "But if you ever need a brain surgeon, look me up."

Dan stood and shook her hand. "I'll keep that in mind. Safe flight."

He walked her out and leaned against the doorjamb as she walked down the stairs. Beryl and Kat walked up behind him. Beryl held out his mobile phone. "You want to take this."

He looked at her, puzzled, then took the phone and put it on speaker. "McGinnis speaking."

"I'll give it to you, Dan, you're good," said Mel. "Really fucking good."

"Where are you?"

"Don't worry. You're not on my radar. I'm not that stupid. Just wanted to thank you. With Rand gone, this is my show now."

"Should we expect an increase in civility?"

"Not likely. I need to make money." She paused. "But it'll be tame for a little while."

"Remember I know your game, now. Fuck with me, my team, or anyone

I know and that recording -"

"Yeah, fuck. Jesus. Okay."

"Keep your nose clean, hey? Deal?"

"Arsehole." Mel hung up.

Dan smiled and pocketed his phone.

"This was fun," said Kat. "What's next?"

About the Author

Tony McFadden is a displaced Canadian now calling Australia home. He and his wife and two children live near the beaches where he spends as much of his time as possible writing.

More about Tony and his writing can be found on the interwebs at TonyMcFadden.net/mybooks
and Twitter (@Tony_McFadden)

Also by Tony McFadden

G'Day LA
G'Day USA

Matt's War
Daly Battles: The Fall of Pyongyang
Target: Australia

Book 'Em - An Eamonn Shute Mystery
Unprotected Sax
Family Matters

Have Wormhole, Will Travel
Killing Time

Mac D: Private Investigator
A Step Too Far (A Mac D Mystery)
Hunter/Prey (A Mac D Mystery)

www.ingramcontent.com/pod-product-compliance
Lightning Source LLC
Chambersburg PA
CBHW021415110726
47901CB00008B/2178